"I'd be a fo...
"to pass up...
me the moon and the stars."

"I'm not that man," Race whispered. "I'm not who—or what—you think I am."

"I know you're a good man, an honest man. It's just—"

"You don't know *anything*!" He hated himself for doing it this way, sharply, in anger, but it was the only way he could make his determination hold out long enough. "I'm not good *or* honest, Kit Cameron."

She drew back from him a little, looking at him with a sudden wariness that clawed at him even more.

"Then what are you?" she asked tightly.

He set his jaw. "I'm exactly what you thought I was that day the sheriff showed up here."

Her eyes widened, and she shook her head, slowly, uncomprehendingly. "What do you mean? What are you?"

He met her gaze levelly. "A killer, Kit. That's what I am."

Dear Reader:

We at Silhouette are very excited to bring you this reading Sensation. Look out for the four books which appear in our Silhouette Sensation series every month. These stories will have the high quality you have come to expect from Silhouette, and their varied and provocative plots will encourage you to explore the wonder of falling in love – again and again!

Emotions run high in these drama-filled novels. Greater sensual detail and an extra edge of realism intensify the hero and heroine's relationship so that you cannot help but be caught up in their every change of mood.

We hope you enjoy this Sensation – and will go on to enjoy many more.

We would love to hear your comments and encourage you to write to us:

Jane Nicholls
Silhouette Books
PO Box 236
Thornton Road
Croydon
Surrey
CR9 3RU

JUSTINE DAVIS
Race Against Time

Silhouette Sensation

First published in Great Britain in 1994
by Silhouette Books, Eton House, 18-24 Paradise Road,
Richmond, Surrey TW9 1SR

© Janice Davis Smith 1993

Silhouette, Silhouette Sensation and Colophon are
Trade Marks of Harlequin Enterprises B.V.

ISBN 0 373 59118 7

18-9405

Made and printed in Great Britain

Other novels by Justine Davis

Silhouette Sensation

Hunter's Way
Loose Ends
Stevie's Chase
Suspicion's Gate
Cool Under Fire

Silhouette Desire

Angel for Hire
Upon the Storm
Found Father

With admiration and thanks
to Leslie Wainger
Indeed the "greatest of the great!"
Here's to the next ten books, and the next, and
the next.

Chapter 1

"'**O**ughta just shoot him when they catch him."

"Nah, shootin's too good for him. Just string him up from the nearest tree."

Kit Cameron glanced at the couple who owned the small Lakeview general store, not knowing whether to cringe or laugh. The Porters were a kindly older pair, but they sounded quite serious, almost vehement.

"Isn't the death penalty a little extreme?" she asked. "All he—or she—has done is steal a little food."

"Sure," Hank Brodie put in from the shoe section of the store, where he was trying on a pair of boots. "By breaking into half the cabins on the west slope in the last six days."

Well, not exactly *breaking into* all of them, Kit thought.

She wasn't surprised at Hank's interjection. No one made any pretense of not eavesdropping in the store that was a central gathering point for the small California mountain town; it was accepted that any conversation that took place here was public domain.

"But he's never taken anything else," Kit said. "Even from the Simpson place, where Sherm has all that video gear."

"You're too soft, girl," Jack Porter said, not unkindly.

"Just like your daddy," his wife put in. "Always telling us to walk a mile in the other man's—" The woman broke off suddenly, her hand rising to cover her mouth. "Oh, I'm sorry, dear. I just up and forgot."

"It's all right, Olive." Kit changed the subject abruptly, knowing they would let it pass. "Could I have a jar of Able's honey, too?"

"Of course." The woman bustled off to the shelf behind her as Hank approached the counter, boots in hand.

"Ring these up for me, will you, Jack?" The tall heavy man in the red plaid shirt leaned one elbow on the counter, reaching to lift the lid of one of the glass jars there and take out a piece of licorice. "I tell you," he said as he bit off a segment, "we've got to do something about this damned thief."

"He seems . . . very careful not to confront anyone," Kit began.

Hank snorted. "'Course. Coward, that's what he is. Lousy sneak. Wish I'd been there when he hit our place, I'd have blasted him to kingdom come. Why, he could be an escaped convict, for all we know."

"What would an escaped convict be doing here?" Kit tossed the thick, dark braid of her hair back over her shoulder, then tried again. "Besides, if all he's taken is a few cans of beans—"

"Don't matter. Thief's a thief. Even if he only takes beans," Hank said with another snort. "Martha's been after me to lock up her silver and all that antique jewelry of hers. Damned nuisance."

The thief had had a chance to take it all, Kit thought, and he hadn't. But she knew Hank wouldn't see it that way. Yes, she muttered inwardly, you're most definitely swimming upstream here.

"About time the sheriff got off his a—" Hank stopped, glancing from Kit to Olive before amending quickly, "Er, off his duff and did something."

"I'm sure he will," Kit said, "as soon as he can. I imagine he's a little busy right now."

"My, yes," Olive said as she added the jar, pieces of the comb still visible in the golden honey, to the big box on the counter. "Terrible thing, that man being run over like that and just left to die."

Kit shivered; the week since it had happened had done nothing to lessen the horror of the brutal hit-and-run that had occurred on the lake road. She had scrupulously avoided learning any of the grim details; she'd had enough of a sudden, unexpected death to last her a lifetime.

"That all, dear?"

Kit nodded. "How much?"

"Well, let's see here, you bought more than usual this week." After quoting the total, Olive smiled at her. "Our mountain air's bringing your appetite back, I hope. You could use a few more pounds."

Not exactly, Kit thought again, although she couldn't argue that she'd lost some weight she couldn't really afford. But the real reason she'd bought more food than usual had nothing to do with her weight.

"Thanks," she said as Olive handed her her change. "See you next week."

"Don't forget, Len will be out with that wood for you on Wednesday," Jack put in.

"I won't."

"Sure you don't want him to chop it for you?"

"I'll probably wish I'd said yes when I'm about a quarter of the way through, but no."

Not that she didn't plan to hire someone to do it for her, Kit thought, the Carter boy maybe, but having Len Porter around for as long as it would take him to chop a cord of wood was more than she wanted to deal with. The only thing he was denser about than her desire to be left alone was her lack of response to, in his view, his considerable appeal.

"I'll carry that out for you," Jack said, moving to come out from behind the long counter.

"No, thanks. I need the exercise," Kit said as she hefted the bulky box.

"All right," Jack agreed reluctantly. "Now, if you need anything else, you let us know."

"I will."

"We're so sorry, Olive and me, about your dad."

"I know."

"Think of him every time we drive by the Ag Center. Never understood what he did there, but it sure don't seem the same anymore, knowing he isn't there."

"No, it doesn't." The University Agricultural Center and Dr. Christopher Cameron, world-renowned mycologist, had been linked together so long in her own mind that she could barely stand to even drive by the facility; it just brought home even more brutally the finality of his death.

Steeling herself against the creeping pain, she tightened her grip on the box. She was tired of being treated as if she were fragile enough to shatter in a stiff mountain breeze, and it was time she put a stop to it.

Brilliant time to declare your autonomy, Kit told herself moments later as she tried to lever the heavy box into the back of her Jeep.

"Hush, Gus," she said to the big dog that was barking in vociferous acknowledgment of her return. "Hey, quit it," she yelped as the animal nosed the box, nearly knocking her over. "Okay, as long as you're in the back, stay there. This is going in your spot, pal."

Having given up on getting the box up over the back lip of the open vehicle, she carried it around to the passenger side and dropped it gratefully on the seat. She would have to watch it all the way up the hill, but it was the best she could do.

"Sorry, old buddy," she teased as the dog cocked his head and looked at the box that had supplanted him. "It's only till we get home."

Letting out a rumbling sound that sounded thoroughly disgruntled, the dog sat down in the small space behind the driver's seat. Kit reached out to scratch the animal affectionately behind the ears. He was a huge mixed breed that looked part German shepherd and a larger part Irish Wolfhound, and Kit had fallen in love with him the moment he'd turned his woeful, brown-eyed gaze on her from his cage at the animal shelter. That at the time she'd had no more room for him than she'd had for a grand piano had made no difference.

And she would have given anything to still be trying to make room for him in her small apartment, she thought with a sigh as she started the Jeep. Instead, Gus had all the room he wanted and more, and she was living in the home she'd always loved but never wanted.

She knew by the way Gus leapt out of the Jeep before it even came to a halt and went racing first up to the door and then out to the edge of the clearing in front of the cabin, that she'd had another visit.

She slid out of the Jeep, knowing also by Gus's actions that it was safe to pick up the box and go on inside. If anyone had still been around, the dog would have alerted her.

"You're a fool, Kit m'girl," she muttered to herself as she stepped up onto the porch. "Not just soft, but soft in the head. This guy could be an ax-murderer for all you know."

Balancing the heavy box precariously on one slim hip, she nudged the door open. She didn't bother with her key; she knew it would be unlocked. She'd left it that way. Again.

The box hit the big oak table with a thud; she'd barely managed to carry the heavy thing that far. With a sigh she rubbed her stinging hands on her snug, worn jeans before she stepped around the table to begin unloading her supplies. And stopped short the moment she lifted her hand.

An odd emotion she couldn't quite put a name to tugged at her as she stared at the jar that sat in the center of the table, caught in a shaft of spring sunlight streaming through the window. It was a duplicate of the jar in the box. But rather than the thick, amber liquid of Able Caldicott's honey, this one held a rich array of bright wild-flowers, cheery Shasta daisies, the bright orange of California poppies and the tall spires of blue lupine rising above the rich green of the pine sprays that framed them.

It was lovely. It brightened the room. It soothed her grief-weary heart. It brought the sweetness of spring right inside. And it hadn't been there when she'd left this morning.

Kit leaned forward, reaching out to stroke the petal of one brilliant poppy with a slender finger. Only then did she see the piece of paper protruding from beneath the jar. Slowly she drew it out.

The feminine curve of her own writing met her eyes. "You must be tired of beans." She remembered the impulse that had made her leave the note between the apples and the cans of hash and chili she'd left out on the table. She still wasn't sure she understood it. Then she saw the marks showing through between her own letters from the other side and turned the page over.

"I was. Thank you."

Her breath caught in her throat. Somehow, until now, he had been a sort of phantom ranging the mountainside above Lakeview, never being seen, never leaving any trace. Even when she'd known he'd chosen her cabin as a target, it hadn't seemed quite real, despite the evidence. And somehow she hadn't been able to find it in herself to begrudge him the one can—of the ubiquitous beans—he'd taken.

It had been two days later that the idea had first occurred to her. Dusted with flour, kneading a loaf of her favorite bread as another baked, she had drawn a deep breath of the luscious aroma wafting from the oven.

"I think I could smell that for miles," she told Gus, who had a decided affinity for the process; whenever she began to bake, the big dog took up residence in the kitchen, waiting patiently for whatever scraps she might toss him.

Her own words had given her pause, and she'd glanced through the kitchen window to the pine-covered slope rising behind the cabin. She'd looked back at the oven, then at the already baked golden loaf that sat on the counter beside it. As usual, she had overdone it, but she loved the baking as much as the product and found it hard to resist.

She hadn't realized what she'd decided until she called Gus for their daily hike. At the last second she carefully wrapped up one of the still-warm loaves and left it out on the table. And when she and the gamboling dog left the cabin, she left the door unlocked.

She knew when he succumbed to the luscious smell; Gus told her. The shaggy, golden-brown dog had gone suddenly still, his head cocked back toward the cabin. A low growl rumbled up from his throat, and she had to soothe him with a quiet word.

"Not now, Gus. But don't go getting the idea he's a friend, boy. Not yet."

Even then he had seemed unreal, some illusory shadow that had no more substance than the barely palpable clues he left behind, his presence proven only by the reaction of the huge, woeful-eyed dog. But now, as she stood staring at the note in her hand, he was as real, as substantial, as Gus standing warm and solid beside her.

And it was a he. Any doubts she'd had about that had vanished with the first look at the bold, strong strokes of his writing. It was a man, and they were wrong about him. Surely no plain thief, no escaped convict of the kind Hank had mentioned, would have bothered. He would never have made the lovely gesture of the flowers to begin with. Nor would he have taken what was obviously barely enough food to survive. Not when he could have walked out of Sherman Simpson's luxurious, sprawling home with any of a dozen pieces of video equipment whose price would have fed him for months.

But in the darkness of the ensuing night, it was easy to convince herself that she was a fool. Anybody who survived by breaking into people's homes to steal food was not someone she should be helping. Lord knew how this unknown man might interpret her silent assistance. What he was doing was wrong, no matter what the reason. No more, she told herself sternly.

When she awoke in the morning to a heavy spring rain, she had to lecture herself again when her first thought was to wonder where he was, if he had anyplace to get out of the wet. Stop it, she ordered herself, and made herself go up to the loft, telling herself she had to stop procrastinating and get on with the task she'd set.

The loft took up almost half the upper area of the cabin and was open to the single spacious room below that her father had called the "great room." She'd slept up here as a child, but now she had converted it into a workroom to take advantage of the excellent light. She slept now in the big four-poster in the bedroom downstairs. The bed her parents had slept in, and where, her father had once told her laughingly, she had been conceived.

"We'd had a doozy of a fight, your mother and I," he'd said with a reminiscent smile. "But the making up was worth it, Kit. Especially since it brought us you."

Once more she found herself wiping away tears as she looked at the big table that now held his vast array of papers. She couldn't face them now, she thought. She just couldn't. She went back downstairs, wondering if the pain would ever go away. Even thoughts of the mysterious visitor were preferable to this.

And so it was with a tiny sigh of surrender that she admitted she was making a pot of stew much larger than she needed for just herself that afternoon. It was miserable out, she rationalized. And if he was out in this without shelter, he would need a hot meal.

"So what are you going to do?" she muttered as she paused in her stirring of the thick stew to put another log on the fire in the big, fieldstone fireplace. "Send him an engraved invitation to dinner?"

Gus made a low, whining sound, and she turned her head to look at him.

"Sorry, sweetie. Don't mind me talking to myself." She sighed, and the big, brown head tilted attentively. "Maybe they're right, maybe I am too soft."

Like Daddy. Her eyes began to sting, and she blinked rapidly to stop the tears that were always so close now. He would have considered everything. He always gave anyone a chance to explain, then weighed what he was told against his own generous but exacting scale of fairness.

He always *had*. Kit made the correction she hadn't yet grown used to, even after nearly a month.

"Too soft," she whispered. "Nowadays it's don't trust the people you know, let alone strangers. Was it really that simple for you, Daddy? Are things so much more horrible now, or did you just refuse to believe it and keep on trusting?"

Gus whined again, lifting his ears, recognizing the questioning tone if not the words. Kit smiled at the shaggy beast and sat down on the hearth to pat his head.

"I'm really rambling, aren't I? I'll say this for you, old friend, you're a heck of a listener." The heavy, plumed tail wagged, and the whine became a whimper of pleasure. Kit smiled and gave herself a mental shake.

"So, if I can't invite him in, what do I do?"

She compromised by ladling a huge serving of the stew into a heavy pan, topping it with a thick slice of bread, placing a spoon across the bread and covering it all with the pan's tight-fitting lid. Then she went for her slicker, pulled it on and called for Gus. The dog looked through the open door at the pouring rain, then back at her face.

"I know it's wet out, but it doesn't look like it's going to stop, so it's now or never. Let's go, mutt."

She left the covered pot on the porch, then followed the loping dog across the clearing. Either he wasn't around, she thought, or Gus had decided he wasn't a threat after all. Or perhaps the heavy rain had blunted even Gus's sharp senses.

Their usual hour of rambling over the mountain was more than Kit wanted to tackle in this weather, and Gus was ready to head back the moment he'd taken care of matters, but she made the big dog wait anyway. Maybe her instincts were right and she had nothing to fear from this man, but she wasn't sure enough to risk a confrontation. Even the gentlest animal could be dangerous when it felt cornered, and man was the most dangerous animal of all, her father had often told her.

When they finally went back, the pot was gone.

"Guess he's moved on," Jack Porter said as he carried the huge bag of dog food to the Jeep.

"Len?" Kit asked, puzzled. Jack had been trying again to convince her to let Len help her with the cord of wood he'd delivered yesterday. But the time she'd spent fending off Len's efforts at flirtation as Kevin Carter unloaded the firewood—heaven forbid Len should do such manual labor himself, she thought sourly—had convinced her that the last thing she wanted was to have him come back.

Not that he wasn't attractive; the big blonde was considered quite a catch in Lakeview, probably in the whole county. An eligible young man with a law degree was a rare find in this rural area. And if Kit found the fact that he was apparently in no hurry to put that degree to any use a sign of the laziness she suspected was a large part of his makeup, she kept it to herself. She just wished he would latch onto any of the dozen local girls who would love to be the recipient of his attentions.

"I meant that sneak-thief. You want this in the back?"

"No, on the seat, please. I'd never get it out of the back," she admitted, eyeing the fifty-pound bag. "Come on, Gus. If you want to eat, get out of the way."

The big dog scrambled to the back of the Jeep with a heartfelt sigh. Jack laughed as the bag of food landed on the seat of the Jeep with a thump and a creak of springs, and the big dog stretched out his neck to sniff at the bag and yip eagerly.

"Glad you have to feed him, and not me."

Kit laughed. She reached out and tugged the corner of the bag clear of the gear shift. She bit her lip, then asked, "What makes you think he moved on?"

"Sheriff was by this morning. Said he hasn't gotten any more reports of break-ins all week."

"Oh." Kit schooled her face to blankness.

"Good thing, too, Harve said. He's got enough on his plate with that hit-and-run."

"I hope he finds whoever it was," Kit said grimly as they walked back into the store. "*That's* who ought to be shot."

"I'm with you there, girl."

Olive was placing a large package wrapped in white paper into the box Kit had brought back to reuse. "An awful lot of hamburger there, dear," she said curiously.

"Uh, Gus eats a lot," she said hastily.

"Gus? You spoil that big galoot, Kit. Hamburger, indeed! Dog food's plenty good enough for him."

"I was only kidding." Why did I say that? Because you're a lousy liar, Kit answered herself. Then she said carefully, "I'll probably freeze any I don't use right away."

"Oh, I forgot, dear. Chris did buy that big freezer a few years back, didn't he?"

"Yes. I'll be stocking up now and then."

That should satisfy her, Kit thought as she climbed into the Jeep and started home, warning Gus severely of the dire consequences if he so much as looked at the package of meat. Olive's curiosity was a formidable thing; all of Lakeview knew that if you wanted to find something out, just nudge Olive in the right direction and you'd soon have your answer. She hoped she'd held her at bay, at least for a while.

It had continued to rain off and on all week, and she had to be careful on the rougher patches of road. There were drawbacks to living so far out, she thought, but the advantages far overwhelmed them. She'd never expected to find as much peace of mind as she'd found since she'd made the decision to accept the gift she hadn't wanted. Her heart had a ways to go yet, but for the first time she was beginning to think it might make it.

The soaring peaks, the sweet, pine-scented air, the openness of the high mountain meadows were all things she'd loved since as a child, her parents had first brought her to their cabin in the Sierras of eastern California. Their too infrequent visits held the most precious memories of her childhood: the freedom to run, the freshness of air unclouded by smog, and the wonder of the deer who came to taste the salt lick her father had placed at the edge of the clearing.

"Darn! The salt lick!"

Gus looked at her, as if startled by her exclamation.

"I meant to get a new one. The rain's practically washed away the old one. Guess it'll have to wait until next week, though. I'm not driving back down now—"

Her words broke off as Gus growled suddenly, menacingly. Before she could react, the dog leapt out of the back of the Jeep. All signs of the friendly, cavorting animal he usually was vanished as he streaked across the clearing with quick, darting glances. Gus was nowhere in sight. She called him. Nothing.

She raced into the house, rummaging in a drawer of the big, rolltop desk until she drew out a thin metal cylinder. It glinted silver in the sun as she ran back outside, lifting it to her mouth.

The faint sound of a distant bark wafted to her on the breeze. She waited a long moment, then blew again. Another bark, closer. He was coming back. She breathed a sigh of relief, thankful now for the time she'd spent teaching Gus to respond to the silent dog whistle. The people in her apartment building had been aghast enough when they'd seen the size of the animal she'd brought home from the shelter; she hadn't wanted to add to their disapproval by disturbing their peace every time she had to call him.

Something moved behind her. Her head snapped around, and her heart leapt as she tensed. She nearly laughed at her reaction to a harmless piece of fluttering blue cloth and took a deep breath to try to steady her racing pulse. Then her eyes narrowed. She walked toward the piece of cloth, which was apparently caught on the logs Len had unloaded on Wednesday.

It was a shirt. Or had been, she thought, looking at the mud stains that marked it, and the tear in one sleeve.

Her first reaction was to wonder what it was doing there. She didn't wonder whose it was; she knew who that shirt belonged to as surely as she knew that the scrambling sound she heard was Gus's big feet as he crossed the gravel drive.

But why had he left it here? Why had he been over here at the woodpile in the first place?

It came to her then, with the suddenness common to the conscious realization of something you'd been looking at for a time without really seeing it. She'd been staring at the shirt, but her peripheral vision had been registering other things: the ax now buried in the tree-stump chopping block instead of in its place in the toolshed, the pile of new kindling beside the stump, and the considerable pile of fireplace-size logs that had been neatly added to the winter-depleted stack.

Oddly, her first thought was that he'd managed to chop an awful lot of wood in the two hours she'd been gone. She felt that same, odd little tug that she'd felt when she'd come home and found the flowers. He must have worked up a sweat, even in the cool mountain air, and taken the shirt off, she mused. Then, as Gus skidded to a stop before her, her mind at last kicked into gear.

"What happened, boy?" She looked at the big animal; he seemed unhurt and unruffled except for the panting that accompanied his long run. She glanced again at the shirt. "He must have taken off in a hurry when he saw you coming. The proverbial hound of hell, that's you."

She scratched his ear, and he wriggled in pleasure. It should have been a ludicrous sight in such a huge dog, but coupled with those soulful brown eyes, Kit thought it was adorable. She looked at Gus carefully, not sure what she was looking for. Blood, maybe, she thought with a rueful chuckle.

"You didn't kill him, did you, Gus?" The dog barked. "So what did you do? Tree him?"

Gus barked again. Kit eyed him thoughtfully. Perhaps her joke wasn't far off the mark; she doubted if any human could outrun Gus if the dog's mind was set on catching him. She took a step forward and picked up the shirt.

The mud stains she'd noticed were faded, as if he'd tried to wash them out as best he could without soap. She held it up, noticing the breadth of the shoulders; if the shirt fit him, he was a strongly built man, she thought. She lifted the left sleeve, wondering what he'd torn it on.

She'd found the blood. And it was no longer funny; the brown mark she'd thought was just another mud stain was blood. It had soaked nearly the entire forearm of the shirt sleeve around the tear; obviously, whatever had torn the shirt had torn his flesh, as well. Her eyes flicked to Gus, then discarded the idea; she'd made sure Gus never confronted the man either. And he would hardly keep coming back if he'd tangled with the protective animal and gotten bitten.

He couldn't have been too badly hurt, she told herself, or he wouldn't have been able to chop wood at all, let alone do it at the pace he must have done to get so much accomplished. So he must be all right. Assuming, of course, she amended wryly, that Gus had left him in one piece just now.

"Hope you have another shirt," she murmured. "A warmer one," she added as she fingered the thin cotton cloth. Along with the rain this week it had been cool; this spring was shaping up to be a brisk one. And at night it was downright cold, especially up here on the mountain.

She walked back to the Jeep, holding the shirt thoughtfully. After she'd unloaded her purchases, she sat on the hearth, rekindling the fire that had burned down to embers since this morning, all the while staring at the shirt she'd draped over the back of her father's chair.

She got up, walked to the big picture window that looked out on the meadow in front of the cabin and peered at the threatening sky. It was going to rain again, at the least, she thought, and an early spring snow flurry wasn't out of the question at this altitude. She looked back at the shirt.

She determinedly went to the kitchen and began to gather the ingredients for the meat loaf she'd planned to make with the ground beef she'd bought. She'd never done as much cooking as she had since she'd moved here; she found, to her amazement, that she enjoyed it. Especially since she seemed to be cooking for three lately, she thought wryly: herself, Gus, and the man who left her flowers and chopped her wood.

When she had the meat ready for the oven she put it in the refrigerator, then went back to the fireplace and put on another log; it was going to be cold tonight. And when she turned around, there was the shirt again.

"Stop it," she muttered. "It's not your problem."

Gus lifted his head from where he sprawled before the fire.

"Oh, I know, if it's not my problem, why am I keeping you inside instead of letting you go chase this guy into the next county, like I should?"

Gus cocked his head, looking at her intently.

"I don't know why. And I'm not going to think about it. I," she said determinedly, "am going to take a nice, long, hot bath, and not think about anything!"

An hour later, when her toes and fingers resembled the rough surface of the logs the cabin had been built from, she tugged on a thick velour robe, pulled her damp hair up into a loose knot atop her head and padded out to the main room of the cabin. And came face to sleeve with that damned shirt again.

"All right!" she exclaimed, and ran upstairs to the loft. When she came back down, she set the sewing basket she'd brought on the table beside the big chair, then picked up the shirt. She took it to the kitchen and hand-washed it carefully, not trusting the heavy-duty washer not to rip it even more. Then she tossed it in the dryer she rarely used; she preferred the smell of clothes and sheets dried in the sweet mountain air. When the dryer buzzed, she knew the shirt was as clean as it was going to get and sat down to carefully mend the tear.

When she was done, she stepped out onto the covered porch to drape the shirt in plain sight over the railing. She drew a quick breath of the cold-tinged air; it definitely smelled like snow, she thought. She looked again at the cleaner but still thin cotton shirt, then went back inside to do what she'd known she would, although she'd tried to resist.

It took her a while before she found the box she wanted among those stacked in the storeroom. She bit her lip at the sight of her father's winter shirts and made herself pick a thick, heavy woolen one of blue plaid.

"I know you wouldn't mind, Daddy," she whispered. "It's just what you'd do."

The wind was beginning to pick up, so after she'd laid the heavy shirt out beside the mended one, she quickly got dressed and called for Gus. Making a noise that for all the world sounded like a grumble, the dog reluctantly followed her outside.

The wind was howling fiercely by the time they reached the end of the drive, and they had only gone a few yards down the paved county road when her guess proved right and it began to snow. Tiny flurries at first, but with all the bitter promise of a harsh spring blizzard.

"Come on, Gus!" she called after ten minutes. "Enough of this! We'll take the shortcut back."

The minute she turned to cut through the thick copse of pines, Gus leapt the split-rail fence in a single bound and raced off into the trees. She clambered over the fence and followed, wondering as the wind picked up even more whether it had been a wise choice. She had to dodge wind-whipped branches and more than once had to hold up her hands to protect her face and eyes from wind-driven pine needles and bits of debris.

She could hear Gus barking up ahead as she made her way slowly up the hill. Snowflakes began drifting down through the thick trees, got caught up in gusts of wind and swirled around her. She guessed that it was even worse out from under the protection of the trees; it had been the right choice after all.

Her breath caught in her throat as Gus's barking suddenly dropped to that low, threatening growl. She tried to hurry, but it was hard in the face of the unexpectedly strong wind. She was close enough now, she thought, that she could cut through the trees straight toward the cabin instead of following the path to where it came out at the base of the slope behind it.

She heard the ominous crack even as she turned to carry out her thoughts. She had time only to let out a tiny scream before the huge, wind-broken limb came down on her.

I wish Gus would hush up, Kit thought groggily. It can't be time to get up yet. I'm still too sleepy. I'm so sleepy I'm almost dizzy. And I'm cold. But I should be warm, and—oh, my head hurts, why won't Gus be quiet?

"Quiet, dog."

Ah, she thought at the sound of the low, male voice. Dad was up. He'd keep Gus quiet. She could go back to sleep now. Until her headache went away. But something was wrong, she thought vaguely, something she couldn't quite put her finger on. She shifted, but her legs were apparently so tangled in the covers that she couldn't move them. She tried again and felt that odd wave of dizziness sweep her again.

She heard a noise close by and tried to open her eyes, wondering why her eyelids seemed so very heavy. A shape swam before her, tall and solid and clad in familiar blue plaid. She knew then, and reassurance flooded her. Still, her voice sounded tiny and far away, even to her, when, as the big shape came closer, she whispered to it. "Daddy?"

The big shape stopped short, and she heard an odd sound. Then it bent, crouching over her. "Are you hurt?"

You sound funny, Dad, she tried to say, but no words came out. She blinked, wishing the world would stop spinning. She shook her head, sending a sharp pain knifing behind her eyes. She moaned despite herself, but the pain cleared her mind and her vision; when she opened her eyes again, she was looking up into the face of a stranger.

And she knew she'd better pray that her instincts had been accurate, because she was helplessly in the hands of the man the entire mountain was hunting.

Chapter 2

"**D**on't move."

Kit stared at him. Had his words been an order or a warning? Not that it mattered. Moving was impossible, even had she been so inclined. Her heart might be hammering as if trying to break free, but her body was pinned by the long, heavy branch. She couldn't speak; her mouth was too dry.

He knelt beside her, this man in her father's shirt, looking at the limb that held her down. She wondered if he was going to leave her there, then thought she might be better off, compared to several alternatives she could think of. God, she'd been a fool. They were all right about her.

She smothered a little cry as he moved quickly, grasping the thick branch at a spot just clear of her side. She saw the plaid shirt tighten over his broad shoulders, saw the strong hands and wrists flex as he lifted the heavy limb with an ease that made her feel small and fragile. Then he was back kneeling at her side, reaching out with one hand.

Gus growled warningly, and she saw the man jerk back. She was surprised the dog hadn't taken a chunk out of him already; he usually didn't let anyone get this close to her unless she told him it was okay. She tried to sit up, but her head began to spin again, and she fell back.

The man in her father's shirt glanced at the dog, then back to her. He let out a compressed breath.

"I guess you've got a decision to make."

His voice was low and deep, and it made her feel funny, like she'd felt when she saw the flowers and the chopped wood. She met his gaze. His eyes were blue, she thought as her vision steadied once more, although blue seemed an inadequate adjective for the clear, intense color that seemed even more vivid next to the thick fringe of dark eyelashes. They seemed to hold concern, as if he were worried about her, but she told herself she was being ridiculous. But there was no denying that they were eyes shadowed with weariness, and she had a distinct impression of a man on the edge of his strength, running on sheer nerve.

He waited, but she was so wrapped up in her study of him that she didn't realize what he was waiting for. His hair was just as dark and thick as his lashes, she thought. His jaw was shadowed with several days' growth of beard, but it didn't disguise the leanness of his face. Natural leanness, she wondered, or the result of skimpy rations lately?

Finally, when she didn't respond to his words, he spoke again.

"Can you move?"

Startled out of her reverie, Kit tried to sit up once more. A little cry escaped her, and her hand went to her head.

"It seems you don't have a decision to make after all," he said grimly.

Kit looked up at him, wide-eyed now, shivering a little from the cold.

"Look, I know you don't trust me. I don't blame you. But I won't hurt you."

His voice was so quiet, so soothing, his eyes so gentle, that Kit wanted to believe him. She wanted to believe she'd been right all along, but face-to-face with the reality of this man who had clearly been living on the run, she found it hard to cling to that instinctive feeling.

Her doubt must have shown on her face, because he repeated, "I won't hurt you." He glanced down at the shirt he wore and added softly, "I owe you too much."

Kit wondered where her voice had gone. It seemed all she could do was stare at him. He watched her for a moment; then it was as if a shutter had come down over the blue eyes, cutting off all emotion and warmth. It was as if, she thought incredulously, she'd hurt him somehow, and he had to close himself off from the pain.

"You're afraid of me."

It wasn't a question. And quite suddenly it wasn't true. She couldn't be afraid of someone who could look like that.

"All right, I'll go. Stay here." His words were short, clipped and emotionless. "Don't try to move. I'll call someone from your phone. They'll come for you."

At last Kit found her voice. "Wait."

He stopped.

"I was . . . just startled. And a little groggy. I'm not afraid."

He looked down at her for a long moment. "Maybe you should be."

Bitterness tinged his voice. She held his gaze levelly, despite her shivering. "No. I don't think so."

Something flickered in that blue gaze, something alive and vital, banishing that flat, dead look. And once more he knelt beside her.

"You've got to get inside and get warm." He glanced at the watchful Gus, sitting on his haunches close beside her. "But you're going to have to call off the moose," he finished wryly.

"He's . . . a little protective."

"A little?" Unexpectedly, a glint of humor lit his eyes for a split second. Then it was gone, and he said softly, "I can understand that."

Kit felt her cheeks heat and was instantly furious with herself. She tried a third time to sit up; this time she was stopped by a strong but gentle hand on her shoulder. Gus scrambled to his feet, a strange sound that was half growl, half whimper issuing from him.

"Easy, boy," Kit soothed, knowing the animal was confused. "It's okay. Shh now." The dog subsided, although he still eyed the man suspiciously.

Kit had expected him to help her to her feet and barely suppressed a cry of surprise when instead he simply slid his arms beneath her knees and shoulders and lifted her easily.

"I can walk," she protested.

"Sure you can," he said easily. "But why should you?"

Kit wasn't sure she liked this turn of events. Not because it made her uneasy, but because it was too comfortable. Because the arms that held her were strong and steady. Because he was cradling her so carefully, so gently. But most of all because she felt an almost irresistible urge to rest her head against his chest. For the first time since her father had died, she didn't feel quite so bereft, quite so alone. . . .

She stiffened sharply at her own treacherous thoughts. She was still groggy, that was all, she told herself firmly, and resolutely kept her head upright.

His long strides seemed to cover the distance in a remarkably short time, and she remembered how tall he had looked as he'd stood beside her. At least six feet, probably more. And she guessed he was as broad in the shoulders as his shirt had suggested, although it was hard to tell beneath the thick wool of the overshirt.

The snow was coming thickly now, but he seemed to ignore it as they crossed the clearing. Gus was at his heels, obviously not convinced of the trustworthiness of this man who held his beloved mistress.

He carried her inside, and Kit noticed that he held the door an extra second to let Gus in. He saw her glance and gave her a wry look.

"I figured if I shut him out, he'd just take the door down."

Kit laughed, a little surprised that she was capable of it under the circumstances. He set her down on the sofa and flipped on the lamp on the end table. Before she could move, he knelt before her and pulled off her wet boots. Quickly he helped her shrug out of her heavy shearling jacket, then took the thick, brightly patterned Navajo blanket from the back of the sofa and tucked it around her. He adjusted two of the throw pillows behind her as easily as if he did this every day, then leaned forward to look at the side of her head.

"Didn't break the skin," he said at last, "but it's a nasty bump." He paused. "Are you still groggy?"

She started to shake her head, then thought better of it. "No. I'm fine now."

He let out a breath. "Maybe you should see a doctor."

Kit started to answer, then stopped as all the ramifications struck her. If she could drive, she didn't really need a doctor, and if she needed a doctor, she shouldn't drive. But if she couldn't drive, there was no way to get to the small clinic in town; he certainly couldn't take her, not when the whole town was looking for him. And she knew when he met her eyes, then quickly looked away, that he knew exactly what she was thinking.

"I'm fine," she repeated.

She meant it. She was steadier now, although her head was still aching. He looked at her, doubt showing in his eyes. And just before he looked away again, she saw a flash of pure misery darken the brilliant blue.

"The dizziness is gone. All I need is a couple of aspirin," she said lightly.

She saw him take a deep breath; then his head came up. "Do you have any?"

She pointed. "Over in the desk. Middle drawer."

"How about ice?"

"In the freezer, out in the kitchen." She started to gesture toward the door, then stopped, remembering. "Never mind. You know where it is."

He looked at her, as if trying to determine whether there was any sarcasm in the words. After a moment he only nodded. After getting the aspirin from the desk, he walked toward the door she'd been about to indicate. When he came back he had a glass of water, the aspirin, and several cubes of ice wrapped carefully in a towel. He gave her the pills, and she took them dutifully. Then, urging her to lean back against the pillows, he placed the icy bundle carefully over the bump on her head.

She offered to hold it, but he shook his head. She let him then, relaxing against the pillows, her eyes drifting closed. The silence stretched out, and she had nearly dozed off when she felt his touch on her arm. She opened her eyes.

"Maybe you shouldn't go to sleep," he said softly.

"Afraid I won't wake up?"

He lowered his eyes. "Something like that." He stood up quickly. "I'll get some more ice."

This time, although she still lay back against the pillows, she watched from him from under half-lowered lashes. Here in the light she could see that he was younger than she had at first thought, or perhaps it was just that the look of strain had eased a little now. Not much older than her own twenty-three, she guessed, twenty-five or six perhaps. Unless you looked at his eyes, she thought. Then he looked old, and utterly weary.

A shock of tousled dark hair fell over his forehead in counterpoint to the hard, stubbled line of his jaw and chin. Thick, dark hair lay softly against the back of his neck, in vulnerable contrast to the strong, corded tendons of his throat. Boyish, yet undeniably an adult male. It was a potent combination.

And you, Kit told herself sternly, are letting your imagination run away with you. She opened her eyes fully and sat up. He drew back the towel, wet now from the melting ice, and looked at her questioningly.

"No, I'm fine, really. It barely aches now."

After a moment he nodded, then frowned when she made as if to stand up.

"I just want to try. If I get wobbly, I'll sit back down."

He hesitated, then backed up enough to give her room, yet staying close enough to reach her if she faltered. She noticed it, and her eyes went to his face. There *was* concern there, she admitted, wondering why that made her feel so odd. He watched her as she slowly stood up. She was only slightly light-headed, and only for an instant. When the feeling faded, she smiled.

He pulled back, staring at her, then drew a deep, almost harsh breath before looking away. "I'll put this back," he said hastily, holding up the towel.

"And now that I'm reasonably sure I won't fall over, I can finish dinner, even though it's a bit late."

She said it casually, cheerfully, and it was a moment before his gaze snapped back to her.

"What?"

"Meat loaf. I fixed it earlier. It just needs to go in the oven for an hour."

He looked at her blankly.

"You don't like meat loaf?"

"No. I mean yes. I—" He shook his head sharply, his expression that of a man who hoped the movement might jog his tired brain into functioning just a little longer.

"Might as well eat inside for a change, then."

She started for the kitchen, fully aware of him staring after her. She put the pan in the oven and set the temperature, then called Gus. After she'd fed him, the dog took up his usual station in the corner of the room, tolerating, if not welcoming, the presence of a stranger in his domain.

Their meal started out very quietly. He'd commented on the luscious smell as the meal cooked, asked if he could help, but after he'd taken the plates and silverware to the big oak table, he'd fallen into silence.

His only action was to periodically walk to the window and look outside. She didn't know if he was restless or truly worried about what—or who—might be out there. He hadn't taken off the heavy plaid shirt, although it was more than warm enough in the house; she wondered if he'd been cold so long that he enjoyed the excess heat. Or maybe he was just afraid she'd want it back.

As she cut thick slices of bread, Kit heard his stomach growl loudly, and when she looked over her shoulder she caught him glancing at her furtively, embarrassment clear on his face.

"Good thing I made plenty," was all she said, but her mind was busy. A burglar who blushed? Not a chance, she thought. There was more to this, to him. Much more than everyone assumed.

"Water? Coffee? Beer? Or something stronger?" she asked after she'd taken the steaming, savory meat loaf out of the oven.

His head came up sharply; he'd been toying with a fork as if it had come from a collection of fascinating antiquities. "I—anything."

She read his look. "What?"

His mouth quirked. "I—do you have a Coke?"

"Coming up," she said lightly. A blushing burglar who turned down beer or booze for a soda? With every minute that passed, she was becoming more and more certain her instincts had been right; she had nothing to fear from this man.

The way he attacked the food she set before him told her worlds about the way he'd been eating until now. Then he caught himself, and she could see him make a conscious effort to slow down.

"Don't stand on ceremony on my account," she said. "I can guess what you've been living on."

"You gave me most of it," he muttered, but he dug in without any further pretense at manners or refinement. He finished a sizable portion, along with all the remaining bread she'd sliced. He savored the bubbling cola as if it were the finest of champagnes. He glanced at the clock on the stove, which registered nearly nine-thirty. And at last, setting down the empty glass, he looked across the table at her.

"Why?" he asked.

Kit knew what he meant, but since she hadn't figured out an answer, she stalled. "What?"

"Why?" he repeated, the look in his vivid blue eyes telling her that he knew she knew what he meant.

"I . . . I'm not sure."

"You took a hell of a chance, helping me."

Kit's mouth quirked involuntarily as she remembered the hours she'd spent pondering that very fact. "Believe me, I know."

"Why?" he asked a third time.

"Maybe I just couldn't get as riled up as the others did over a can of beans."

His expression grew bleak. He got up and once more walked to the window to peer out into the oddly whitened night. When he spoke, his voice was as tired as his eyes. "I didn't want to.... I knew they'd be upset, but I hoped..." He let out a tightly held breath. "Of course they're angry. I broke into their homes, stole from them...."

"Only food," she said quietly when he broke off.

"It's still stealing."

So her burglar had a conscience as well, Kit thought. "You sound like them," she said with an ironic little laugh. "Up in arms, as if you'd taken the family heirlooms instead of baked beans they probably wouldn't have eaten anyway."

He turned around to look at her, a grimace twisting his mouth. "It did seem to be what everybody had the most of. And you were right. I was sick of them." He walked back to the table and looked at the considerably depleted meal. "I guess it shows," he admitted. "I'm sorry. I didn't mean to eat you out of a week's worth of food."

Kit shrugged. "I was going to leave most of it for you anyway."

He stared at her, then opened his mouth as if to speak, but no words came out. At last he shook his head. "I don't understand you."

"I don't understand me, either." She gave him that wry smile again. "But then, neither does anybody else."

His dark brows lowered. "'Anybody else'?"

"Any of the up-in-arms contingent."

"You...told them?" he asked tensely. "That you were...helping me?"

She sensed his tautness and said quickly, "No. They already think I'm half crazy anyway, and that sure wouldn't help."

"Why do they think that?"

Kit grimaced. "They think I'm too soft, like my father. He always said there are a lot of throwbacks in the people around here. Back to when you minded your own business and stealing a horse—'' she gave him a sideways glance '' — or a can of beans, was a hanging offense.''

''You don't agree?'' he asked quietly.

''Let's just say I take more convincing than they do. My father always taught me to consider extenuating circumstances. He—''

She stopped abruptly, aware simultaneously of the oddity of talking so openly to this possibly dangerous stranger and of the relief of it; had she isolated herself too much, for too long?

He looked at her for a long, silent moment. When she didn't go on, he looked away and walked back to the window, looking out at the snow that was still coming down. And at last he pulled off the heavy overshirt, and Kit realized it had been more a matter of lack of inner fuel to keep warm than anything else that had made him wear it even in the warmth of the oven-heated kitchen.

Without the concealing bulk of the wool shirt, she could see that he was as broad and strongly built as she'd thought. His back and shoulders filled the shirt, then tapered down to a slim, taut waist and hips emphasized by the close-fitting jeans that were worn, grubby and torn at one knee. That reminded her, and she lifted her gaze to the mended sleeve of his own shirt, and the stain around the tear that she hadn't quite been able to remove.

''What happened to your arm?''

He jerked around, then glanced down at himself as if he'd forgotten. ''I cut it,'' he said shortly.

''On what? It must have been deep. There was a lot of blood.''

''It looked messier than it was. It's fine now.''

''But if it was something rusty, you might need a tetanus shot.''

''I've had one.''

''Lately?''

''Yes. My boss made sure I kept up—''

He broke off suddenly, as if realizing he had nearly let something slip that he didn't want to. Kit felt a flicker of irritation; apparently it was okay for her to trust him without knowing a thing about him, but he wasn't about to trust her any more than he had to. But then her irritation faded as she realized that, of the two of them, he had considerably more to lose if he misplaced his trust.

"I'm sorry," he said softly, startling her. "I can't."

He'd read her perfectly, she realized ruefully. Her father had always said she utterly lacked a poker face; obviously it was true.

"I've got a decent first-aid kit, if you'd like me to look at it."

"Really, I think it's all right. I cleaned it out at the lake, down by the flats, and it stopped bleeding fairly quickly."

"Let me look anyway. If you've been sleeping out in the rain and mud, it could be infected."

Chagrin flashed across his face. "Actually, I've been sleeping in your toolshed the last couple of nights."

Startled, she glanced at Gus. Then she realized it was her own fault for giving the dog such mixed signals. No wonder he'd been confused about what to do when the man he'd known had been around had suddenly appeared close up.

"Well, if you've been sleeping in there, I'd definitely better get the first-aid kit," she said, "because I *know* that place is filthy. I don't think it's been cleaned in a year."

"But it's dry." He smiled a little crookedly. "And it cuts the wind."

My burglar also has a dynamite smile, Kit thought, then groaned inwardly at this habit she'd picked up of referring to him as "my burglar." He was looking at her steadily, and something in that bright blue gaze unsettled her. She hastily began to gather the dishes.

"I'll get the first-aid kit as soon as this is cleared," she said.

"I'll do that."

"But—"

"I'll do it."

Surrendering, and grateful to get away from that intense gaze, she scurried into the bathroom and got out the well-stocked white box marked with a red cross. The dishes were soaking in hot soapy water when she got back, and he was rinsing the glasses he'd already washed.

"It's waited two days," he said when she tried to get him to abandon the task. "It can wait a few more minutes."

Only when he'd thoroughly finished the last dish did he let her lead him into the great room. He sat in the desk chair she indicated and rested his arm on his knee as she pulled the desk lamp over and turned it on.

She smothered a gasp when he rolled up the sleeve she'd mended. A nasty, crooked cut ripped across his muscled forearm. But he'd been right, it looked relatively clean, and thankfully free from infection.

"What did you do this on?" she asked again as she dug out antiseptic. It might not do any good at this late date, she thought, but it couldn't hurt.

"Barbed wire." He winced as she swabbed the length of the cut; it had already begun to heal, but the antiseptic was still painfully strong.

"Able's place?"

He looked at her quizzically. "I don't know. Why?"

"He's the only one around that uses it. To keep livestock away from his bees."

"Bees?"

"He's got several hives," she explained as she set aside the antiseptic and the ball of cotton she'd used. "He's the local honey entrepreneur."

"Then I'm glad it kept me away, too. The last thing I needed was to stumble into an apiary."

She laughed lightly. "Able's bees don't have much tolerance for anyone but him," she agreed. "As soon as it's dry I'll wrap it up," she said, reaching for the box of sterile gauze.

He nodded. Then he glanced from the rolled back sleeve to her face. "Thanks for fixing my shirt."

"Sure."

She didn't look at him as she opened the box and unrolled a length of the gauze. He had put his other elbow on the desk and propped his head up on his hand, as if he were too weary to hold it up any longer. She reached for the scissors in the kit. She cut the gauze, then reached for the roll of adhesive tape. And nearly dropped it when he spoke.

"That's a good picture of you."

She looked up, puzzled. He was looking at the familiar cherished photo in the antique silver frame that she had loved to hold as a child.

"That's not me," she said with a laugh. "That's my mother."

"Oh. I thought it was you."

"Are you sure *you* aren't the one who got knocked in the head? I don't look anything like her."

"But you do. Your hair is thick and dark and silky, like that—" he gestured at the picture "—and you have the same upturned nose. Your eyes are that incredible color, too, like amber flecked with gold. And—"

"You're being silly," Kit said a little breathlessly, telling herself he was only saying those things to be kind to someone who was helping him. "I'm just plain old me. She was beautiful."

His head snapped around sharply. "What?"

"She was beautiful," Kit repeated. "I'm too tall, and my mouth is too big. She was tiny and sweet and delicate. Like an old-fashioned tea rose."

"And you don't think you are?"

"Me, a rose?" She laughed again. "A sunrose, maybe."

"A sunrose?"

"A tough little guy. Leathery leaves, and flowers so bright and garish they make you blink. Nothing subtle or delicate or beautiful about 'em."

"Where do they grow?" he asked softly, and she had the oddest feeling there was more to his question than a desire for a gardening lesson.

"Anywhere you plant them," she told him. "They make do with about any conditions you can throw at them."

"I think I could have guessed that."

His eyes told her he wasn't talking about flowers anymore, and she couldn't stop the color that crept into her face.

"You said 'was.' Your mother's dead?"

"Yes."

After a moment he asked, "When?"

"A long time ago. And it was a relief for her in the end. She'd been sick a long time, and she knew how hard it was on my father and me."

"I'm sorry." He glanced back at the photograph. "It's just the two of you now, then? You and your father?"

She didn't think her expression changed, but when he spoke again, his voice was as soft as a caress.

"Him, too?"

She made herself say it. "A month ago."

"Ah, little sunrose, I'm sorry."

Kit's breath caught at the gentleness in his tone. The stinging began anew behind her eyelids, and she blinked rapidly, desperate not to cry in front of him. She didn't even understand why she was telling him this, except that it felt so good to talk to someone who didn't have any preconceptions about her father, someone who was sympathetic without being pitying.

Admit it, she told herself ruefully. You're as vulnerable as a seedling that's just cleared the surface right now, and he's a good listener. Too good a listener.

"It was his shirt you left for me, wasn't it?"

She nodded. "I . . . He was really why I did it. All of it. It was . . . the kind of thing he would do."

"Helping a . . . thief?"

"No. Helping a man who was desperate enough to steal food to live, but honorable enough not to touch other things much more precious to their owners."

She heard him suck in a breath, but no words came. After a long, silent moment, she looked up at him. Those vivid eyes were fastened on her intently, unwaveringly.

"Your father," he said slowly, "must have been an exceptional man."

"He was." Unexpectedly, just when she thought she had them controlled, the tears spilled over. "I'm sorry. I still miss him so much."

He reached out, brushing at the tears with a touch so gentle it only expanded the emotional tide.

"You always will, sunrose. Something like that never goes away. But if you're lucky, it gets so you can live with it."

He spoke with the bleakness of bitter experience. But it was what she'd needed, to hear the acknowledgment of the pain and her right to it, instead of the platitudes that insisted time would heal, that she should put it behind her. And she knew that somehow she must have sensed that he knew that kind of pain; it was why, she supposed, she'd opened up to him like . . . like a sunrose to a spring rain.

She looked at him, her eyes still wide and wet from tears, her lips quivering a little with her effort to stem the flow. And suddenly she saw that shutter drop in his eyes, again cutting off all warmth and emotion. It was as if the door had suddenly blown open, letting in a blast of chill snowy air.

"If you'll finish that, I'll get out of your way."

His voice was flat, inflectionless, and Kit stared at him. What had happened? It was like looking into some carved immobile mask, as if the last few minutes had never been. It was the most implacable face she'd ever seen, and she knew instinctively it would do her no good to try to change it. Perhaps she'd brought it on herself, she thought as she began to neatly bandage his arm. She'd given him warmth and shelter, had fed him, and now he had his strength back, the strength that enabled him to look like that.

"Thank you," he said formally when she'd finished. "You're very good at that."

She looked down at the arm covered with neat, spiral turns of gauze. "My father taught me a lot of things." She didn't know what else to say in the face of his sudden coolness.

"He should have taught you that you're as lovely as—"

His gruff words stopped abruptly. He stood up, and walked quickly toward the front window. Kit couldn't help staring at him, wondering foolishly what the rest of his words would have been.

"What's your name?"

The quiet, unexpected question, coming with his back still to her, caught her off guard. She answered without thinking. "Kit."

He looked over his shoulder, one brow lifted. "Kit?"

"For my father. His name is—was Christopher." He turned around at the catch in her voice, and seeing the softness in his eyes, she risked the question. He owed her at least that much, she thought.

"Do you have a name?" The moment she said it, she saw in his face that he wasn't going to tell her. "All right," she said stiffly. "I guess I'll just call you what the rest of the town's calling you."

He winced, his eyes closing as if she'd slapped him. When he opened them again, it was to look over his shoulder into a world still white with blowing snow. She saw him shiver, then saw him consciously stop it. Then he looked back at her. The chill that had overtaken his eyes was gone.

"I'm sorry...Kit. I can't. But once I get out of here, you'll be all right."

She'd be all right? Of course she would, she thought. Why wouldn't she?

"Thank you. For everything."

"You're welcome," she answered automatically, absurdly, as if this were a normal conversation, under normal circumstances.

He was looking at her intently, as if he were trying to memorize her every feature. That look sent a little frisson down her spine, and she nearly shivered as he had done.

"Goodbye, Kit," he said softly.

"Good—are you crazy?" she cried, suddenly realizing that he had every intention of walking out that door into a bitter spring snowstorm.

"Probably."

"You can't go out there! There's practically a blizzard going on out there, in case you hadn't noticed."

"I noticed."

Of course he had, she thought. He'd been going back and forth to every window since he'd been in the cabin. He'd

been as restless as a caged cougar, as watchful as a field
mouse with a hawk circling overhead.

Watchful. It came to her then, and it surprised her with
its sting.

"Are you afraid I'll turn you in?"

His dark brows rose. Then he smiled, a crooked, sheep-
ish smile that testified to the sincerity of his words. "That
was the one thing that *didn't* occur to me."

She didn't want to analyze the solace she found in that
declaration. "Then why are you going out there?"

"Is that an invitation to stay?"

He said it with a raised eyebrow and Kit felt herself
blush.

"I wish I could, sunrose." His voice was low, serious
now. "But it's not safe."

"Not safe?" Realization flooded in; for a moment,
amazingly, she'd forgotten. "But it is," she told him, remembering Jack's words. "They're not looking for you
around here anymore."

He froze, staring at her. The chill she'd seen before was
a heat wave compared to the ice that glazed over his eyes
now. He crossed the room in three long strides and grabbed
her by the shoulders. She nearly cried out, his grip was so
fierce.

"What do you mean?"

His voice was harsh, and as menacing as the look in those
frozen eyes.

"I . . . The sheriff," she gasped out. "He thinks you're
gone."

For one long, tense moment he stood there, rigid, his
fingers digging into her shoulders with a strength that made
his earlier gentleness seem even more incredible. Then,
slowly, she saw the thaw come, as thoroughly and inexorably as spring. And when it reached his eyes, he let go of
her.

"The sheriff," he muttered, as if the thought had never
occurred to him. "Of course. The sheriff." He expelled a
harsh breath. "I—I'm sorry, Kit."

She stared up at him, still shaken.

"I scared you. I didn't mean to. I just thought..."

"Thought what?" Her voice was barely a whisper.

"I..."

"What?"

"I thought...you were one of them." It broke from him as if against great resistance.

"One of who?" Her voice was stronger now, steadier, as her mind regained control of her sudden fear.

"I... Nobody."

"If you didn't mean the sheriff, then who?"

"Never mind."

Irritation flickered in Kit again. How could he say something like that and expect her to just forget it? How could he—

His words came back to her then. *It's not safe.* What kind of words were those from a man prepared to thrust himself out into conditions that could quite likely kill him? Unless...

"Just whose safety are you worried about?" she asked softly. She saw the answer in his weary eyes before he could avert them. "Then there is someone else, isn't there? Besides the sheriff? I wouldn't have anything to fear from him."

"Kit, don't. The less you know, the better. I've got to go."

"And leave me to explain your frozen body when the storm is over? Thank you."

"I'll be all right."

She just looked at him.

"Kit, I've got to get out of here."

She glanced at Gus, who was watching them with interest from near the crackling fire. "He could stop you."

He looked at the big dog. "He probably could. But he'd have to chew me up to do it, Kit. And I don't think you'd let him do that."

It had been a bluff, anyway, so Kit didn't argue with him. "Why go out there? No one is going to be out in this." She gestured toward the window.

He sighed. She'd never heard so exhausted a sound. "I wish I could believe that."

She stared at him in disbelief. "What could make anyone risk this?"

"Kit..."

"What could be so important?"

He let out a low, compressed breath, then looked at her face, his blue eyes holding her amber gaze.

"Me," he said at last. And then, bluntly, he added one more word. "Dead."

Chapter 3

She couldn't doubt him. There was too much certainty in his voice, too much grim knowledge shadowing his blue eyes. Still, all she could do was whisper, stunned, "What?"

He shook his head. "No, Kit. I've already told you too much."

"You haven't told me anything! Not even your name!" she burst out. "You expect me to believe someone's out to kill you over a few cans of—"

"It has nothing to do with that."

That silenced her. For the first time she had a sense of being far beyond her depth, grappling with some unknown, dark menace with enough power to drive even this strong man to desperation. She watched as he walked to the door. His hand was on the knob before she found her voice again.

"You'll freeze to death out there tonight."

Her voice was as flat as if she had already fallen victim to that icy fate. He looked back at her.

"I'm sorry, Kit. I never should have stopped here. I should have kept moving." His shoulders slumped as he drew a long breath, then said quietly, "But I was so damned tired."

"You still are. Too tired to slog through that. Too tired to keep moving, like you'd have to. Hypothermia can hit awfully fast." She looked out the window at the frigid night. "You might as well just go down to the lake and jump in. Make it quicker." She smothered a chuckle, knowing that if it escaped, it would sound harsh and bitter. "Save them the trouble, whoever they are."

"Kit..."

"You know what's crazy? I should be wondering why someone wants to kill you. I should be wondering if maybe they have good reason, if maybe you've done something horrible..."

He stiffened, icing over once more, his face tightening into harsh forbidding lines that made him look as if he were carved out of the same granite as the mountain.

"But all I can think of are those flowers, and the wood, and you washing the damned dishes...."

She turned back to him then, knowing that her eyes were bright with moisture and not caring. She saw the ice leave his eyes, saw the blue darken. When the words came, they were in the strained tone of a man who had lost the battle not to speak.

"I've...done some horrible things, Kit. Maybe enough to...deserve it. But not now. Not this."

She believed him. Perhaps she was a fool, or perhaps she trusted too much in her father's ways, but she believed him. And now that she'd decided that, the rest of her choices were easy.

"Even if they are crazy enough to be out in this," she said after a moment, "they'd never make it up here. Not until the snowplow clears the road tomorrow. The snow always drifts up because of that grove of trees, and no one can get through."

He looked at her for a long, silent moment. Then he shook his head. "If you're wrong...if anything happened to you, I..."

"I may not have the slightest idea of what's going on, but I do know this place and how isolated it is in a snowstorm." Her mouth quirked. "It was what my mother hated about it. And besides—" She snapped her fingers. Gus leapt to his feet and was at her side in an instant. "—I've got him."

He smiled, but it was halfhearted. "Sunrose, he may be a moose, and I've no doubt he'd die for you, but he can't stop a bullet."

She paled a little but answered steadily, "But he can warn us."

An odd expression flitted over his face at that last word. "And then what do we do?" he asked softly.

Her mouth was open to tell him about her father's guns in the bedroom closet, but, perhaps a bit tardily, her common sense kicked in. Or a belated sense of self-preservation, she thought wryly. She knew so little about him; telling him about what could be a last line of defense seemed a bit foolhardy. Wondering at the strange limits her mind drew, she shrugged.

"We improvise."

He shook his head in wonder. "They're wrong. You're not half-crazy, you're certifiable."

"If that means I don't want to feel responsible for you dying out there, then yes, I am."

"You wouldn't be—"

"But I would feel that way."

He stared at her. Then his mouth twitched at the corners. "Tell me," he said conversationally, "are sunroses stubborn?"

"Try and get rid of them and they'll just grow back," she countered sweetly.

"I thought so." He shook his head again. "Okay, Kit. I'm too tired to fight you anymore."

"You were too tired in the first place," she told him. "You were just too stubborn to admit it."

"Me? You're the—"

"Sunrose, remember?" she said quickly, cutting him off. "There's a folding bed upstairs, if you want, or the couch down here isn't too bad."

The look he gave her then made her feel oddly warm, but he answered easily enough.

"The couch is fine. It'll be a featherbed, after where I've been sleeping."

"I'll get you a pillow and a blanket."

"Thank you." She turned to go. "Kit?"

She looked back.

"I—" He stopped, and when he went on, she knew it wasn't what he'd been going to say. "Could I borrow your shower?"

"No."

He looked so taken aback that she couldn't keep a straight face.

"I don't have one," she said with a smothered grin. "You're welcome to the bathtub, though."

His mouth twisted sardonically. "Thanks. I didn't figure you'd mind if I smelled a bit less like a wet skunk." He sniffed expressively. "Matter of fact, neither would I."

"Good thing I have a huge water heater."

At her smile, that odd look flitted across his face once more. But he only nodded.

"I may take all of it."

"Save some and I'll throw your clothes in the washer."

"Just get them close," he said ruefully. "They'll be able to jump in on their own."

Later she checked the stitching she'd done on his shirt sleeve, then gingerly picked up the grubby jeans from where he'd abandoned them outside the bathroom door. She heard a small splash from inside, followed by a sigh of utter bliss.

A smile curved her mouth; she knew that feeling, that luxurious sensation of heat and relaxation as the steaming water wrapped around you. It was why she had never bothered to add a shower. The antique, claw-footed tub was perfect, deep enough to let you soak clear up to your neck—although he was probably too tall for that, she thought—and shaped so that the curved lip was the perfect place to rest your head.

"Don't fall asleep," she warned teasingly through the door, remembering all the times when she'd done just that.

"If I'm not out in a hour, come get me."

His voice was low, husky, vibrant with a low note she didn't recognize. It was the pleasure of the hot water, she told herself sternly. Poor man probably hadn't washed in anything but cold lake water for days.

She gathered his clothes and carried them to the washer. Automatically she checked the jeans before she put them in, finding only a battered pocket knife, which she set on the counter. She reached for the soap, fighting the images that suddenly rose before her eyes. Images of a strong, male body stretched naked in her tub, skin glistening with water, vivid eyes veiled by thick, dark lashes half-lowered in enjoyment. It didn't take much of a leap for her mind to change the pleasure of a soothing, hot bath to pleasure of another kind, equally hot, and color soared into her cheeks.

Kit Cameron, you cut that out right now!

She emphasized her inward censure with the slam of the washer's lid. She pushed the buttons with unnecessary fervor, added a healthy dollop of soap, and then a bit more. She hit the button to start the cycle, then turned smartly on her heel.

"There!"

And no more silly thoughts, she told herself. Maybe you are too isolated here, when you let the first attractive man who comes along do this to you. Well, not the first, she supposed. Len Porter was attractive enough, but he'd certainly never set her to speculating about what he'd look like lolling in her bathtub.

But then, Len probably wore baggy boxer shorts, too, not snug, blue briefs like the ones that were twirling in her washing machine right now.

Stop it! No more, she ordered herself fiercely. No more bathtub scenes going on in your head, no more imagining what he looks like in only those blue cotton briefs, no more

ridiculous wondering what it would be like if his invitation
to come get him had been meant as sexily as it sounded.

"I *am* going crazy," she said mournfully to Gus when he
came to nuzzle her hand as she sat at the kitchen table.
"Sitting here watching that stupid machine like it was the
movie of the week."

Gus yelped, and Kit shook her head.

"Pretty silly, huh? Okay, out of here, pal. We'll go read
a book or something. This won't be done for half an hour
anyway. I'll just—"

Uh-oh, she thought. No matter how she added this up,
she had one set of wet clothes and one naked man. Who
would most likely not hide in the bathroom until his clothes
were dry. Not when there were perfectly good towels in
there to wrap himself in. Towels that, in view of her re-
cently overactive imagination, were not nearly big enough.

Gus's toenails clattered on the floor as he followed her
dash to the storeroom.

"No, Gus, you can't come in. It's tight enough as it is in
here."

She found the box she wanted, and inside it the thick,
terry cloth garment she'd been looking for. A faint trace of
menthol shaving cream and a touch of a woodsy after-shave
clung to it, and for a long moment she clutched it to her,
drawing in deep, comforting breaths of the loved, familiar
scents. Then, before the memories and the sadness could
overwhelm her again, she gathered up the robe and hurried to drape it over the bathroom doorknob.

She was just beginning to wonder if she was truly going
to be faced with the task of rousting him out of the tub
when she heard the door open. She turned her attention to
the book in her lap, staring at it as if she'd been raptly involved instead of listening for any sound from the bathroom.

"I almost did fall asleep in there. That's quite a tub."

She looked up then, and her breath caught. The pale blue
of the robe turned his eyes the color of the mountain sky on
a summer morning. He was taller than her father had been,
and his strong, leanly muscled legs were visible to the knees.

The neck of the robe showed a deep vee of sleek tanned skin, with only a slight scattering of dark hair in the center. He'd used the razor she'd set out for him; his strong jaw was smooth now. His hair was wet, slicked back, emphasizing the long, taut cords of his neck. The boyishness had vanished, and he was making her heart tumble in her chest. All the images she'd beaten off came roaring back.

"I feel much better. Thanks."

She nodded, unable to speak.

"And thanks for this," he said, indicating the robe. "I know it must... bother you to let a stranger use your father's things."

She shook her head slowly. She told herself to look away, but it did no good.

"I... He wouldn't mind."

He sat down on the sofa, leaning forward to rest his elbows on his knees and looking across to where she sat in the big recliner. He just looked at her silently, until she said hurriedly, "Your clothes should be almost dry now. I'll get—"

"I'll get them later. Thanks."

She closed her book with a snap. "I'll get out of your way, then, so you can rest."

"You're not in my way, Kit. It's your house."

She bit her lip. "Er... I put a big log on, so the fire should be set for most of the night. I usually don't use the heater until morning, but I can turn it on if you—"

"I'm fine. I told you, this is the Ritz after the last week."

"Well, then..."

"Relax, sunrose."

She blushed furiously and scrambled to her feet. "Stay here, Gus," she blurted out.

The big dog sighed and lowered himself heavily to the floor in front of the fireplace. Kit felt her guest's gaze and turned to see a raised brow. As clearly as if she could read his thoughts, she knew he was wondering if she'd told the dog to stay here to guard against whoever might be outside, or to guard him. But he only looked at her and asked simply, "Gus?"

"It's short for Argus." She smiled, though it was a little wobbly. "I know he's just a mutt, but—"

"No. It fits. He would know you, no matter how many years you were gone."

If the fact that he knew the reference to the mythical Argus, the loyal dog who was the only one to recognize Homer's battered traveler after his legendary odyssey, surprised her, she tried to hide it.

"He's used to you now. It will be all right." She barely restrained herself from scampering away. "Good night...er...good night."

She clutched the book to her and turned to go. She'd taken only a few steps when he stopped her.

"Kit?"

She looked back at him.

"My name's Race."

After a startled moment she nodded. And dove for the shelter of her room.

The first thing Kit saw when she woke up was the gun. The dark metal caught the pale morning light and glinted with the deep color that gave it the name blue steel. Like his eyes, she thought sleepily, eyes that could darken to— She bolted upright, suddenly and completely awake. She sat there in the big four-poster, staring at the gun resting on the nightstand.

She didn't know exactly what had compelled her to get the revolver from the closet last night. She hadn't pondered it even as she loaded the big, lethal .45 caliber bullets into the cylinder. She didn't want to ponder it, didn't want to analyze whether she was doing it for protection from the outside danger, or from the danger that slept on her couch. She only knew that on some deep, inner level, she felt threatened in a way she'd never known before.

A glance out the window over her bed confirmed that it had stopped snowing; the quiet whiteness made it very hard to believe what he'd told her, that there were people out there who wanted to kill him. Violence of any kind seemed impossible in this pristine, lovely world.

Slipping out of bed, she tugged on her jeans and an old sweatshirt. After adding a pair of heavy wool socks, she padded over to the door and opened it quietly. When she heard no sound except the occasional snap of the fire, she walked carefully out into the great room. Gus was immediately there to greet her. Even he, it seemed, was walking carefully; the usual clicking of his toenails seemed oddly muted.

She couldn't stop herself from looking. And for a moment she forgot to breathe as her eyes swept over the lean, muscled lines of her visitor's bare back above the tangled blanket. She swallowed tightly as she thought of him beneath the thick wool, wearing only the blue briefs. Or less. Then she caught sight of one leg, a newly washed gray sock extending below faded denim. She could breathe again.

Had he dressed out of some sense of propriety? she wondered. Or had it just been a survival instinct, to be that much readier to run if his hunters appeared? She saw that his shirt was draped over the arm of the couch, close at hand, and that his lace-up boots were nearby on the floor.

He lay on his stomach, his body twisted on the couch that was too short for him. His head was resting in the crook of one muscled arm, the one not swathed in the bandage she'd applied. His dark hair was tousled and falling over his forehead. The semicircles of his thick, lowered lashes shadowed his cheeks, cheeks that looked less drawn, less gaunt, now.

Her gaze drifted back to that gray sock. It made him seem vulnerable somehow, although she couldn't say just why; there certainly wasn't anything vulnerable about those broad shoulders, or the muscular curves of his back and arms.

Whew, she thought, it's a good thing he's not a mind reader. If he was, he'd . . .

Oh, Lord. Maybe he was. Or maybe he didn't have to be, maybe all he'd had to do was read her silly open face, read the spicy, risqué thoughts she'd been having. Maybe that was why he'd dressed. Color flooding her cheeks, she turned away and hurried as quietly as she could toward the kitchen, struggling to collect herself.

She thought about it for a minute before she let Gus outside, then realized she didn't have much choice; the way he was eyeing the back door despite the snow told her that. At least he would be back quickly, she thought with a grin as she watched the big dog mince his way through the snow.

She started the coffeemaker; although she didn't drink coffee much, it wouldn't hurt to have it ready if he wanted some. Race, she amended silently, remembering that she now had something to call him besides "he" or "my burglar."

Was Race his first name? Not that it mattered, she thought dryly. Considering how long it had taken before he'd entrusted her with even that bit of information, she would probably never know.

An eager scratching at the door sent her hurriedly to open it.

"Shh," she cautioned the dog, who scrambled to get back into the warmth of the kitchen. "And hold still."

She grabbed a towel and rubbed his damp fur before he could shake himself and soak the entire room. She ran the thick cloth over the big paws, thinking with a smile that anyone who came across Gus's tracks in the snow would probably be looking over his shoulder for wolves at least.

"Maybe even a small bear," she teased the dog, who swiped a pink tongue over the tip of her nose.

Tracks, she thought suddenly. She stood up, the towel clutched in one hand. She tiptoed back into the great room and over to the picture window. The thermal double glass enabled her to leave the window undraped and open to the view of the meadow and the slope below; now it also allowed her to see the smooth expanse of white, unmarred by tracks of anything larger than a rabbit caught off guard by the sudden spring storm. Still, she searched again, just to be sure.

"Kit?"

She whirled. "Oh! I'm sorry. Did I wake you up?"

"It's all right." He sat up, running a hand over his di-shevelled hair. He glanced at his watch, and his brows low-ered as he frowned. "It's late."

"You needed the rest. And it's only seven-thirty."

"I meant to be out of here as soon as it stopped snow-ing."

It was a mutter, low and soft, and Kit wasn't sure she'd been meant to hear it. But she did, and was startled by the stab of pain that knifed through her at the thought that he'd meant to just disappear without a word. She would have come out this morning to find him gone, she thought, probably with the blanket neatly folded and stacked by the pillow. And a note, perhaps, as short and concise as his thank you for the food she'd left out for him.

So what did you expect? she asked herself. He had a lot more on his mind than polite niceties. She would not let him see her silly hurt feelings. She set her jaw in determi-nation and kept her voice casual.

"Nobody's been around at all. There's not a track out there except for maybe a rabbit. And—" she gestured at Gus "—he's been out, and he would have set up a racket if anybody was nearby."

He looked at the shaggy animal. "I'll bet you would, wouldn't you, Gus?" he said softly.

The dog's plumed tail wagged at the mention of his name. And then, to Kit's amazement, he walked across the room and rested his chin on a denim-clad knee. Race lifted a hand and tickled the big dog behind the left ear.

Kit gaped at the pair. Race caught the look and smiled awkwardly. "We...came to an accord of sorts last night."

"But he never... The only person he ever let pet him so quickly was my dad."

Her voice caught on the last word. Sympathy, warm and soothing, glowed in Race's blue eyes for a moment. But he said nothing, and she was grateful for it; the look eased the inner ache a little, but any soft, kind words would have brought her to tears. In this, at least, she'd been right to trust him, she thought. In a moment she was able to go on.

"He's usually standoffish for a long time with strangers."

"Then I'm flattered." He scratched Gus's ear again, and the dog sighed.

Kit studied them for a moment and couldn't help thinking of Gary. Gus had detested Gary, and the feeling had been mutual and obvious; Gary had growled at the dog nearly as loudly as the animal had snarled at him. It had been his autocratic demand that she get rid of Gus that ended their brief engagement. Gus, she'd decided, was much nicer. He had more personality, too. And, she'd thought with self-deprecating wryness, he was smarter. He'd seen right through Gary's practiced, smooth facade to the petty shallowness of the real man.

Yes, she thought as she watched Race's long, supple fingers rub the dog's head, Gus was definitely smarter. He would never be fooled by a three-piece suit and a perfectly styled head of hair. He knew class when he saw it.

Race's dark head came up. "You're awfully quiet, sunrose."

"I was just . . . thinking." Dangerous thoughts, she told herself. Thoughts that had no basis in fact. Because she had no facts about this man. Nothing but a name and a dog's instinct. And her own foolish reaction to his powerful male presence.

Race slowly got to his feet. "About what? Why you let yourself get into this?"

He was looking at her steadily, his eyes somber with understanding. But Kit barely noticed. All she could do was stare at him. At the broad, muscled expanse of his naked chest, the flat, ridged plane of his stomach, and the trail of dark hair that began at his navel and arrowed down to disappear below the waistband of the jeans that rode low on his narrow hips.

"N-no. Not exactly," she finally managed to stammer. "I . . . I think I'll fix breakfast. I'm so hungry. . . ."

When she realized how her last words must have sounded when coupled with her avid perusal of his body, she flushed. His eyes narrowed a little, but then he shook his head as if in denial of whatever he'd been thinking.

"Kit," he began, "I have to—"

"You have to eat before you do anything."

She turned and started toward the kitchen. She half expected him to stop her, or to protest that he had to leave immediately. But he didn't, and when he came through the door after her, she looked back to see him wearing an oddly bemused expression, as if he didn't quite understand why he wasn't doing exactly what she'd been thinking he would.

As she collected the ingredients for the meal, he quietly went about gathering plates and utensils. He toasted the bread she'd gotten out, then buttered it. He spoke only to ask if she wanted coffee, and when she declined, he got her a glass for the milk she'd requested instead.

She watched him dig into the steaming cheese-and-mushroom omelette as if the enormous meal he'd eaten last night had never been. He didn't even slow down enough to take a sip of coffee until the omelette was half gone. Then he looked at her a bit sheepishly over the rim of the cup.

"I guess I was hungrier than I thought."

"There's enough for a second, if you want."

He shook his head. "I've already taken too much of your food."

"Better mine than someone else's."

He looked at her quizzically. "Someone else's?"

"Who would have reported it."

"I'm still not sure why you didn't."

She held his gaze for a moment. "My father again, I suppose," she began slowly. "He never formed an opinion until he was sure he had all the facts."

"Some people would say what you did know was enough."

"Most, I suppose."

He studied her for a moment. Then he asked softly, "Except your father?"

She swallowed against the lump in her throat. "He could be as harsh as anyone, if he was certain someone was irretrievable. But it took an awful lot to convince him to give up on people."

"He sounds...very special, sunrose," he said softly. He glanced around the room. "Did you live here with him?"

She shook her head. "He wanted me to, after he retired a couple of years ago, but I was...busy with my own life. So I put it off." A touch of bitterness crept into her voice. "I put it off too long."

"'The thief of time,'" he intoned softly.

"Procrastination?" she asked, recognizing the quote.

"Yes." She bit her lip, blinking rapidly.

"I'm sorry, Kit."

"So am I. It's just not fair. He was only fifty-two."

"No. It's not fair."

She seemed to draw herself up, as if shaking off the sad memories. She took a bite of the omelette, then another, but barely tasted it. She forced herself to down at least half of it, then set down her fork as he stood up.

"What are you going to do?"

"Get some more coffee."

Kit looked startled; then her mouth quirked. "I meant in general, not this minute."

He looked back at her as he refilled his cup, a rueful smile curving his mouth. "I wish I knew. Who was it that said wisdom is not in knowing what to do in the ultimate, but knowing what to do next?"

"I don't know. Who?"

His brows furrowed. "Herbert Hoover, I think."

"Oh. So what are you going to do next?"

He sat back down, running a hand over his hair. "I'm running real short on wisdom these days. I—"

He broke off, going suddenly rigid in the chair, his head snapping around sharply.

"What...?" she began, trailing off when she realized what he had heard. "It's the snowplow," she said quickly. "It's early. They must have known the storm was coming and been ready."

She had been about to ask again, but she had seen the look that came and went in his eyes, and knew that leaving here was high on his list. She didn't repeat the question after all. At least he wasn't jumping up to leave this instant, she thought. And she didn't let herself wonder why it mattered so much.

She began to eat again, and, taking his cue from her silence, he said nothing more until he'd finished his meal. Then, hands wrapped around the mug of coffee he'd refilled, he spoke.

"Did you go there?"

She blinked at him. Then he gestured at her with one finger, and she realized that she had put on her Stanford University sweatshirt this morning.

"Yes. I graduated two years ago, in the fall."

He looked down at his coffee, lifted the cup for a sip, then set it back down. When he lifted his head and looked at her again, there was a touch of wistfulness in his eyes that startled her.

"What was it like?"

The quiet question caught her as off guard as the look in his eyes had.

"I . . . It's a good school."

"I know. But what was it like?"

"Stanford?"

"College."

Her brows rose. "You didn't . . . ?" She stopped. She'd gotten the idea that he'd had more than just a basic education; just the way he spoke, the quotes he'd known, his familiarity with Homer's *Odyssey*, seemed a bit beyond the average high school curriculum.

"No." He shrugged, but Kit sensed sorrow beneath the casual dismissal.

"I thought . . . I mean, the way you talk . . . the things you know . . ."

"I just read a lot."

She blushed. "I'm sorry. That was very presumptuous of me, wasn't it? Not to mention snobbish."

He shrugged again and took another sip of coffee. And then, as if to atone for her gaffe, she found herself talking at length about her years in college; he seemed to drink it in like a man starved for the first spring wildflowers after a long cold winter.

"An English major?" he asked when she paused. "Are you a teacher?"

"Sort of. I've been working with a reading program for adults down in Sacramento. But really I did it so I could help my father. He was going to write a book."

"A book?"

"Based on his work. Twenty years' worth. He had started the outline, and I was going to help do the writing to tie it all together." She sighed. "Now I'll have to try to do it without him."

"What did he do?"

"He was—"

The faint sound of tires on gravel stopped them as effectively as an unexpected mountain landslide. Race was on his feet in an instant, every muscle tensed. Automatically Kit glanced at Gus; the dog's head was up, his ears alert, but no warning growls or trumpeting barks of warning issued from his throat.

"It's someone he knows," she said quickly, but Race didn't look at all comforted. He took two quick steps to the window and looked out, twisting so that he could see the driveway. She heard him suck in a harsh breath, saw him go rigid, every muscle taut with strain. He started edging toward the back door.

Kit got up and ran across to see what he'd seen, then smothered a tiny gasp when she spotted the four-wheel drive Blazer with the light bar across the roof and the county sheriff's seal on the door.

"It's Harve Brooks. I'll go see what he wants."

She looked over her shoulder as she spoke; Race had his hand on the knob of the back door. Gus was looking at him, his big head tilted quizzically.

"Just wait. Let me talk to him."

She saw him start to shake his head.

"Race, please."

The moment his name left her lips, she saw something flicker in his eyes, saw the muscle along his clenched jaw jump.

"Kit—"

"I won't give you away."

He let out a long breath, looking at her. Then he lowered his gaze. "I know," he said softly, his dark lashes hiding his eyes from her.

"Then stay here." The knock on the front door was muffled by the closed kitchen door. "I'll find out what he wants. Just wait," she repeated.

His head came up. He stared at her, shaking his head slowly in wonder. "Why? Why are you doing this?"

Her mouth twisted wryly. "When I figure that out, I'll let you know."

All she could do as she walked across the great room was wonder if he would be there when she got back.

"Harve!" She feigned surprise as she looked at the rather corpulent man in the green uniform. "What brings you up here?"

"Well, Miss Kit, since you're about the only one on the west slope I haven't heard from lately, I figured I'd check in on you."

"I'm fine." Kit's mind raced. Was he really here just to make sure she was all right? It wasn't unusual, but...

"No problems? No unwelcome visits?"

Her first instinct was to pretend she didn't know what he was talking about, but she knew he wouldn't believe that. She decided to play it lightly.

"You mean the man with the bean fascination? I thought he'd taken off for greener pastures."

He ran a hand over thinning silver hair. "Maybe. Or maybe he's just lying low. Maybe he knows everyone's on the lookout for him. He's broken into about every place but yours."

Kit didn't know if guilt was making her imagine the speculation she thought she saw in his eyes, but she didn't want to take the chance. She spoke quickly.

"Why do you suppose he hasn't hit me?"

Harve looked startled. "I was hoping you might be able to tell me that."

She'd been right, she thought. He was suspicious. Maybe somebody had mentioned to him that she wasn't a charter member of the shoot-him-on-sight club. She fought to keep her tone casual.

"Only thing I can think of is Gus."

Harve's graying brows lowered. "I forget about him. Guess he would scare off 'most anybody."

"Anybody with any sense," she agreed.

"Where is he, anyway?"

"Uh...out playing in the snow," she lied; Gus hated snow.

"Oh. Well, you keep him close by from now on. I got a feeling this guy is still around."

"Well, he's out of luck," Kit quipped, hoping her tension didn't show, "because I'm out of beans." *I gave Race the last of them,* she thought.

"I mean it, Miss Kit," he said seriously. "This guy may be getting desperate."

Bothered by his solemnity, Kit gave a little laugh that sounded forced. "Desperate enough to take on Gus?"

"Maybe," Harve said grimly. "Especially if he's who I think he might be."

Kit's eyes widened at his tone. "Who...?" She couldn't finish the question.

"My hit-and-run driver. And if he is, he's already killed once. In my book, that makes for a desperate man."

Chapter 4

Kit couldn't look at Race when she walked back into the kitchen. After the rest of her conversation with Harve, she didn't dare look at him, afraid her every tangled emotion would show in her eyes. Doubt, fear—and an absurd sense of betrayal that she told herself she had absolutely no right to feel.

Disappointment, she corrected herself silently. She would allow herself that. The only thing she didn't know was if it was disappointment in him, or in herself and her apparently incompetent judgment.

"Kit?"

His voice was tight, strained. She looked up. The moment their eyes met, she saw him wince, as if he indeed could read her every thought, as if he could feel the fear that laced through her.

"Sunrose…" He trailed off, shaking his head like a man at a painful loss for words.

For one long, silent moment she continued to look at him; then she looked away and snapped her fingers. Gus uncoiled from the kitchen floor and scrambled over to her. Race stiffened, and Kit knew that the simple action of call-

ing her protector to her side told him more than any words
could have.

"What did he tell you?"

The words broke from him like water breaching a dam.
Kit's fingers threaded through the shaggy fur on Gus's
neck. Her voice quavered when she spoke.

"You already know that, don't you?"

He looked as if she'd punched him. He stared at her, his
jaw tight, his skin a touch paler, stark beneath dark hair.
Pain flickered in his eyes. And, in a brief but unmistakable
flash, guilt. Then his expression went flat, emotionless, yet
somehow utterly, completely exhausted.

Oh God, Kit thought as that look shattered her last hope.
Only then did she realize that she had been hoping, desperately hoping, that he would deny it. That he would tell
her something she could believe, something that would
make everything all right.

Even a lie, she thought with bitter self-realization, would
be preferable to this. God, you're such a fool, she told herself scornfully. You justified what you were doing by telling yourself it was what your father would do. But you
forgot one important little detail, Kit Cameron. You obviously don't have the judgment or the instincts your father
had.

"So it's true," she said, unable to keep the bitterness
from her voice.

She saw him shudder, then make a tremendous effort to
stop the convulsive movement. He said something under his
breath, something she couldn't quite hear. Then he lifted
his head to meet her condemning gaze.

"I... I told you, I...I've done some things I'm not very
proud of."

"'Not very proud of'?" Kit stared at him. "That's what
you call it?"

He winced, started to speak, then stopped. Silence
stretched between them like a worn rope between mountain climbers, with the same potential for damage when it
snapped.

"Why didn't you . . . turn me in?"

"I may yet," she said grimly.

"Why didn't you now?"

"Because I said I wouldn't give you away." And, fool that I am, I always keep my promises.

He laughed, a short harsh burst of sound. "And you didn't think that my being a . . . that what he told you was worth breaking a promise for?"

She told the truth softly, too humiliated to deny it. "I hoped he was wrong. That you hadn't done it. But I guess you've shown me what a fool I am, haven't you? So don't think that I won't call the sheriff right back here the second you're—"

She stopped suddenly, realizing that if he was the killer the sheriff had labeled him, she'd made a very big mistake. She stared at him, her eyes wide with dawning fear.

She knew he saw it in her eyes, that he couldn't help but see it. Pain flashed in the tired eyes once more. He lifted a hand, stretched it toward her awkwardly, as if he were fighting the movement. When she drew away from him as far as she could without taking an actual step back, his hand fell to his side. And, impossibly, he looked even more weary.

"I would never, ever, hurt you, sunrose," he whispered, as if he'd read her thoughts. His voice was soft, with a taut, pleading undertone that pulled at her in a way she refused to acknowledge. A way that made her want desperately to believe him.

You've already been enough of a fool, she told herself. But she couldn't seem to help herself. Whatever else he'd done, she couldn't make herself think that he would intentionally hurt her. She couldn't look at him, couldn't look at his weary face and those haunted blue eyes, and believe it.

"No," she said tiredly, "I don't think you would. Although I don't know why hurting me should be any different than hurting that man was."

"I had no choice," he ground out through clenched teeth. Then he let out a choking breath, shutting his eyes as if in pain. "At least, that's what it felt like. Then."

Gus made an odd, almost whimpering sound, as if he could sense the tension in the room and it was making his hackles tingle. He sat quivering on his haunches, looking from her to Race in obvious distress. Race opened his eyes.

"Kit—"

"How could you?"

It burst from her, an impassioned plea for an explanation she could understand. He let out a long, compressed breath and shut his eyes again, this time as if he couldn't look at her, couldn't stand the expression of pain on her face. She couldn't help it; it was too strong to hide, even knowing what it told him about how much she had come to feel so quickly. As did the tremor in her voice as she asked him again.

"How could you just leave that man there to die?"

"Kit, I—"

"He might have had a chance, but you just left him there on the road, like he was no more than some rabbit you'd run over."

"I was scared! I was just a kid. I—What did you say?"

A kid? She stared at him, brows lowering in angry confusion. "What?"

"What did you say? About . . . on the road?"

"You know what I mean! God, to think I helped you, when I can't think of anything more loathsome than a man who would hurt someone like that and then just leave them alone to die!"

"Kit, wait—"

"You left the scene, so your car must have been running. You could have taken him to a hospital, even if you didn't stay until the police—"

"Kit, stop! What are you talking about?"

Something in his fierce tone got through to her, and her anger changed to bewilderment.

"The hit-and-run, of course."

"What hit-and-run?"

She just stared at him, baffled.

"There was a hit-and-run? A fatal one? Somebody was killed?"

"It's been the talk of the mountain," she said suspiciously.

"And the sheriff told you it was me?" he asked, looking utterly astonished.

"I..." She trailed off, staring at his bewildered expression. Hope rose in her, and she tried desperately to tamp it down. Don't be any more of a fool than you've already been, she ordered herself severely again. He's probably lying. He's probably been lying all along.

"What exactly did he say?"

Afraid she hadn't stifled that forlorn hope, she didn't dare answer. He took a step toward her, but stopped when she tensed and Gus shifted uneasily.

"Kit, please. I don't know anything about any hit-and-run. Did he actually say it was me? Use my name?"

"No," she said slowly. "He just said that the driver was probably the same man responsible for the break-ins. They started at the same time, and there's been no sign of anyone else around, no strangers. And they just found the car involved in the hit-and-run near where the first burglary was. He said that you must be hiding out on the mountain until you could get away...."

She trailed off, staring up at him, her eyes searching his face, trying to decide if she dared believe him.

"I don't know anything about it," he repeated. "I don't even own a car."

Each word was bitten off with a fierce intensity that was almost frightening. Her instinct—or perhaps her heart, she admitted—told her to believe him, but her newly revived common sense was trumpeting the knowledge that he would no doubt say that anyway.

"It was stolen from down below," she said slowly.

He groaned. "Of course it was. And you think I..." A sharp breath escaped him before he said bitterly, "God, why wouldn't you think I did it?"

Kit's mind was racing as she tried to sort things out. If he hadn't lied before, she thought, if it wasn't the sheriff that he was worried about, after him for the break-ins, and if he truly didn't know anything about the hit-and-run, then who on earth could be hunting him, and for what? Then his words came back to her whirling mind.

"But you said . . . you left because you were scared."

A short harsh breath escaped him. "I thought . . . That was something else. A long time ago."

Her brow creased. "But you thought that was what Harve was here for?"

He gave her a wry, pained smile that was decidedly half-hearted. "There are some things you never quite leave behind."

She studied him, biting her lip.

"Kit," he said urgently, as if suddenly overwhelmed by a fierce need for her to believe him. "I would never do something like—"

He broke off, his eyes going dark and shuttered; whatever self-defense he'd been about to offer, he'd changed his mind. Because he knew it was a lie? Kit wondered. But if he'd truly done it, if this was the horrible thing he'd alluded to, why would he quibble about one lie? But then, why would he have admitted to doing anything at all? She shivered under the force of her chaotic thoughts.

Race straightened, taking a deep breath as if bracing himself. His eyes were cool and withdrawn, and when he spoke, his words were stiffly formal.

"I'm sorry, Kit. But thank you for not telling him I was here. I know you didn't like lying to him."

"I didn't lie. I just didn't tell him anything."

The words were even, neutral, but the look in his eyes told her that he knew she was quite aware of the fineness of the line she'd drawn. He swallowed, as if the thought of her lying for him disturbed him. Which was ridiculous, she thought, if the rest were true.

"Kit," he began slowly, looking oddly haunted, "did he say . . . Do you know who it was, that was . . . killed?"

"No," she said, wondering why it mattered. "A man. From down below, I think. I haven't been paying much attention to the local news lately." It was an understatement, she thought. Since her father's death, she hadn't been paying much attention to anything except survival for herself and Gus.

He seemed to relax a little, but his voice was still taut. "I can only tell you that I honestly don't know anything about that accident. I promise you that I'm not lying, Kit." His mouth quirked. "But I'd say that anyway, wouldn't I? To keep you from calling him the minute I walk out of here."

Kit fought to hang on to the sour, cynical part of her that had leapt to life with the sheriff's accusing words. It was hard, very, very hard, as she stood there looking at him, remembering how gentle he'd been with her when she'd been hurt, remembering how worried he'd been that he had somehow put her in danger. And most of all, no matter how silly it might be, remembering how quickly Gus had accepted him. But somehow she found the strength she needed and spoke with forced evenness.

"I think you'd better do that now."

"Walk out of here?" The smile shifted crookedly as his jaw tightened. "Yes. You're right."

He turned as if to go, then turned back.

"I don't blame you for...thinking the worst. I've caused you a lot of trouble, but I never meant to. You're sweet and kind and generous, and you don't deserve to have someone like me taking advantage of that."

He seemed to shiver a little, glancing out the window as if to assure himself that the marked vehicle was gone. Then he walked over to the back door. This time she made no effort to stop him. He twisted the knob, but looked back at her before he pulled it open.

"You'll be all right now. Safe," he said quickly.

He opened the door. Kit felt the outside air invade the warmth of the kitchen, wrapping snow-chilled tendrils around her ankles. She was a little surprised she could feel it at all, she felt already so cold inside.

"I'm sorry, sunrose," he said softly. Then he opened the door and walked out into the snow.

* * *

Kit sat at the table in the loft, staring down at the piles of papers. Her father might have a meticulous mind, but his filing system left much to be desired.

He'd *had* a meticulous mind.

And there it was again, welling up to overtake her in a consuming tide of pain and yearning. If only she hadn't postponed her trip here, if only she'd come when he'd first retired, as she'd wanted to. But he'd told her to continue with her commitment to the reading tutor program she'd helped set up down in Sacramento, and she hadn't arrived until February. And two days later she had come home from the Porters' store to find him lying amid a scattering of tools, the ladder still leaning against the newly repaired roof. At her first touch she'd known it was too late. He was already cold, and so very far away.

She stifled the cry that always rose in her when she thought of it. No, it wasn't fair. Life wasn't fair. But if nothing else, her father had taught her not to whine; it would dishonor his memory if she continued to surrender to the urge.

But it was so hard not to think about it, when it hovered over her constantly. There was only one thing powerful enough to drive it out of her mind, and she didn't want to think about that either. It was all she'd done through the long hours of last night. She'd turned the whole situation over and over in her mind until she was exhausted, and none of it made any more sense.

If Race had been the hit-and-run driver, why hadn't he just kept on going? Harve had said the car had been abandoned, not broken down. And, naturally, wiped clean of any fingerprints.

If he wasn't the driver, then why *was* he up here roaming the mountain? And if it wasn't the sheriff chasing him that he was worried about, who was it? And why? And if he wasn't lying, if he hadn't done whatever the mysterious "they" were after him for, what was the horrible thing he had virtually admitted doing? The thing from "a long time ago," the thing so horrible that he thought the police might still be after him no matter how long it had been?

And why on earth had he left her flowers, chopped her wood? And, and, and . . . it seemed to go on endlessly.

Stop it, she snapped at herself. He did it because he's a clever, manipulative man, and you're a gullible fool. You believed him because you wanted to. You took one look at those eyes, at that strong, lean body, and fell like a ton of mountain granite for that no doubt well-practiced, hesitant charm.

This mountain was a quiet, peaceful place, a serene retreat with a slow, even pace that was rarely disturbed by ripples of disorder. Yet the past week had seen, relatively speaking, turmoil. And with an instinctive knowledge she would have preferred not to have, she was certain it all centered somehow on the man called Race.

A man she had spent far too much time thinking about, she told herself firmly, then turned her attention back to the task at hand.

She riffled through the papers again, trying to decide on a method of sorting twenty years of work. Her father had wanted to write this book so badly, she thought, badly enough to take an early retirement from the work that had been his life. She owed it to him to finish the task somehow. Especially since it was her own procrastination that had delayed the project until for him, it was too late.

Not that he had pushed her, she admitted. He had been very casual about it, thinking, of course, as she had, that they had all the time in the world. True, he'd seemed more fervent in their last phone call, but she'd thought it was more about the curious thing he'd mentioned, some oddity that had cropped up, something connected to his job. But since he had already retired by then, she didn't understand that either. And he hadn't spoken of it again after her arrival, no doubt still thinking there was plenty of time. If she'd only come sooner, if she'd only . . .

If, if, if. Much too powerful a word to be only two letters long, she thought painfully.

She sighed, and Gus, sprawled behind her chair, lifted his head. She reached back and tickled his ears.

"Oh, Gus, why do we let the most important things go too long?"

He whined, an oddly comforting sound, and his big tongue swiped over her fingers. She turned determinedly back to the clutter before her.

"Lord," she muttered after a futile hour, "I'll never be able to do it."

For the first time she doubted her ability to complete the task she'd set for herself. He'd written a rough outline, but when she had gone to his notes, she had found chaos. Everything seemed scrambled, with bits of documentation from the stack for each section of the outline pulled out, apparently haphazardly, and clipped together in a separate pile for a reason she couldn't fathom.

"I don't know enough," she said glumly to Gus. "I'm a reading teacher, not a botanist."

She needed help, she admitted at last, although she'd suspected it from the moment she'd felt emotionally stable enough to confront her father's files. They had planned to go through them step by step together, with him there to answer all her inevitable questions. She wondered if there were any of his colleagues, people she might have met over the years, who might be willing to help.

A vague memory stirred, of a man coming to the cabin while she'd been here on a visit a year or so before her father had retired. He'd been, she recalled, the man her father had said would someday be his replacement at the center. And he'd seemed nice; her father had seemed quite pleased that he would eventually take over in the research lab. She'd been introduced, but had left the two men to talk shop while she and Gus went off on one of their long summer rambles, and now she couldn't recall his name.

"He's a good man," her father had told her that night after the man had gone. "He's bright, inventive, and I like the program he set up, to find the 'sparks of brilliance,' as he calls them, that might have been overlooked. He's already found some excellent people through that mentor program.''

She hadn't paid close enough attention that night, she thought. She was sorry now; if she had, she would at least be able to remember the man's name. The man who might be patient enough to deal even with me, she thought.

That was the kind of person she needed, if he would be willing. She would check her father's personal phone book tonight; maybe the name would ring a bell if it was in there, and if she could find the book at all in the disorder of the desk downstairs.

She lifted several pages held together with paper clips, then stopped as a piece of paper fluttered down to the table. She looked at it, puzzled, wondering what this news clipping was doing in with a stack of notes on plant pathogens. Another piece of confusion, she sighed, setting it aside.

It was afternoon when it happened, the sharp, short snap that made her jump. She stared glumly at the light bulb that had given up, only now remembering what she'd forgotten on her last trip to Porters'. She couldn't even pirate a bulb from another lamp; this desk lamp used a long, tubular bulb unlike any other in the cabin.

I could just move another light up here, she thought, then sighed. Why bother? She wasn't getting anywhere anyway, not in this sea of notes on obligate parasites and swimming zoospores. Maybe if she got out, went down to Porters' to get the light bulbs she knew they had stocked for her father, the fresh cold air would clear her head. And even driving down the mountain road in the snow couldn't be anywhere near as frustrating as trying to wade through this.

She pulled on her sheepskin coat and called Gus. Her mouth twisted into a wry grimace as she tugged on her insulated snow boots. Dangling participles she could handle; a detail-intensive study of root rot was beyond her. She was going to need that help, and as soon as she got back she was going to track down that phone book and go through it until she found the name she wanted. She was sure she would recognize it when she saw it.

She was halfway into the Jeep when, as her gaze swept over the small toolshed, she stopped short. She stared at the small building for a moment. He wouldn't, would he?

Why not? she asked herself sourly. What was a little trespassing, next to murder? Or manslaughter, she supposed, technically speaking. Not that it made a dog's hair's worth of difference. Either way it made her ill. And it was the crime itself, she insisted silently, not the fact that *he* had done it, that made her stomach churn.

Slowly she climbed back out of the Jeep. Gus looked at her, his head cocked as if in puzzlement. But when she began to walk toward the small building, he scrambled after her, his big paws sending up little puffs of snow.

"And just what," she muttered to herself, "do you think you're going to do if he *is* there?"

It was, she had realized by then, a moot point; Gus had ambled past her to sniff casually at the door of the shed. Even though she doubted that the dog would be on the offensive against the man he'd accepted, she knew he would at least give some sign if he were inside the small structure.

Still, she found herself kicking away the snow so that she could open the wooden door, driven by an urge she didn't quite understand. She felt an odd, inward tug when the first thing she saw was the pile of tarps, once stacked on a shelf, now folded neatly on the end of the wooden bench that graced the meadow in front of the cabin on the sweet-smelling summer days.

The bench took nearly all of what little floor space there was, yet she knew that it was still too short for his long body. And hard, she thought; the pads that normally cushioned the solid oak boards were in the cabin awaiting an hour or so of her time to repair the wear and tear of last summer. She shivered slightly. There was nothing in the way of insulation in the small building; at night, it couldn't have been much warmer than the body-numbing cold outside.

With a sigh, she backed up a step and reached for the door to pull it closed, still not certain why she had felt compelled to look at the place where he had slept. She stopped mid-motion as something else registered.

The ax she had last seen dug into the tree-stump chopping block was hanging neatly back in its place. But what had caught her eye was the edge of the blade, buried earlier in the wood of the stump, but now obviously bright with the stroke-marks of a fresh honing.

She took a closer look then. Not just the ax, but everything, was neatly in place. Boxes she didn't even know the contents of were carefully stacked. The tools were in perfect order, from the smallest hammer to the shovel to the big tree pruner with the broken blades.

Had he done it as a favor, in return for the food she'd given him? Out of sheer boredom? Just to make room for himself? Or perhaps because of some need to burn off nervous energy, born of knowing he was being hunted?

No, she thought, that couldn't be. The exhaustion she had seen in him had been real; he'd had no energy to spare. But would a man who had heartlessly left an injured man to die beside an empty road worry about a nebulous debt owed to a stranger?

It was more likely that he'd been looking for some kind of weapon, she thought; even unspoken, the words had the bite of acid. And if he had been looking for a weapon, Lord knows there'd be no shortage of possibilities in here. But everything seemed to be accounted for, as far as she could tell.

Her mouth quirked at the sudden image of Race armed with a pair of hedge clippers. And then the expression faded when she realized she had an equal amount of trouble picturing him armed with anything else either. Or using a car as a lethal weapon.

"You're kidding yourself." The words broke from her in a self-deprecating, almost angry tone. "You just don't *want* to believe it, that's all."

No, she added silently, you'd much rather believe he was telling the truth, that it was all a mistake. And just because... because...

Because why? Because he was gentle, almost tender, with you? Because you spilled your heart to him? Because you don't want to believe that anybody with eyes like that could be a coldhearted killer? Or simply because he's the only man who has ever made your stomach feel like it does when you stand on the edge of the lake overlook? The only man ever to send your heart into free-fall?

"Because you're a fool," she snapped, and a low whine rumbled up from Gus. "Sorry, sweetie. It's me I'm angry at, not you. Let's go." She backed out of the sled, slamming the door shut hastily and flipping the latch.

It was only because she was feeling vulnerable, she told herself as she wheeled the Jeep out onto the road. If her emotions hadn't been so battered already, if the wound of her father's death hadn't been so very raw, she wouldn't have been so susceptible. She wouldn't have reacted like that to him. And she wasn't going to waste any more time on him.

"And that," she told herself firmly as she negotiated the drifts of new snow that were already beginning to melt in the bright spring sun, "is the end of that."

After a trip that made her grateful more than once for the Jeep's studded tires, she arrived at Porters'. When she went inside, she wasn't surprised to see Hank Brodie in the store again. He hung around constantly, gathering town news like one of Able's bees gathering pollen. Her father had always said that if Hank had been a woman, he would have been called a gossip and a snoop, but since he was a man he was merely sociable and inquisitive. One of the many inequities in this man's world, he'd said. And as she remembered his half-joking, half-serious expression, sweet, sad memories rose up to buffet her like the confused early spring winds that had preceded the snow.

Kit stared at the various bolts of cloth that lined one wall of the store, not out of interest but to give herself time to control the tears that were so near the surface lately. She'd thought she had her emotions in check, that she had cried all the tears there were in the month since her father had died, but now it seemed to be beginning all over again, with the least thought of him starting the moisture brimming in her eyes.

Several minutes passed before words began to penetrate her roiling emotions.

"—took care of that problem once and for all." Hank's voice was, as usual, boomingly audible, and today, for some reason, colored with an obvious undertone of pride.

"It certainly sounds that way," Olive was agreeing. "But weren't you frightened?"

"Me?" Hank chortled in that superior way Kit had always found so irritating. "Course not. Now, the wife, she was mighty upset, him comin' so close again."

"I should think so."

"Man's got to protect what's his, right, Jack?"

His, Kit muttered to herself. His property, his house, his wife . . . it's a man's world, all right, Daddy.

"Sure," Jack agreed mildly. "You call the sheriff?"

"Yep. He's gonna put the word out. He should be easy to find now. That'll teach him to come sneaking around my place." Hank rubbed his hands together in satisfaction. "Yep, I was ready and waiting for him this time."

"Well, that's— Oh, hello, Kit." Olive interrupted herself when she spotted Kit over Hank's shoulder.

"Hello, Olive, Jack."

She gave Hank only a nod of recognition; sometimes his primitive notions of male possessiveness and territorialism grated fiercely on her. And he rarely spoke to her at all unless it was to criticize her "softness," as he called it. He stopped short of criticizing her father for it; whether it was because the entire town had liked Christopher Cameron or out of respect for the dead, Kit neither knew nor cared.

Her lack of a greeting seemed to irritate the man, although she couldn't imagine why; he certainly couldn't care what she thought of him, or of whatever heroics he had performed and felt compelled to brag about. But she knew it had. She'd seen the annoyance that flashed in his muddy brown eyes. But after a moment the temptation of a new audience overtook him.

"You missed all the excitement, girl," he said expansively. "I was just telling Jack and Olive here that it'll be safe around here again soon."

"Thanks to you, I'm sure." Her sarcasm was lost on the big man.

"Why, I suppose, though I'm not one to need thanks," he agreed modestly. "A man's got to do what a man's got to do, you know. To protect—"

"—what's his," Kit interrupted wearily. "Yes, I heard." Then, in resignation, "So what is it, Hank? Did you finally catch that big, ferocious raccoon that's been eating Martha's garden?"

"Well, no..." Hank looked at her for a moment, as if some of her mockery had penetrated this time. But his ego steadied him, and he went on. "Wouldn't waste my time on a little thing like that."

"Of course not."

He gave her a smug, satisfied smile. "Tell you what I did catch, though."

With all the enthusiasm of a captive audience, Kit waited. Annoyance flashed in Hank's eyes again when she didn't ask the question he was waiting for, but, as Kit had known, it didn't stop him.

"Caught that damned cabin thief, that's who I caught."

Kit's eyes widened in shock. "You...what?"

Pleased that he had at last gotten her full attention, Hank nodded importantly.

"Yep. Caught him right on my property. Probably on his way to break in again. But I was ready for him this time, by God."

"What..." Kit had to stop to wet her lips before she could go on. "What did you do?"

"Why, what should have been done a long time ago. What any self-respecting man would do."

"What?" she repeated a little faintly.

"I shot him, of course."

Chapter 5

Kit shivered as she drove down the mountain at what was, for the slick road conditions, a breakneck pace. It took every ounce of driving skill she'd ever gained to keep the high-profile vehicle on the pavement. More than once Gus whined in frightened protest. She tossed him some words of reassurance, but she didn't dare take her hands off the wheel to pet him.

Hank's mocking words still echoed in her ears. "I didn't kill him, only winged him. Too bad. Girl, you've got to toughen up if you're going to live around here. Things ain't like they are down in the flatlands. You've got to—"

She hadn't stayed to hear what she had to do. She'd run out to the Jeep, wondering every step of the way what "winging" someone with a 12-gauge shotgun meant.

Her first instinct had been to go home, hoping he might have come back—if he'd been able to make it. When she found no sign of him, she had sat silently for several long, precious minutes, her mind racing. At last, a memory stirring, she threw the Jeep back into gear and began the careering trip back down the mountain.

She reached the lake road in what would have been a re-
spectable time even in perfect weather, though it seemed to
her that it had taken forever. Somewhere in the back of her
mind was the rueful awareness that all her self-lecturing had
done no good whatsoever; she'd never even entertained the
possibility of just letting it go, of letting whatever would
happen, happen. Her common sense might tell her that he
deserved whatever he got, but her emotions were in charge
right now, and they were running too high to be easily
stopped.

She didn't even feel the usual qualm as she passed the
gated entry to the Agricultural Center; she drove past the
place where her father had worked for twenty years without even a glance.

The sharp honk of a horn made her eyes flick to her
rearview mirror in surprise; surely no one would want her
to speed up, not at this pace. She didn't recognize the big
white car, but the grinning blond man behind the wheel,
waving madly for her to pull over, was all too familiar.

She contemplated ignoring him, but she knew Len was
too pigheaded to give up. And she certainly didn't want him
following her, especially if her hunch was correct. So, reluctantly, she pulled over.

"Hey, baby!" Len called as he got out of the car and
swaggered toward her. She heard Gus's low growl; he'd
never liked Len, although the man rarely even noticed the
big dog.

"Hello, Len."

"Going a little fast, weren't you?"

"Er... Gus likes to go fast," she said quickly, casting an
apologetic glance at the dog for the lie. "What are you doing around here? These aren't your usual stomping
grounds."

It was true, she thought. Len tended to frequent the clubs
and restaurants that attracted the tourist crowd—and an
ever-changing assortment of young ladies—to the other end
of the lake. Which was no reason for him to look so startled. Or so guilty, she thought.

"A change of scene," he said, and abruptly reverted back to his original subject. "But you'd better watch it, Miss Speedster. Harve's got a couple of new deputies on, you know, and they've got some funny ideas about how things are."

He leaned against the side of the Jeep as if settling in for a long, cozy chat. All Kit could think about was precious time ticking away; she had to get rid of him.

"Well, if I get a ticket, I know a good lawyer, don't I?" she asked brightly.

Len looked startled. She didn't blame him; she'd never gone in for catering to his already sizable ego. Then his eyes narrowed suspiciously.

"Where are you off to in such a hurry?"

God, why am I such a lousy liar? she moaned inwardly. "Just out for a spin," she fibbed again, wishing desperately she was better at subterfuge. Then something about the big white car caught her eye, and she seized on it like a mountain skier grabbing a tow rope.

"Looks like you're out for a spin, too. A new car?"

The smug grin that spread across his face told her that her distraction had worked.

"Yep. Isn't it a beauty? Always wanted a Cadillac."

"It's . . . big."

The grin widened. "That's what I like about it. Looks expensive, doesn't it?"

"Yes," she said honestly, keeping her thoughts about Len's concern with looks to herself. But she couldn't hold it all back. "Does this mean you're working now?"

Annoyance flashed across Len's face. "Geez, you sound like my folks."

Kit lifted a brow. "They worked hard to put you through law school. It's only natural for them to want to see you use your education."

"And now you sound like your old man, always trying to see both sides." The grin came back. "Well, I'll tell you. I've got a few irons in the fire. Enough to buy this little toy, anyway."

Only Len could call a car that had to be over fifteen feet long a toy, she thought wryly. But no matter what he wanted to call it, she had to get going.

"Look," he went on, "that's why I stopped you. Thought you might want to take a little ride in the new carriage."

"Len, I can't—"

"Come on, how can you resist? It rides like a dream."

She *had* to get rid of him. "I can't now." She gave him the most flattered look she could manage. "But I'd love to sometime. Rain check?"

He frowned at her words, but her look must have been more successful than she'd expected; he capitulated.

"Okay. Later then, baby. I'll call you."

One of the great lines of modern male humanity, Kit thought as she watched him drive away in the long coupe, hoping that this time it meant the same thing it usually did. The last thing she wanted was to hear any more from Len Porter.

The moment he was out of sight, she scrambled back into the Jeep. The tires spun a little on the slushy shoulder, then grabbed, and she had to wrestle with the wheel to stay straight.

The flats, she thought, her eyes watching for the turn-off, even though she knew it was at least a couple of miles away. He'd said that he'd gone to the flats when he'd hurt his arm. It was the part of the lake that was the easiest to get to on foot, but it was usually deserted because of the soggy footing and the lack of any facilities. The tall water reeds would give excellent cover near the water's edge, and the trees were thick enough to hide any approach.

She had to slow down when she made the turn onto the flats road; it was narrow, and the snowplow had apparently only made one pass. She went to the end, then pulled the Jeep carefully off the road behind a thick stand of pines where the snow wasn't quite so deep, concealing it from any unlikely but possible passerby. Shutting off the motor, she sat for a moment, just listening. She heard nothing.

After a while Gus whined restlessly, and she reached out to rub his head.

"Wish you were a tracker, my friend."

He whined again. Kit looked at him thoughtfully. It was true, the big dog had no experience in tracking, but he did know the meaning of "find." He'd often led her to her father when he'd gone so far afield on one of his specimen hunts that he was out of earshot when dinnertime rolled around. So wasn't there a decent chance that, if given the command, he might lead her to the only familiar thing around—Race?

You're stretching it, Kit m'girl, she told herself. But what other choice did she have? It could take hours to search this place, even presuming she was right in thinking he might have come back here. And Race might not have hours.

The thought of him out here somewhere, alone and hurt, put all other considerations out of her mind. It didn't matter what he might have done; she just couldn't walk away. And if she was being a fool, then so be it. She climbed down and whistled to Gus.

"Can you do it, boy?" The dog whimpered eagerly, dancing a little on the uneven ground that was more wet than snow-covered this close to the lake. "Can you find him? Find Race?"

The big dog cocked his head, his ears coming up alertly at the familiar word.

"That's it, Gus. Find. Find Race."

With an excited yelp, the big dog gamboled off as if it were a game. Resolutely Kit started after him, hoping that in his canine mind there was some rhyme or reason to the rambling, spread-out pattern he was describing across the marshy land.

It was heavy going, and before long Kit's feet were aching with cold; only the thought of how much colder Race must be kept her going. She slogged on. Twice Gus ambled down to the lake itself, apparently unaffected by the icy chill of the water, but both times he struck out more up to dryer—relatively—land. The minutes ticked away. Ten, twenty, forty minutes, an hour. After she'd clambered over another of the seemingly endless fallen trees, she fell back to rest for a moment and get her bearings.

They'd been going uphill for a while; although the slope was slight, it had put a familiar ache in her calves. And east, she thought, checking the position of the rapidly falling sun. They were probably halfway back up to the lake road, she thought sourly; she could have parked a lot sooner and started right here.

She shivered and realized she'd better get going, to get her blood pumping again if nothing else. She drew her lips together to whistle for Gus, who had wandered out of sight. She was startled when, at the instant she'd been about to issue the summons, the dog barked excitedly from off to her right. She laughed it off, remembering the same odd feeling she got when, reaching to dial the phone, it rang under her hand. The bark came again, and she slid off the fallen tree and headed toward it, not allowing herself to hope.

When she saw that Gus had cornered something on the lee side of a huge log, she began to run. When she got close enough to see the ridiculously proud expression on the dog's face, her heart began to hammer in her chest. When she saw Gus lower his head and lick something, when she heard him give a worried little whine, her heart seemed to stop. Filled with dread, she clambered over the fallen tree.

She could have walked within ten feet of him and never have noticed him. Either he'd done it on purpose, as camouflage, or he'd fallen so many times and become so coated with mud and leaves that he blended into the surroundings perfectly. He was wedged into a hollowed-out part of the big log, his broad shoulders effectively holding him there, even while unconscious.

He was only unconscious, she told herself firmly, refusing to allow the other possibility into her mind. Still, it was a moment before she could bring herself to touch him.

He was alive. He was cold, but it wasn't the unforgettable, frigid feel of death; she remembered that far too well. And when she probed with shaking fingers, she found his pulse, strong and steady, beneath his jaw.

With a tiny cry of relief she sat back on her heels. She clenched her hands together, shivering with the sudden release of fear as she stared down at him, tears threatening to cloud her vision.

His hair was damp and clung darkly to his head, matted with mud on one side. He was pale, the dark semicircles of his thick lashes standing out starkly on his cheeks. He had his arms wrapped around himself, his hands trapped beneath his muscular biceps for warmth against the surrounding snow.

Warmth. She had to get him out of here. She had to get him warm again, and fast. She didn't know how badly hurt he'd been, but if he'd hung on this long under these conditions, it couldn't be as bad as she'd feared. Right now hypothermia was her biggest fear. She stood up.

"Guard him, Gus. Stay and guard."

The dog yelped. She knew he understood the command, and knew that despite the way he whined in protest when she began to walk away he wouldn't move an inch.

She made her way to the road, just a short distance away through a break in the trees, and began to run. It seemed much longer this time, although her watch told her it was only minutes before she was back to where she had hidden the Jeep. She blessed the sturdy vehicle as it started at a touch, and she drove it at a reckless pace back up the hill.

She heard Gus's bark as she backed as far as she could into that break in the trees. Then she jumped down and ran back, crooning to the big dog as she knelt beside him.

"Good boy, Gus, you sweetie."

The dog whimpered his pleasure at her hug, but Kit froze at another, oddly strangled sound. Her gaze shot downward and met a pair of dazed blue eyes.

"Su . . . sunrose . . ."

"Shh." She hushed him gently. "Save your strength. You've got to help me get you out of here."

He closed his eyes, and she saw a slight, negative motion of his head.

"Race, don't be crazy. You're half-frozen already, and it's getting late. You'd never make it through the night outside."

"N-not s-safe," he stuttered, proving her words with his chattering teeth.

"Let me worry about that. I've got the Jeep in as close as I can, but it's still a good twenty feet. I can't carry you, so you've got to help."

She reached for his shoulders to help him out of the curve of the log.

"K-Kit—"

"You don't have any choice, so shut up and move!"

For the moment at least, she was stronger than he was, and he gave in. He rolled free and came out on his hands and knees. Only then did she see that his left hand was crusted with blood; she bit back the sound that rose to her lips.

It was a clumsy, staggering trip, but they made it. She took as much of his weight as she could, although she doubted he was leaning on her as much as his battered body wanted to.

"You should be able to fit in the back if you curl up just right," she told him. "I'll put Gus's blanket over you. It'll probably smell like wet dog, but it'll hide you."

She felt his eyes on her again and met his gaze evenly. Dazed as he was, she could still read the question in them.

"No, I don't know why I'm doing this, so don't bother to ask. Just get in and be quiet."

It was a hellish drive. Kit spent every foot of it expecting disaster, and when it didn't come it only strung her up tighter. She drove carefully, both to avoid jarring the man lying ominously still behind her, and to avoid drawing any undue attention. She didn't now how she managed casual return waves to the few mountain people she passed, or how she kept herself from crying out when one of the new deputies Len had mentioned gave her an interested look as she made the turn onto her road. Only when she saw him go in the opposite direction did she begin to breathe again.

Race was shivering violently as he climbed, with her help, out of the back of the Jeep. She'd pulled up close enough to the front door that all he had to do was step from the bumper to the porch, but the shaking of his chilled body nearly turned the simple move into a tumbling disaster.

"Sorry," he muttered.

"Hush," she ordered, and led him inside and straight to the bathroom. He leaned against the wall, eyes closed, arms still wrapped around himself as if he could ward off the shudders that wracked him. She tried to get him to sit down, but he only muttered something about never getting up again, so she let it go.

She leaned over and turned the bath taps on full blast; the hot water heater was directly next to the bathroom, so she knew the steamy water would begin to fill the big tub in short order. Then she turned to look at him again.

"Did he really shoot you?"

The dark, thick lashes lifted. He tried to shrug, but it became another shiver instead, so he stopped.

"Did he?" Her voice was sharp with worry.

"A li'l," he finally managed.

"A little? How do you shoot someone 'a little'?"

"Bird shot. If he'd been usin' double-ought buck, like mos' folks 'round here..."

He didn't have to finish it; she knew what kind of lethal damage that kind of round could do. Her father had taken apart one of the shells once, to show her the twelve .33 caliber pellets it held. It had made her shudder then, just as it did now.

"'S'okay, sunrose. Jus' peppered me a little. Stung, mostly. Bled a little."

She pulled herself together. "Good," she said briskly. "Then it can wait till we get you warm."

She reached down and tested the water. Too warm, she thought. It was going to be a painful shock to his chilled body as it was. She turned down the hot tap and let the tub fill the rest of the way.

"Okay, it's ready."

He didn't move.

"Come on, you've got to get warm. Get your clothes off and get in."

He blinked, then looked away from her. Kit stared at him. An explanation for his reluctance occurred to her, and she felt heat rise in her cheeks. She tried to convert her embarrassment to anger.

"You're half-dead with cold, what do you think I'm going to do, jump your naked body?"

"Should be so lucky," he muttered.

Kit stared at him, wondering if the implied first word was "I" or "You." You know what it was, she told herself sternly. You just didn't expect him to be nasty about it. It stung and made her words sharp with what she hoped he would take for exasperation.

"Look, keep your shorts on if you're feeling shy. I'm sure the mud's soaked through, but it won't matter, we're going to have to refill the tub a few times to get you back to normal anyway. And as soon as you're soaking, I'll get you the robe."

In the end, she had to help him. He couldn't manage the wet, clinging clothes alone. He tried to get his fingers to work the buttons of her father's shirt and then his own while she tugged at his boots. The rawhide laces were wet and the knot wouldn't give.

"I'll have to cut them," she said. "I'm sure I have another pair." He merely nodded and continued his shaky-fingered battle with the buttons.

By the time she returned with a small, sharp pair of sewing scissors, he was bare-chested and leaning against the wall next to the tub again, as if the fight with the shirt had drained what little energy he had left. For a split second she didn't move, a little stunned by the sight of that naked, muscular expanse.

The bandage she'd wrapped around his arm that night that seemed so long ago was grubby now, and more than a little ragged. Giving herself a mental shake, she gently cut it off. Despite the ominous appearance of the gauze, the cut beneath was clean and healing nicely. Then she quickly knelt to snip the wet laces, and tugged off both boots and socks, shivering herself at the icy feel of his feet.

She stood then, and keeping her mind strictly on the urgent business at hand reached for his belt buckle. She undid it quickly, then the snap of his jeans, then reached for the tab of his zipper. His sudden stillness made her lift her eyes to his face. Something glittered for a moment in the depths of his eyes, something that made an odd kernel of heat kindle inside her. His mouth, a little less blue with cold now, quirked slightly.

"Not 'xactly how I pictured it," he said, either not trying or too weary to hide the wry, rueful note in his voice.

"How you...pictured it?" Kit wondered if she sounded as stunned as she felt.

"Often. I—"

Another shiver overtook him, bringing Kit abruptly out of her astonished state.

"You've got to get warm," she repeated, and was proud that her fingers barely shook as she finished unzipping his jeans. She tugged them off quickly.

He hesitated at the edge of the tub, staring down at the water as if he knew exactly what it was going to feel like to lower his shivering body into it.

Kit didn't push, not that she wasn't anxious for him to get into that lifesaving warmth. But she seemed to have lost her voice, had lost it the moment he stood before her clad only in the blue briefs. Had lost at the moment she realized that he was even more beautifully put together than she'd imagined, from the flat, ridged belly to the long, strongly muscled legs, from the sparse scattering of hair over his breastbone to the thick, dark trail that began at his navel and led her eye downward...

If he hadn't moved then, she didn't know what she would have done. Only when he shifted himself to sit tentatively on the edge of the tub did she realize that she actually lifted her arm, her hand stretched out as if desperate for the feel of him.

Her cheeks heated again. What if he'd looked up then and caught her staring at his nearly naked body so hungrily? Caught her reaching for him, her fingers curling of their own volition, as if they wanted to feel the taut curve of his buttocks, caress every hard, masculine line of his lean frame?

"Maybe...jus' sit in the steam..." His voice was still rough, although he was able to speak more clearly now.

He needs help, and your mind's in never-never land, Kit told herself severely. She composed herself and her expression, but her voice was another matter; since she didn't trust it at the moment, she merely shook her head.

"Not good 'nuff, huh?"

His mouth twisted into a grimace, and she saw him suck in a breath as he swung his legs up to the rim of the tub. He was shaky, she could see that, and she took a quick step to grab his arm and help him balance. He braced himself with his other arm on the other edge of the tub.

Kit cringed inwardly, remembering the time as a child when she'd played too long in her first real snow and her father had had to thaw out her nearly frostbitten feet, it had been agony, and that had been only her toes.

"You want to ease into it?" she asked him gently.

He shook his head, a little fiercely. And with a sudden, quick motion, he lowered himself into the water.

A strangled sound that Kit knew would have been a scream if he hadn't throttled it rose from his throat. His eyes snapped shut as every muscle went rigid; the expression on his face screamed louder than any noise he could have made. Her stomach knotted as if she were feeling the pain herself. She had to look away.

They were on the third tub of water, each hotter than the last, before she thought he was warm enough for her to worry about the rest.

"Where did he hit you?"

"Shoulder," he muttered, moving his left arm tentatively. "Back in a couple of spots, too, I think."

"Hank...shot you in the back?"

He gave her a rather wan, crooked smile. "I didn't exactly stick around after I saw him come out of his house with that shotgun."

She bit back whatever she'd been about to say and replaced it with "Lean forward."

Slowly, he did, raising his knees and looping his arms around them. The angry, red wounds were obvious, three of them, one just below the shoulder blade, two more lower down on his side.

"Race?"

"Mmm." His voice was muffled as his head rested on his arms.

"I . . . don't know what to do about these."

"Tweezers."

"What?" It came out a little sharply, but the thought of digging into his already wounded flesh had tightened her throat. His head came up at the sound of it. He looked back over his shoulder at her.

"Or my knife, if you don't have any." She gave a little gasp at the thought. "It's all right, sunrose. Think of them as splinters or something."

"Splinters? Race, these are bullets."

"Little ones. Not even BB sized."

"But they could be in deep—"

"Not at the distance he shot them." Still she hesitated. "Believe me, Kit," he said wryly, "it couldn't hurt any more than getting in this tub did."

She couldn't argue with that, and five minutes later she found herself doing what she would never have thought possible, digging into living flesh with a pair of needle-pointed tweezers sterilized in boiling water.

He never made a sound, although several times she saw his knuckles whiten as his hands clamped around the edge of the tub. At last the horrible job was done, and three small, bloody lead pellets lay in her palm. Race leaned back in the tub, resting his head on the edge as he looked at her. Slowly he raised one hand and gently cupped her face. Her stomach did a little tumble as his hand slid to the back of her neck. She was sure it was from what she'd done, not from his unexpected touch.

"More hot water," she directed a little gruffly; obediently, he raised one strong leg and turned the tap with his foot, never releasing his hold on her. Slowly he eased her closer, then lifted himself until his lips brushed softly over hers.

She heard him suck in a breath, and it was as if it had come straight from her own lungs; she could hardly breathe. She knew the tiny sound she heard must have come from her, although she didn't remember making it. Just as she didn't remember ever feeling anything like the little dart of fire that had shot through her at the feel of his firm, warm lips on hers.

"Kit," he said hoarsely. "Kit, I—"

He broke off, releasing her suddenly. He sagged back into the tub. A little dazed, she saw him swallow tightly, as if it hurt. Then, steadily, lightly, he smiled at her.

"Thanks, doc."

"I . . . Of course," she stammered.

When she realized she was staring at him, the water in the tub no barrier to her avid eyes, she scurried out of the room. She tossed the shotgun pellets in the trash and scrubbed her hands at the kitchen sink, trying not to think about the fact that it was Race's blood she was washing off. And the fact that he had kissed her.

In thanks, she told herself doggedly. Remember that. She tried. She tried to concentrate on more mundane things; she would apply antiseptic when he got out of the tub, and bandages to protect the wounds she'd reopened with her probing. But first she would fix some hot food, then build a fire. Thinking herself successfully diverted, she set about the tasks.

When the fire was going and the last of the beef stew that she'd frozen was heating, she went back to the bathroom.

"Race?"

He didn't move. His head was lolling back on the rim of the tub, the steam gently rising from the water. He looked, at last, utterly relaxed. He was, she saw when she got closer, sound asleep.

She went back to the kitchen and took the stew off the stove.

Kit sat up on the couch, wrestling with the afghan to keep it wrapped around her to fight the morning chill. She tugged at the soft, comfortable sweats she'd slept in, straightening them. Groggily, she padded in sock-feet over to the fireplace and stirred the coals, adding three more logs and watching until the flames caught. Then she tiptoed over to the bedroom door, inched it open quietly and peered inside.

He hadn't moved. He still lay sprawled face down, head buried in the pillows, one bare foot over the edge of the bed. She doubted if he even remembered staggering into the bedroom and collapsing; if he'd been even partially aware, he would have given her more of an argument over sleeping in her bed while she took the couch. She closed the door silently.

She stood in the great room for a moment, yawning. Then she walked over to the desk, flipped on the lamp and began the search she'd postponed from yesterday.

She found the phone book in the third drawer she checked, its pages filled with her father's untidy scrawl. She began to thumb through it, her eyes scanning the names quickly, hoping something would trigger her memory. By the time she was halfway through, all she'd managed to do was make herself feel guilty; most of the names in this book had sent messages of condolence, and she had yet to answer them. Wallowing in self-pity, she told herself accusingly.

She began to read again. The name Park caught her eye, until she realized it was "The Park," a new restaurant her father had taken her to on her last visit. With a little laugh at herself she went on. And found the name Richard Parkson on the next page.

That was it. All the memories fell into place with the missing piece of the name of the man who had taken over her father's position at the center. And he had, she realized only now, been at the funeral. She'd just been so devastated that she hadn't realized she'd met him before.

There was only one number listed, but then she realized her father would hardly have needed to write down a phone number that had been his own for so long. So this must be a home number, she thought. She glanced at her watch. If Richard Parkson kept the same hours her father had, he'd been at work for an hour already. She reached for the phone.

It felt decidedly odd to phone that familiar number and ask for the extension that had been her father's. When a female voice answered, she asked for Dr. Parkson. And got silence in answer.

"Hello? Are you there?"

"Er, yes, I'm sorry."

"I'd like to talk to—"

"I heard you, but I'm afraid that's impossible."

Kit's brow furrowed. "Look, my name is Kit Cameron, my father used to—"

"Oh, of course, Miss Cameron. I remember your father."

"Then may I speak to Dr. Parkson?"

"I'm so sorry, but I'm afraid not. You see he ... he's no longer here. Would you like to speak to Dr. Whitney?"

If there was a name she recognized from her father's ruminations about the center, it was that of Dr. Martin Whitney. "A politician, not a scientist," her father had said. "Hasn't done any real research work in years."

"No," she answered. "Not now. Could you tell me where Dr. Parkson is now? I was hoping he would help me with some of my father's notes."

"Oh, dear." The woman sounded genuinely distressed. "I'm afraid not. We're not supposed to talk about it."

And despite Kit's efforts, the woman wouldn't budge. When Kit hung up she was mystified. What on earth had *that* been about? For a moment she just looked at the phone. Then she picked it up and dialed the number written in the book. The hollow ring went on and on, until at last she gave up, her puzzlement growing.

With a sigh she began to fix coffee, wondering if it would clear her head and help her make some sense out of things. She knew that she was clinging to the strange call and her problems with her father's notes to avoid thinking of the other problem lying quietly asleep in the bedroom.

Her bedroom. In her bed. Gloriously, sleekly naked: a fact she had tried very hard not to dwell on. It was difficult; she remembered too clearly the moment when, about to leave the room, she had turned back just in time to see him drop the robe wearily on the floor. She'd had a brief glimpse of his strong, naked body, the curves of muscle and taut, flat planes painted in shadow and silver by the moonlight streaming through the window, before he dropped to the bed in a semi-controlled collapse. Her cheek seemed to burn with the memory of his touch, her mouth tingling with the recollection of his lips brushing hers.

With an effort she pushed away the vivid picture and reached for a heavy mug from the cupboard.

She was curled up on the couch, sipping at the streaming, fresh brewed coffee, when the phone rang and nearly made her spill it. Quickly she set the mug down and hurried to the desk where the phone sat, trying to get to it before it woke Race.

"Miss Cameron? This is Dr. Whitney, head of the Agricultural Center. I believe we met a few years ago?"

Startled, Kit took a moment to reply. "Yes, Dr. Whitney, I remember." She said no more; it had been at a Christmas party held by the center, and she had guessed Whitney's identity by his self-important air long before her father had pointed him out to her.

"I was told you called."

Efficient staff, she thought. It had only been an hour ago. "Yes, I did. I called to ask—"

"Miss Watson told me you wanted to speak to Dr. Parkson. I'm afraid that's impossible. But I'm sure *I* could help you, Miss Cameron. I know about all the projects we've undertaken here at the center."

Something about his tone set her teeth on edge. "I'm sure you could, but I'd rather—"

"Miss Cameron, I hate to be the one to tell you this, but since you obviously haven't heard..."

"Heard what?" Exasperation tinged her voice.

"There was...a terrible accident. Hit-and-run."

"Of course I heard. I—" Kit broke off with a gasp. "Are you saying he was the man...?"

"Unfortunately, yes."

Kit shuddered. The man whose image had come back to her at the name in her father's book, that tall, thin man with the kindly smile, had died so horribly?

Whitney cleared his throat. Wasting no time on the niceties, he launched into an immediate campaign to be the one to assist her with her father's notes, offering to come over immediately and begin.

"Thank you, Dr. Whitney, but no. Not yet."

"But I truly would like to see *all* of his notes. And soon."

Something about his very insistence bothered her, and she found herself stalling him without really knowing why.

"I'll let you know. I've barely started."

She hung up rather abruptly, not ready to deal right now with his continued persistence. The realization that the victim of the hit-and-run had been a man she'd met, a man her father had liked and admired, had shaken her greatly. And the knowledge that the man responsible for it could be at this instant asleep in her bed...

A noise made her whirl around, startled. He wasn't asleep. He was standing in the doorway of the great room. And in his hand, dark, deadly and leveled right at her, was her father's gun.

Chapter 6

"You're one of them." Race's voice was low, strained. "God, I'm stupider than I thought. Here I am trying to protect you, and you've been one of them all along."

"Wha—?" Kit's throat was so tight as she stared at the gun he was holding that she couldn't force out the question. She didn't understand what he was saying, but the cold, shuttered look on his face made her shiver inside, and accusation turned his eyes icy.

"You and Whitney," he muttered, shifting his shoulders under the blue robe. "I never would have guessed you'd—" He shook his head, as if in self-disgust. "So tell me, exactly what is it that you've barely started? Making a fool out of me? Convincing me you're as innocent as you look?"

He knew Dr. Whitney? He'd obviously overhead her, but what he was saying made no sense. Kit struggled to find her voice, but she couldn't seem to make it work. All she could see was the gun, and she didn't know if it was the weapon itself or the fact that it was Race aiming it at her that made her mouth feel like dry pine needles.

"What do you get out of it?" His voice was sharp, angry, and Kit couldn't tell if the anger was directed at her or at himself. "A percentage? I know you didn't work at the center, so how did they hook you into this, Ki—" He stopped as if he couldn't bear to say her name, then finished, "Miss... whatever your name is?"

"Cameron."

It came out in a low, quavering voice, but it came out. It was all she could think of to say, and she didn't understand why Race's brows rose sharply.

"What?"

"My name is Cameron."

He looked stunned. He stared at her, wide-eyed. "Cameron... Kit Cameron?"

She felt as if she'd begun to read a book with the first half missing. Slowly, she nodded.

"Your father was... Chris Cameron? *Doctor* Christopher Cameron?"

She nodded again. Something had changed in these last seconds, and she didn't know what it was. All she knew was that the anger and condemnation in his eyes had been replaced by utter bewilderment. The gun wavered, but he didn't lower it. He just kept staring at her.

"Race," she began softly.

"I don't get it," he whispered. "Dr. Cameron... everybody said he was so... He couldn't have been involved in this...."

Realization slowly penetrated Kit's shock. "You know... knew my father?"

Race shook his head a little dazedly. "No, I... heard about him.... My boss always said..."

"What about your boss? What are you talking about? Involved in what?"

As if her words had been the mental shake he'd needed, he steadied himself. "That was Whitney on the phone, wasn't it? Martin Whitney, from the Ag Center?"

Slowly, Kit nodded. His voice was still tinged with suspicion, his words carrying a definite edge, and it did nothing to ease her alarm. Then the familiar nickname he'd used for the center registered. "Do you . . . work at the center?"

He made an odd sound, half sour laugh, half rueful sigh.

"Race, will you put that gun down? You're scaring me."

His gaze flicked to the weapon, then back to her face, but he didn't put the gun down. "Why were you talking to him?"

Something hot and surprisingly fierce flashed through Kit; it took her a moment to recognize it as anger. Your timing was always great, she muttered inwardly to herself. You wait until he's holding a gun on you to stop being a softhearted idiot. But she'd rather be angry than scared, she thought.

"If you're not involved, why were you talking to him?" he repeated.

As if he weren't holding her potential death in his hand, she lifted her head and met his gaze squarely. "If you already believe I'm . . . involved in whatever it is you're talking about," she said coolly, "then it won't do me any good to deny it, will it?"

"I don't . . . I can't believe you would . . ."

He trailed off, shaking his head once more. Something about his expression, about the look of confusion and doubt on his face, a look she'd worn so often herself in the last few days, drained her anger away as quickly as it had risen.

"Believe me," she said quietly, "I know exactly how you feel."

He let out a breath, short and compressed. Then, slowly, he lowered the gun.

Kit let out a breath of her own, and her taut muscles relaxed. "Does this mean you've decided to trust me?"

He made that odd, low sound again. "It means that if I can't trust you . . . I don't care anymore."

The words were so lost, so desolate, that Kit had to bite back a tiny sound of dismay. She'd never heard anyone sound like that. It was horrible. Then, when he reversed the gun in his hand and held it out to her, with a flat, dead look in his eyes that told her he wouldn't be surprised if she took it and used it on him, she knew that the grim weariness in his voice was merely the outward sign of an even more battered soul.

Gently she took the weapon and set it on the arm of the chair beside her. Her knees suddenly unsteady, she sank down in the cushioned softness.

"What is it, Race?" she whispered.

He walked past her, hands shoved deep into the pockets of the blue robe; she could see they were clenched into fists. He turned, then sat on the sofa across from her.

"Why did you call Whitney?"

She looked startled. "I didn't. He called me."

"Why?"

"What has that got to do with anything? What's going on? How do you know Dr. Whitney? *Do* you work at the center?"

Race sighed and ran a hand through his hair. "Kit, I can't tell you any more now than I could before."

That anger, bright and hot and energizing, flowed through her again. She leapt to her feet. "You! You are the most stubborn, pigheaded, contrary, exasperating man!"

He blinked, startled. "That was . . . quite a mouthful, sunrose."

"You haven't heard anything yet!" she snapped, leaping up and stalking over to stand in front of him. "I've spent a week calling myself every kind of idiot there is for wanting to help you instead of siccing the sheriff on you. I've cooked, baked, loaned you my father's clothes, used up more hot water than I normally do in a month, practically killed myself racing down the mountain thinking you were dead or dying, made myself practically flirt with Len, trudged all over those damned wet, cold flats looking for you, made a fool out of myself over one stupid little kiss, and you just sit there and say you can't tell me anything?"

His look of surprise had changed to one of chagrin during the unexpected tirade, until her last words, when the oddest expression crossed his face.

"You made a fool out of yourself over what?"

Kit's cheeks flamed; out of it all, it was just her luck that he would pick that one slip of the tongue to respond to.

"Forget it," she said hastily, starting to turn away. He reached up and grabbed her hand, tugging her back. She fought him, but he wouldn't release her.

"Sunrose," he said softly.

"Let go," she said, avoiding his eyes.

"Was it really a stupid kiss?"

She made another sound of protest as he inexorably pulled her closer.

"It didn't feel stupid to me," he said softly. "It felt . . . wonderful."

Without knowing quite how he'd done it, Kit found herself toppling over into his arms, coming to rest solidly against his chest, her legs draped sideways over his. His heat rose around her, and she was suddenly, fully aware that he was no doubt naked beneath the blue robe. The image of him from last night, silvered by moonlight as he stood beside her bed, shimmered in her mind and made her dizzy with its power.

"You can't have made any more of a fool out of yourself than I have, dreaming about this," he whispered, the low husky note in his voice sending contrasting ripples of heat and chill down her spine. She ordered herself to move, to get off his lap. Somehow the command never made it to her muscles; they had gone lax and useless at his soft admission that he had dreamed of this just as she had.

"Ahh, sunrose," he murmured, gently pressing her head down to his shoulder, then creating a soft path of kisses over the silk of her hair. When his lips, warm and firm, reached her neck and began to trace a path to the curve of her ear, she shuddered in his arms.

"No." The protest was weak, without strength.

"You're right," he said, his breath warm and soft against her skin. "This is crazy. I have no right. . . . I'll stop, Kit, really, in just a minute. . . ."

And then his lips found hers. Kit had a brief moment to wonder how such a soft, gentle touch could spark such fire. And then there was no room for thought, no room for questions, there was only the feel of his mouth on hers and the astounding realization that her body was capable of its own decisions, no matter what her mind said.

She felt him shift under her and whimpered a little in fear that he was going to pull away, going to put an end to this sweet flowing heat she'd never known before. She heard a low, growling sound rise from him in the moment before his tongue slipped past the yielding barrier of her lips to probe hotly into her mouth.

She was melting, her every muscle slack as she sagged against him, wishing there was a way to wrap herself around him, to feel this lovely warmth everywhere. His hands were moving, stroking her back, then coming up to cup her face, to thread long, supple fingers through her hair.

She twisted in his arms, unconsciously searching for more of his heat with her body. Her breasts pressed against the solid bulk of his chest, and her tiny gasp mingled with the echo of his groan. His arms tightened around her, crushing her to him. She felt his hands cupping the back of her head, adding their pressure to the driving heat of his mouth on hers.

Then she was moving, and she didn't know how. Her muscles weren't solid anymore; they were some liquid, heated mass that had forgotten its boundaries. All at once she realized that the pressure on her shoulders was from his hands, and that he was tearing his mouth from hers. She opened her eyes to look at him dazedly.

"Race . . . ?"

"You didn't tell me sunroses were so…potent." His voice was thick, and he was dragging in air as if he was finding it in as short supply as she was. His eyes had darkened to sapphire, and she could see his chest rising with his quickened breathing, could see the knot that held the robe on his lean, muscled body. And could see that one quick tug would loosen it . . .

Blushing, Kit ducked her head against his chest. His hand came up and gently stroked her hair, and she snuggled against him with an unconscious little wiggle.

This was crazy, she thought in some tiny, still functioning part of her mind. Bare moments ago, this man had been holding a gun on her, accusing her of who knows what, and now, here she was, kissing him with more passion than she'd ever known she possessed.

"I didn't know," she whispered, not really meaning to say it aloud.

"What?"

She made a small sound of denial at the words that told her she had indeed spoken her wondering thought. As if he'd read that thought, Race smiled at her bowed head. He lifted a hand and tilted her chin back with a gentle finger.

"That," he said with emphasis, "was not a stupid little kiss."

Her color deepened, but she held his gaze. "No. No, it wasn't."

He looked at her quizzically. "You sound...surprised."

"I've never been kissed like that," she said simply.

Race stared at her. "You? As beautiful as you are? And you're...what, twenty-two? -three? And you're saying nobody's ever kissed you?"

She reddened furiously then. "You don't have to say that. Besides, I didn't say I'd never been kissed. I'm not some...some naive little virgin. I was even engaged, once. But...no one's ever kissed me...like that."

"Who the hell were you engaged to, a eunuch?" he muttered.

"Hardly."

"Then what was wrong with him?"

"Nothing. What was wrong with me, however, could fill a book, as he'd be the first to tell you." She sighed; she hadn't fallen into this rut of bitterness in a long time. "I'm sorry. I haven't let that get to me for a long time. Gary just had...different priorities, that's all."

"He was a fool if you weren't the first of them."

"He was many things, but a fool isn't one of them."

Race snorted. "Damn good thing you didn't marry him, if he never even gave you a decent kiss."

"That has nothing to do with it," Kit said, using flippancy to cover the embarrassment she was feeling at laying her past bare in front of him. "I broke it off because he didn't like Gus."

Race didn't laugh, as she'd expected. "You know," he said softly after a moment, "I think I believe that. Your loyalty runs deep, sunrose."

She searched his face for any sign he was teasing her; there was none. He'd meant what he said. The tension eased out of her muscles. At the gentle pressure of his hands, she relaxed against him once more.

"I didn't have to say what?" he asked after a moment.

She lowered her eyes; she'd been hoping he would forget that part of what she'd said.

"Sunrose?"

She sighed. "You know what I mean. You didn't have to say I'm ... beautiful."

"No. I didn't."

She didn't quite know how to take the quiet answer, so she said nothing. She wished she'd had the idea sooner and kept her mouth shut. She didn't know what it was about him that seemed to loosen her tongue so. She never talked about Gary to anyone. She felt as though she'd once more bared her soul to him, and once more been shut out in return.

"The first time I saw you," he said softly, unexpectedly, "you were walking by the creek just up the hill. I thought you were just one of the local kids, cutting school or something. Until you took off your jacket and sat down on that rock ... and I knew you were no kid. Then you pulled off that hat, and the sun hit your hair ... it was like fire, so warm and red ... but you looked so sad, I wanted to ..."

He trailed off, and she felt him take a deep breath. It shook her, to realize he'd been watching her, but the soft vibrant note in his voice took away any unease. In his way, she realized suddenly, he was giving her the only recompense he could for her openness.

"I didn't realize you were the one who lived here until the day you made the bread. I saw you leave . . . and leave the door open. You meant for me to come, didn't you?"

She nodded, a tiny little movement against his chest. He chuckled, a short, wry sound that she felt begin before she heard it leave his lips.

"A good thing. I don't think I could have resisted that smell." The chuckle came again. "That's when I saw Gus, and realized how lucky I'd been the first time, not to have tangled with him. Although he nearly had me the other day."

"He was only—"

"Shh. I know," he said, gently interrupting her defense of the big dog. "He did exactly what he should have."

She relaxed, savoring the feel of his arms around her. At the same time she felt the tension of their unfinished discussion as if it were a physical thing, hovering over them. She knew how real it was when at last he spoke.

"Kit?"

"What?"

"What did Whitney want?"

She sat up, looking at him. A new tension filled her as she studied his face, wondering if anything had truly changed, if he thought that the fevered moments that had passed between them had diverted her. And on the heels of that thought came another, grimmer one. She drew back, fearing she had guessed all too accurately.

"Is that what this was for?" she asked hoarsely. "So I'd tell you what you want to know, because you . . . you kissed me?"

Race winced. "No."

She just looked at him, waiting, something cold and harsh knotting up inside her.

"Kit, I didn't mean it that way. Lord, don't think that. Not when I've wanted to kiss you ever since I first saw you, that day by the creek."

Her color deepened, but still she waited, the knot tightening. After a long, silent moment, he sighed.

"Kit, please. I've already gotten you into this too deeply."

"Exactly," she said flatly. The knot was making it hard to breathe.

His eyes searched her face, and she didn't try to hide what she knew showed there; if he refused again, it would be the end of whatever had flashed to life between them. She would know that he had used her, was using her still, and that was something it would be impossible for her to forgive. She saw the understanding in the vivid blue depths, even as she saw the anguish that followed.

"Oh, sunrose, how do I choose? How do I decide between putting you in even more danger than I already have, and having you hate me?"

Abruptly, at the sight of the pain in his eyes, and at the taut, agonized sound of his voice, the knot inside her let go. Even if he was using her, she couldn't bring herself to add to that pain. Softheaded, she told herself caustically. But when she spoke, her voice was level and emotionless.

"He wanted to help with my father's book."

Race's brow furrowed. "What?"

"I called the center to talk to one of my father's colleagues, to ask him for help with the book my father had started. Someone must have told Dr. Whitney about it, and he called me."

"Why?"

He sounded stunned. Kit looked at him, puzzled.

"I told you, he wanted to—"

"No. Why are you telling me now?"

She couldn't answer that, not without revealing more than she already had, which was far too much. "Does it matter?" she asked, a little testily. "Do you want to know or not?"

He looked as if it mattered very much, but after a moment he nodded. "He wanted to help you?"

"He said he could help me better than anyone."

He studied her for a moment. "You...don't sound convinced."

Kit shrugged. "My father didn't think much of Dr. Whitney's credentials as a scientist."

"So you told him . . . ?"

"No. I'm not sure why, except that he was awfully pushy about it. And Daddy didn't like him."

"Your father was a very astute man," Race muttered. "Didn't your father retire quite a while ago?"

Kit didn't comment on his knowledge, knowing she wouldn't get an answer. She merely nodded. "Nearly two years."

"Then why would Whitney wait until now?"

"He probably didn't know about the book until I called the center looking for someone to help."

Race grimaced. "And Whitney volunteered?"

"Adamantly."

"Why?"

Kit gave an exasperated sigh. "How should I know? Dad said he hadn't published anything in years. Maybe he wants a credit on the book."

"More likely *all* the credit," Race said sourly.

Kit lifted an eyebrow. "What are you saying?"

"That if Diogenes had come across Whitney, he'd still be looking for an honest man."

Kit opened her mouth, then shut it. Race eyed her warily.

"What?" he asked.

"Nothing."

"Nothing?"

"I'm tired of asking things you refuse to answer."

He winced. "Kit, it's—"

"—for my own good. So you've said."

"It is, Kit. You don't know what you'd be getting into."

She looked down at him. "It seems to me I'm already in it. Whatever it is."

She saw his jaw tighten, saw the shutter come down again in his eyes. She scrambled off his lap, hating the way she trembled slightly as she stood before him.

"All right, if you won't tell me, I'll have to guess."

She started to pace, her movements short and sharp, betraying her annoyance.

"You know who Dr. Whitney is, well enough to make that kind of character assessment—or is it assassination?" She ignored the grimace he made and kept on, ticking things off on her fingers as though checking off items on a list. "You know of my father. That means you either work at or have some connection with the Agricultural Center. How am I doing so far?"

"Kit—"

"From the way you reacted to Dr. Whitney calling here, it's obvious he has something to do with the trouble you're in. You've mentioned your boss, but with respect, so I know it's not Dr. Whitney. But you haven't gone to him."

"I—"

"So whatever the trouble is, it must be something you know he wouldn't help you out of."

"Stop it."

She knew she'd hit a nerve by the snap in his voice. "Is that what it is? Did Dr. Whitney catch you doing . . . whatever it is that someone wants to kill you over?"

"Damn it!" He was on his feet in a movement so violent that Kit took a step back at the force of it. She saw him wince and flex his wounded shoulder, but the pain barely took the edge off the emotion she saw in his face. "I can't stand this," he grated out. "I never should have come here at all, let alone come back. I should walk out now and never look back."

"What's stopping you?" The quietness of her voice robbed the words of any of the sarcasm they could have held. It also seemed to rob him of his own anger. He let out a compressed breath and closed his eyes as his head lolled back wearily.

"Stupidity?" he suggested grimly.

"Try again. You're as stubborn as this mountain, but not stupid."

His head came up, and his blue gaze fixed upon her. Something odd, something almost like gratification, flashed in his eyes, followed by a softer expression.

"Foolishness, then."

"Foolishness?" Memories of her own foolishness over him pinkened her cheeks.

"Yes," he said softly, "because I can't stand for you to think that of me. Because I want to tell you the whole damned rotten story, just to stop you from looking at me like that."

"So tell me," Kit whispered, barely able to get the words out past the tightness in her throat.

He walked across the room and stood looking out the window into the gray morning light. After a long moment he said quietly, "Will you tell me something first?"

"What?" Her voice was carefully neutral, masking the leap her head had taken at his implication.

"Who's Len?"

She gaped at his back. "What?"

He turned around. "You said . . . you made yourself flirt with him. . . ."

"Oh. Well, I ran into him when I was on my way to the flats to look for you. I had to get rid of him somehow." She wrinkled her nose. "That's the only language the golden boy seems to understand. Anyway, he's the Porters' son. You know, from the store in town."

"He works there?"

Kit laughed. "Hardly. Oh, he helps out now and then, but a man with a law degree is above that kind of thing, as Len would be the first to tell you."

Something harsh and pained flickered in Race's eyes, like the glint of silver off one of the lake trout before it dove to the safety of deep water and was gone. But when he spoke, his voice was as neutral as before.

"The 'golden boy'?"

"Just a local nickname. He's big, blond and handsome. The catch of the century, his parents keep telling me."

"Sounds like they're right."

Kit looked at him sharply, wondering if she'd imagined the edge that had crept into his voice. "If you like people who rest on their laurels," she said. "But what has our local Berkeley Law School graduate got to do with anything?"

"Berkeley? He went to Berkeley?"

"Yes," Kit answered, her brow furrowing at his sudden testiness. "Why?"

"I was just . . . curious."

"Curious? Or trying to distract me?" She didn't say "again," but it seemed to hang in the air as if she had.

"No."

"Then are you going to tell me what all this is about? And what it's got to do with Dr. Whitney wanting to see my father's notes so badly?"

His brows furrowed. "Your father's notes?"

"Yes," she said with strained patience. "That *is* what we were talking about, isn't it?"

"I thought it was a book."

"It will be. My father outlined it, but it's very rough, and I can't make it work if I can't understand his notes. There are tons of them, and those are only the ones he brought home when he retired. I can't even begin to sort them without help."

A stunned look came over Race's face. "Dr. Cameron's notes," he whispered. "God, I didn't realize. I still didn't make the full connection that your father was . . . Dr. Cameron. That's what he's after."

"Who? Race, what are you talking about?"

"Whitney. He wants your father's notes. He must think there's something in them, even from two years ago. . . ."

"Race!"

Her exasperated exclamation shook him out of his shock. He looked at her grimly. "Whitney's . . . involved in something at the center. He's using the facilities for his own project."

"So? If he's the head of the center, he's in charge of all the projects, isn't he?"

"This is not something the university would sanction, believe me."

Kit stared at him. "What's he doing, growing pot?"

Race gave a harsh, humorless chuckle. "I wish it was that simple."

"Then what—"

"Let's just say it's on a considerably higher level than that."

"Higher than growing illegal drugs?"

"Much."

"But what could he be doing under the nose of the University of California that's that serious?"

"It's a long ugly story, sunrose. I only stumbled on it by accident."

Kit's mind was racing now. "You caught him at it?"

"Sort of. I...had a few pieces, my boss had a few. When we put them together, we found we had dynamite."

"So you *do* work at the center."

He shrugged ruefully. "I did."

Kit's forehead creased. "But if your boss knows about this, why isn't he helping?"

Race let out a long breath, and she saw that old haunted look come back into his eyes.

"I don't know. He sent me to the UC Davis Ag Center to have them check something out. He was supposed to meet me when I got back, a few days ago, and we were going to decide who to turn this keg of dynamite over to. But he never showed."

"Maybe he acted on his own. Maybe he decided it couldn't wait—"

"Not Rick. He's very thorough. He wouldn't make a move without this last piece of proof."

"Rick?"

"My boss."

A grim certainty was forming in Kit's mind. "Race," she said softly, "who was your boss at the center?"

His brow furrowed. "Rick. Dr. Richard Parkson."

"Oh God," she whispered, and her heart quailed at the sudden, horrible understanding that shadowed Race's eyes.

Chapter 7

"**I** think I knew, deep down," Race said wearily.

Kit sat on the arm of the sofa, looking down at him. He'd been sitting there so silently for so long that she was almost startled when he finally spoke.

"That's why you asked me, after Harve was here, if I knew who'd been killed, isn't it?" Her voice was low, soft.

He nodded. "When you said it was someone from down below, I hoped I was wrong. But the more time that went by with no word from Rick..."

"I'm sorry, Race." She sighed. "I never knew if they'd found out who it was. I tried to avoid hearing about it. I was...too wrapped up in my own grief, I suppose."

"I understand."

"It sounds like you were...close."

His jaw tightened.

"You were one of the 'bright lights' he found, weren't you?" she asked softly. "My father told me about Dr. Parkson's mentor program."

"He was...more than just a boss. He gave me a chance when nobody else would. He sent me to school, taught me himself, made me think I was more than just—" He broke off, his shoulders slumping. Kit saw him blink rapidly, and tears stung her own eyes. This was too close to her own recent pain, and it hurt unbearably.

"Where did it happen?" he asked tightly, after another long silence.

"On the highway, just at the turn for the lake road. I suppose that's why the first rumors were that he was from down below, because it was late and he was headed down the mountain."

"When?" The word was short, tense, abrupt.

"Last Saturday night."

An explosive curse snapped through the air.

"Race?"

"He was on his way to meet me. I'd called him from Davis, to let him know when the bus was getting in. He was going to pick me up there."

She knew the place he must mean; the only bus station within miles was in the rapidly growing town at the base of the mountain. "What did you do? When he didn't show up?"

"I hitched a ride up the hill. When I got to my place at the center, somebody was already there. Searching it."

"You lived at the center?"

He shrugged, avoiding her eyes. "It was easier."

She wondered at his unease, but only asked, "Did you see who it was?"

"Only one of them. A big guy I'd seen around Whitney's office before. I figured Whitney was on to me, so I didn't hang around."

"If he was on to you, then ..."

"I know. He must have guessed I would have gone to Rick. That's why I didn't dare leave. I thought maybe he was holding Rick or ... something." An oddly remorseful look crossed his face, but after a fractional pause he went on. "So I kept going back to the center, trying to find out...."

"That's why you were down by Hank's place," Kit said in a tone of discovery. "You were headed for the center."

He nodded, a rueful smile twisting his lips. "Brodie damned near took care of me for them." The smile faded. "And all the time, Rick was already . . ."

"I'm so sorry," she said softly. "That accident certainly made things easier for Whitney, didn't it?"

"Accident?" Race's head came up sharply. "Ah, sunrose, you are an innocent, aren't you?"

"What do you—" Her breath caught in her throat. "Oh God. Do you mean . . . ?"

"A rather convenient hit-and-run, wasn't it?" he said bitterly. "*Too* convenient."

"My God, Race, you're talking about murder!"

"So? What's the difference between running a man down on a dark road and ambushing somebody in a dark house?"

"What do you mean?"

"After I found them at my place, I walked to Rick's house. Whitney's goons beat me there. They were waiting outside. Same guys, I think, at least the big one. Still never saw the other one. But they had guns. If I hadn't been half expecting them, they would have killed me. That's when I headed up the mountain."

Kit was stunned. Her feelings about the man aside, Martin Whitney was a respected scientist. The thought of him being involved in something criminal, of him having such thugs at his command, was ludicrous. To think of him as responsible for the murder of a colleague was absurd.

"I know," Race said softly. "It's hard to believe. The only good thing is that they couldn't have found the evidence Rick had, or they wouldn't still be after me. And that Rick didn't . . ."

He stopped, his mouth tightening, and suddenly that remorseful look made sense to her. "You thought he'd set you up?"

"I . . . wondered."

God, Kit thought, what kind of life had he led, that he could suspect even the person closest to him of such a thing? No wonder he didn't trust her; he didn't trust anyone. She wanted to say something, to reassure him, to point out that he could trust her just as he could have trusted Rick, but she couldn't find the words. Maybe there weren't any.

She steadied herself, and after a moment she asked softly, "You're sure they're still after you?"

He laughed grimly. "I've been dodging them for days now. Why do you think I kept trying to stay away from you? The last thing I wanted was to bring them down on you."

Kit shook her head slowly. "I . . ."

"I'm sorry, Kit. I never meant to get you mixed up in this."

"I know. But it seems I am."

He nodded slowly, glumly.

"But I don't understand what this has to do with my father's notes. Why would Dr. Whitney want to see them now, after all this time?"

"He must think there's something there that could hurt him." He ran a hand through his hair, wincing as the movement pulled on the wounds in his back and shoulder. He lowered his arm and looked up at Kit.

"I know you're not quite sure you believe me yet," he began slowly, "but . . . could I see the notes you're talking about?"

She looked at him for a long time, studying his face as if she could find all the answers she didn't have there. All she saw was a quiet weariness, along with the dark shadow of grief. You've always led with your heart, Kit m'girl, she thought. Why stop now? She stood up suddenly.

"All right."

He looked startled; then a slow smile curved his mouth. "You're one of a kind, sunrose."

He followed her up the stairs, carrying the lamp she'd told him they would need.

"I . . . keep forgetting to get a bulb for the desk lamp."

He plugged in the lamp, then straightened up to survey the clutter on the desk. He let out a low whistle.

"You can see why I need help."

"It's quite a stack all right."

He pulled up the chair she'd slid over to him and sat down. He angled the lamp shade and began to scan the various stacks.

"I tried to sort it out, but he had it in such a weird order, I couldn't make any sense of it. I know this was what he was using for the book, but it doesn't match the outline at all." She gave him a wry smile. "Not that I would have a clue anyway. For the life of me, I don't know a hyphae from a mycelium."

"One's made up of the other," Race said, not looking up from the sheet of scrawled entries he'd picked up.

"Huh?"

"Mycelium is what they call the mass of hyphae in a fungus."

"Oh." Kit sighed; she'd been wrestling with this for so long, she was beyond hiding her ignorance. "What's a hyphae?"

He looked up at her and grinned briefly. "They're threads of simple cells that tangle together to make a mycelium."

"Oh. Thanks a lot."

She watched as he sifted through the stacks of papers, careful not to disturb the order. She saw his eyes flick over the pages, searching, stopping occasionally, then racing on. It was nothing like her own plodding pace, and she began to realize that much of this was familiar to him. Tentatively, she asked another question.

"What's a zoospore?"

"A reproductive cell that can move on its own," Race answered absently, his eyes still scanning rapidly over her father's pages.

"On its own?"

"Usually by swimming. Fungi that grow in wet conditions produce them."

She tried another question, then another, and got the same result; answers given quickly and simply, even with only part of his attention. He obviously knew what he was dealing with, she thought, much more than she did. She wondered again what he'd done at the center. She knew most of the people there were at the least college students, more often Ph.D's like her father, yet Race had said he'd never been to college.

"California peach rust," Race murmured.

"What?"

He looked up at her from the page he was holding. "I forgot that your father discovered that."

"Oh. You mean the disease they wanted to name after him?"

"That's an honor, you know."

"Sure. Cameron peach rust."

"It took a lot of work, Kit. To isolate it, test it, identify the casual agent so it could be treated—"

"I know. Don't think that I don't respect my father's work. I do." She sighed. "It's a defense mechanism, I suppose, because it's all over my head. I'm embarrassed, because I'm a reasonably intelligent person, yet I can't understand much of his work. But I do know how important that was."

Race studied her for a moment. "You're also a very honest person, sunrose. I envy you."

It seemed an odd thing to say, but Kit wasn't sure why, so she said nothing. He went back to the papers, and she saw him flex his shoulder again.

"Does it still hurt?"

"Not really. Just a little twinge now and then." He glanced up at her. "Nice work, doc."

"Thanks," she said with a grimace. "But I wouldn't want to do that again." She eyed him warily. "You might keep that in mind."

A grin tugged at the corners of his mouth. "I'll do that."

She watched as he went back to the stack of papers, reading, his hands turning over sheets rhythmically, wondering yet again what he was looking for. She was so intent in her scrutiny that her breath caught when the rhythm was interrupted and his hands stopped. Then she saw what it was that had stopped him.

"I don't know what that was doing in there," she said, gesturing toward the newspaper clipping she'd noticed before. "It didn't make any sense, but I didn't want to take it out until I was sure it didn't have anything to do with anything."

It was a moment before he looked up at her, and Kit got the oddest feeling that he had delayed in an effort to compose himself.

"Is this the only clipping?"

"The only one here," she answered. "I haven't gone through his other boxes, only the ones he had labeled for the book."

"Could you look?"

Kit glanced from him to the clipping, then back. "I don't get it. What does this have to do with anything?"

"I'm not sure yet."

With a sigh, Kit turned and went to the other boxes stacked against the wall.

"All those?"

Race sounded incredulous, and Kit smothered a laugh. "You should see what he *didn't* bring home. There must have been a dozen file cabinets full that he left at the center. My father took notes on everything. He— What's wrong?"

"Maybe that's why Whitney waited until now. Maybe he didn't realize there were more notes."

"Until...I called the center," Kit said slowly. She stared at the boxes. "But what could be here? Surely this...whatever it is, wasn't going on back when my father was there?"

"I don't know. But the fact that Whitney was interested is enough to interest me."

Kit looked back at the stack of boxes that was as tall as she was. "If you'd tell me what you're looking for, maybe I could help."

"Just look for more clippings, for now."

With a frustrated sigh, Kit dragged down the top box and sat on the floor. She wished he would just tell her instead of playing this silly game of trying to protect her from a situation she was obviously already in up to her neck.

The time ticked by, and when she was halfway through the third box, she realized that when she had lugged them all up to the loft, she had stacked them in reverse order. Perhaps she should have started at the bottom, which would have been the top before she'd moved them.

She quickly finished the box she was on, then tried to tug the bottom box out from under the rest. She wrestled with it for a few moments, and then Race was there, lifting the others so she could pull it free.

"Thank you."

It came out edged with her frustration, a frustration she knew was visible as she yanked the lid off the box, but she wasn't sure she cared anymore.

"If you're tired, I'll go through the rest of those."

"What I'm tried of," she snapped, whirling on him, "is working in the dark. What I'm tired of is you telling me half a story. What I'm tired of is wondering what my father's notes have to do with any of this, and what that clipping has to do with my father's notes. What I'm tired of is . . . is . . ."

"Me?"

He was staring at her with that shuttered look. For an instant she wanted to say yes, anything to get his disturbing presence out of her life. She had enough to deal with, adjusting to the loss of her father, without the chaos he created in her.

As if he'd read that answer, he drew back, his jaw tightening.

"I don't blame you. But I can't leave yet, Kit. There's a chance there may be something here. I've got to find it. All I have now are the test results from the ag labs at Davis, and that isn't enough. Not without the evidence Rick had."

"But maybe you can get it. You said they didn't find it."

"Rick might not have had it with him. He could have been on his way home first. He lives . . . lived down off the lake road."

Kit's heart twisted at the look on his face as he made the correction she'd had to make so often herself. But, remembering how even the most well-meaning condolences had only made things worse, she said nothing about it.

"Did he keep it at home?" she asked instead.

He nodded. "He didn't want to keep it at the center. We didn't know how many people there were involved."

Kit bit back her frustration at his purposeful vagueness. "That must be why they were at his place," she suggested. "If they didn't find it that night..."

She trailed off, knowing he was probably still wrestling with the realization that his friend and mentor had died such a horrible death. It took him a moment, but when he spoke, it was evenly enough.

The muscle on the side of his jaw tightened further. "They wouldn't still be looking for me if they'd found it. They know I can't prove anything without it."

Again she bit back her exasperation. "So they don't have the evidence."

"No."

"But they think you do."

He nodded. "But I don't."

"But what do you think you'll find here?" She gestured at the boxes and the papers on the table.

"I won't know until I find it."

"Oh!" The exclamation burst from her in an explosive breath. "You are the stubbornest, most—"

"Yeah. I know. You told me."

"All right! I'll sit and go through these damned boxes all day, if that's what you want, until we find whatever it is you think is here. Then you can just go out on your stubborn, one-man crusade and leave me in peace!"

She plopped back down on the floor, swiping a hand furtively over her cheeks. He knelt beside her, his hands on her shoulders, and turned her to face him. She knew that her tears still glistened beneath her eyes, but she wasn't about to humiliate herself further by brushing at them now.

"Oh, sunrose, I'm tearing you up, aren't I?"

"Yes!" She lowered her eyes.

"I'm sorry. I didn't think what it would do to you to have to go through all your father's things."

Kit looked at him blankly. "I didn't mean this—" She cut herself off, blushing.

"Then what?"

His eyes widened, and Kit's blush deepened as she realized that he'd understood as clearly as if she'd finished the sentence; it wasn't going through her father's things that upset her; it was him.

"I . . . disturb your peace?"

She lifted her head then, even knowing what a failure she was at hiding intense emotions. "You know you do."

"Kit," he breathed softly. She felt his hands clench on her shoulders, felt him start to draw her closer. Then he stopped, and she saw that odd fleeting look of harsh pain flicker deep in his eyes again.

"Race . . . ?"

"Kit, I can't. I want—God, I can't."

It was so tortured that Kit couldn't stop herself from reaching out to touch him, to run one slender finger along the firm line of his jaw.

A low, strangled sound broke from him, and in the next instant she was in his arms, crushed tightly to his chest. He was pressing soft kisses on her hair, over her forehead, on her still damp cheeks. She tilted her head back, knowing she was inviting disaster, but unable to stop herself from searching eagerly for his mouth.

She heard another sound, low, soft and somehow hot, but she wasn't sure if it came from him or from her. Then she found his lips, and the only thing she heard was the beating of her pulse in her ears.

He deepened the kiss hungrily, nibbling at her lips, his tongue stroking her mouth, then probing deeply, as if he couldn't get enough. She felt it begin again, that new, wonderful melting sensation, that golden heat that spread through her in ever-widening waves.

She lifted her hands, sliding them around his neck. Her fingers slipped beneath the collar of the robe, and down over sleek, hot skin. His tongue plunged deeper, and she met it with her own eagerly. Her fingers flexed involuntarily, as if testing the strong, hard muscle beneath that sleek skin, and she felt a shiver ripple through him.

She heard him groan low in his throat; then he drew back his tongue. She moaned in protest, reaching to regain the sweet contact. It was a moment before she read the withdrawal for the invitation it was, but when she did, she didn't hesitate to flick her tongue over his lips and then beyond. She searched the new, enticing territory of his mouth, tracing the even ridge of his teeth. Then his tongue surged forward again to taste hers, sparring, dancing, stroking, until she nearly gasped at the growing heat.

He slid his hands down her back, grasping her waist and pulling her against him. They went down to the floor together, Kit draping herself over him as the need to feel that sweet flowing heat everywhere flooded her again. Emboldened by his sound of pleasure, she probed deeper into his mouth, loving the taste of him. Her hands slid over his chest, seeking beneath the robe, and she wondered if he was so smooth and sleek and hot everywhere. She delighted in his quick intake of breath when her fingers found the smooth swell of his chest, then stroked the sparse scattering of hair in the center. She savored the rippling beneath her fingers as she traced the beginning of the ridged musculature of his belly. She reveled in his groan when she found and circled the flat nubs of his nipples. But most of all she rejoiced in the racing hammerbeats of his heart as she laid her palm flat against him; it proved to her that she was not alone on this crazy, reckless flight.

Then she felt his hands slide up under her shirt, first stroking across her back, then stilling to press her hard against him. He shifted until he was completely beneath her, taking her slight weight with a low growl of pleasure. She felt him then, the fully aroused length of him pressing against her belly. Driven by a need she'd never known before, she twisted, caressing him with the movement of her body, his short, sharp groan of her name making her want to do it with her hands, her mouth and any other way she could think of.

The acknowledgment of that desire stunned her. She'd never felt anything like it before, never wanted, never needed, like this before, and the realization shocked her into stillness. My God, she thought, what am I doing?

"Kit?"

"I..." She braced one hand on the floor and pushed away, staring down at him, all her bewilderment clear on her face. "I don't even know your last name," she said in a tiny voice.

It was as if she'd cast him out into the snow that still lingered in the shady places of the mountain. His eyes went from deep, hot sapphire to ice in an instant. He lifted her off him, his hands gripping hard enough to hurt, then turned away from her as if he wanted to hide the fact that his heated, aroused body had not made the change so quickly. She saw a shudder go through him, saw his hands knot into fists as if he were waging some silent battle with himself.

"Race..." she began, not really knowing what to say, only knowing that she felt as if she'd delivered a mortal blow to an already wounded creature.

"You're right," he said, not looking at her. "You don't know the first thing about me. If you did, you'd hate yourself for letting me touch you."

He got unsteadily to his feet. The robe did nothing to hide the evidence that his body was still intent on what her stunned sensibilities had interrupted. And, incredibly, when he realized she had noticed, a dull red flush rose to his face. Then he was gone, his bare feet making little sound on the stairs as he hurriedly left the loft.

Kit sat there for a long time, listening to his movements downstairs, wondering what he was doing. She didn't know what to do. She'd never felt like this, never been so utterly confused.

She heard him mutter something, probably to Gus, she thought. Her hands flicked idly over the file folders in the box beside her, patting at the uneven edges of the papers they held in a halfhearted effort to neaten them. Then something about the texture of those papers got through to her, and she turned her head to look.

He was in the kitchen when she went downstairs, adding another to a small row of cans he had on the counter. He'd dressed in the ragged jeans and shirt she'd washed again last night, his own socks and boots, and her father's heavy overshirt.

He paused in the act of setting down the can he held, and she knew he'd heard her in the doorway. Then he set it down without turning and reached for a canvas sack that she recognized as one of her father's old sample bags from the toolshed. Dampened, it had kept his cuttings fresh until he got home; dry, it was a sturdy tote bag. Which was obviously Race's intention, she saw, as he began to put the cans into it.

"I'll pay you for these. And the other food."

His voice was flat, emotionless, as dead a sound as she'd ever heard. She took a step into the room.

"When I can, I'll send the shirt back."

"Race..."

He turned around, his face as bleak as his voice. "And I have to borrow this for a while. I'll get it back to you somehow."

Her eyes widened when she saw that his fingers were resting on the butt of her father's gun, stuck into the waistband of his jeans. He reached out and picked up his knife, which sat on the counter, and shoved it into his pocket; she wondered vaguely if it had a can opener on it.

"I'm sorry," he said. Remorse flickered across his face, the first trace of emotion she'd seen. "For everything."

Kit had had about enough of this one-man campaign of his. He seemed bound and determined to handle things alone, keeping her out of what was happening even though it was crystal clear to her that she was already involved through her father, even if she didn't know quite how. If there was anything her father had taught her growing up, it was his quiet way of reviewing the situation and making a decision based on the available facts. Well, she'd looked at the facts and she'd made a decision. And if Race didn't like it, that was tough.

"I think," she said coolly, "that you might want to look at this." She lifted the file folder she held, holding it so he could see the newspaper article she'd clipped to the outside. "If you have time, of course, before you take off running again."

He flinched, but Kit got the oddest feeling it was more from her choice of words than her biting tone; he looked as if he'd expected the latter.

"What is it?" he asked after a moment.

"What you were looking for, I presume."

He crossed the room in one long stride and took the folder from her. He flipped it open, his eyes narrowing at the sight of the small stack of photocopied news clippings. She saw him suck in a breath at the sight of the first one, quickly turn to the next, then the next.

"Damn."

It was low, vehement and frightening. As was the way he sank down into the kitchen chair beside him, almost as if his knees had given way.

"Race, what is it?"

"He knew," Race breathed.

"What?"

He glanced up at her, then back at the file. She saw that muscle along his jaw tighten and knew he was gearing up to refuse her again. Without speaking, he reached for a ragged piece of pale green paper that sat amid the photocopied clippings.

"Damn it, Race, those are my father's papers! I didn't have to show them to you. I didn't even have to tell you about them!"

"I know." He tugged the green paper loose. Kit vaguely noticed that it was graph-ruled, like the lab books she'd seen her father use so often; in fact, it looked as if it had been torn out of one, but she was too angry to wonder about it. Her anger increased at his refusal to answer, and her voice rose a notch.

"Don't I at least have the right to know what a stack of articles about some ten-year-long war between two little countries halfway around the world has to do with my father? He only cared about his work, he never followed that kind of thing, why would he save those—"

She interrupted her own tirade; he'd gone starkly pale, nearly as pale as he had at the realization that Rick Parkson had been the man killed on that dark, lonely road last Saturday night. Slowly, she sat down in the chair beside him.

"Race?"

He looked up at her then, the piece of paper shaking a little with the intensity of his grip.

"This is Rick's," he said hoarsely.

She stared at the paper, seeing for the first time the neat, tidy writing, so unlike her father's rather wild scrawl.

"It's not my father's writing," she admitted slowly.

She reached for it, and after a moment's hesitation, he gave it to her. "It's Rick's," he said flatly.

The note was short, merely a reference to an earlier telephone conversation and a brief explanation. "These were pulled from the university files," it said, "and I'm very much afraid of what they may mean. Please consider this carefully. You understand the ramifications."

She looked at him. "Does he mean the clippings?"

"It was fastened to them. The latest is dated two months ago."

Kit's eyes widened. Barely two weeks before her father had died. "I knew he'd been in contact with Dr. Parkson, he mentioned it the . . . day I got here, before he . . ."

Race sucked in a deep breath. "He told me he was going to consult with an expert. I had no idea he meant your father."

"Race, I still don't understand! What does this have to do with anything? With my father's work? With Dr. Parkson's work?"

"It figures," he said under his breath, as if he were thinking out loud. "Who else would he go to but the man who'd been in a position to notice the same things we'd found...?"

He looked at her sharply then, and when he spoke his voice was brusque, almost sharp. "When you last talked to your father, did he say anything about the center? Mention anything... unusual?"

"No, but..."

"But what?"

"Well, it's just a feeling I got. Nothing he said, really..."

"Tell me!"

She drew back at his sharp tone.

"I'm sorry, Kit, but this is important. I can't tell you how important."

"You," she said, a little sourly, "can't tell me *anything*, it seems."

"Please, sunrose." He reached out and took her hands in his. "I know I've got no right to make demands, but I have to know. What kind of a feeling?"

She sighed. "Just something he said in our last phone conversation, before I left to come here. He said something odd had come up. Something that intrigued him. But he didn't mention it again when I got here, and I thought I'd been wrong."

"About what?"

"I got the idea it had to do with his work at the center. I didn't understand why, since he'd retired, but I thought maybe he'd never quite let go. It was his life for twenty years, and he still felt... connected, I guess. I—"

She broke off as something occurred to her. Race didn't miss the look that crossed her face.

"What is it, Kit? You thought of something."

"I remember my father said something about Dr. Parkson coming to see him about some kind of problem. I thought he meant that he'd come for scientific advice, but..."

"When? Did he say when?"

Her brow furrowed as she tried to remember. "I think...yes, it was just after my session wound up at the literacy center. About two weeks before..." She trailed off.

"Before he died?" Race asked gently.

She nodded.

"And about the time this last clipping is dated."

She nodded again. Slowly. Feeling as she had when she first realized her father was truly gone; lost, adrift and utterly bewildered. And the only person who could explain it all, who could help her understand, wouldn't.

"I remember how upset Rick was when your father died," he said, in the quiet tone of one who knew that the words were all he could give, and that they weren't enough. "He felt as if he'd lost not only a valued colleague but a good friend."

She said nothing, but a tiny, whimpering sound escaped despite her efforts to hold it back.

"Oh, sunrose," Race said softly, lifting one of her hands and kissing it gently. "I'm sorry."

"Don't," she said stiffly. "I'm tired of apologies."

He looked at her for a long, silent moment. Then, in a low, almost tender voice that pulled at something deep inside her, he said, "Yes. I imagine you are. And you're right. You have every right to know what's going on."

"So you're going to tell me everything, right, Mr. Who-ever-you-are?" She couldn't help the sarcasm that tinged her voice as she threw his own words back at him.

"Barkley. My last name's Barkley." He looked pained, as if it hurt him to say it. His mouth quirked at her expression. "I don't blame you for not trusting me. Lord knows I've given you no reason to. But believe me, Kit, I was only trying to protect you."

"Then why tell me now?"

Something flickered in his eyes, something dark, shadowed. Worry, she thought. And resignation. As if where he'd once decided he had no choice but to keep it from her, he now had no choice but to tell her.

"You have to know now. Because—"

Gus's trumpeting bark made them both jump, and they stared as the big dog skidded slightly on the kitchen floor, then dug in and raced into the great room.

Kit glanced at Race. He'd gone rigid, staring after the big dog. His eyes flicked to her, and she shrugged.

"I don't know. I'll go see." She got to her feet.

"Kit."

She glanced back to see him watching her intently. "Don't worry," she said ironically. "I have no intention of turning you in until I hear the whole story."

He winced. "I guess I deserved that. But I—"

They barely heard the knock on the door over Gus's new outbreak of thunderous barking. Kit looked that way, then back at Race.

"Go," he said.

She hesitated a second, then nodded and walked into the great room, pulling the rarely used door nearly shut behind her, masking any view into the kitchen from the other room. She looked out the window as she headed for the door, seeing but not recognizing the big gray sedan that was parked in the drive.

Gus was dancing beside the door, emitting low growls. Kit reached out to tangle her fingers in the thick hair on his neck, not sure if it was so she could hold him back or urge him on. For the first time she wished there were a window in the door; she didn't much like living this way, she thought. Then, taking a deep breath to steady herself, she opened the door.

Her eyes flicked quickly from the balding man in the dark blue, pinstriped, three-piece suit who stood on her porch to the huge, brawny man who stood behind him, clad in a pair of green coveralls.

"Miss Cameron?"

Her gaze shot back to the pinstriped suit, to the horn-rimmed glasses that made his eyes seem oddly small and flat. Something about the precise, prim tones made a memory click. Kit's heart began to hammer in her chest.

She fought to control it, to keep the sudden fear that had flooded her from showing. In a voice that was remarkably steady, she answered him.

"Dr. Whitney, I presume?"

Chapter 8

Race crouched behind the kitchen door, straining to hear. He supposed that to most people Kit's voice would sound completely normal. But he'd come to know her rather well in the last few days, and he heard the undertone of strain. And so did Gus; he heard the big dog whine agitatedly. Whitney, he thought. Damn.

"I'm sorry, Dr. Whitney, but as I told you on the phone, I've only begun to go through my father's notes."

"Of course. But that's why I'm here, to offer any assistance I can."

"And your... friend here? I suppose he's here in case I need any furniture moved?"

Easy, Kit, Race thought. Don't fly off the handle now.

"Er, Walt is my driver." Whitney laughed. "I don't care for these mountain roads."

Walt Squires, Race thought. The hulk who'd trashed his place. Damn, he'd brought the muscle. And Kit was out there alone. Every muscle in his body tensed.

"They are rather difficult to negotiate." Kit's voice was smoother, the edge that had crept into it hidden now.

Atta girl, he thought.

"Yes. Er, may we come in?"

Race held his breath.

"If you don't mind, Dr. Whitney," Kit said smoothly, "I don't really feel up to company today. Another time, perhaps."

"Well, then, if I could just take a quick look at your father's notes...?"

"I'm afraid not. Until I go through them, I just wouldn't feel right about anyone seeing them. Even though," she added with a slight emphasis, "I don't understand much of what is there. I may put it off altogether for a while."

Nice move, sunrose. Make him feel safer.

"As I said, Miss Cameron, I'm here to offer my help."

"That's very...kind of you, but I'm not ready to discuss my father's papers. It's too soon."

Whitney cleared his throat audibly. "Surely you could make an exception for me, Miss Cameron."

Arrogant son of a— Gus's whine interrupted Race's silent epithet; the dog clearly didn't like this any more than he did.

"Really, Dr. Whitney, surely you understand my feelings. Those notes are my father's—"

"I'm afraid not, Miss Cameron." Something hard and steely came into the man's voice. "You see, in reality, those notes are the property of the center."

"What?"

Kit's astonished exclamation blended with Gus's short bark. Race tensed, not at all sure what he was going to do, only knowing that if there was the slightest hint of danger to Kit he would think of something. He would go for a knife, he thought, the big one that Kit had sliced the meat loaf with the other day, and—

"You heard me. Anything to do with any of the center's...projects is technically the center's property."

"My father left all of his relevant papers at the center," Kit said stiffly. "He brought only his personal notes home."

"I'm afraid I must verify that, Miss Cameron."

Race stiffened as he heard a thud that sounded like the door being forced against the wall. At Gus's angry growl he was upright, his hand reaching for the kitchen door. Then Kit took matters into her own hands.

"Easy, Gus. Dr. Whitney, you are being unconscionably rude. And your timing is unforgivable. Please leave."

"I'm afraid I must insist, Miss Cam—"

"No, *I* insist, Dr. Whitney. I will decide if and when *anyone* sees my father's notes. And until then, I must ask you both to leave."

Race heard a heavy footstep, and again reached for the door. And again Kit handled things.

"Let me rephrase that, Dr. Whitney. *Gus* and I must ask you both to leave."

As if on cue, the big dog snarled fiercely, menacingly, and Race heard the scrape of his toenails on the wood floor, followed closely by the resounding slam of the door and the click of the lock. He sagged against the doorjamb, only realizing how tightly strung he had been when the tension released him.

When he heard the car start and the sound of tires fading away on the gravel drive, he slowly pushed the door open.

Kit was leaning against the wall, her eyes closed, her face pale. Gus was sitting anxiously at her feet, making tiny whimpering sounds that sounded odd coming from the large animal.

He could see why the dog was worried, he thought as he looked at her. He could see it in the way she moved as she straightened, slowly, hesitantly, with none of the fluid grace that had been the first thing he'd noticed about her when he'd been watching her from the woods. Well, almost the first thing, he thought, remembering how the spring sun had lit her dark hair with fiery highlights, turning it all the colors of autumn leaves.

Her head was down now, hiding from him those incredible eyes that were the color of golden-brown amber held up to the sun, and flecked with pure gold. With her coloring, she had looked that day like some lithe, woodland creature completely at home on her mountain; now she looked like a frightened fawn that had just discovered a deadly threat in her serene meadow.

Another image rose up, unbidden, of the only time he'd heard her laugh, romping with that absurdly huge dog in the meadow in front of the house. Her laughter had rung out across the new spring grass, echoing like wind chimes in a gentle breeze, and it had, for a brief moment, filled all the hollow places inside him.

And now she was standing there shaking, this woman who had given him that unexpected gift. This woman who had braved a killer for him. Race crossed the room in four long strides and gripped her shoulders. He felt the little tremors that were rippling through her.

"Kit, it's okay."

Her eyes fluttered open; they were huge, the golden flecks that had so intrigued him erased by the wideness of lingering fright.

"Kit," he repeated a little sharply as she only stared at him blankly.

"I . . . didn't know what to do," she said.

The quaver in her voice ripped at him, and he couldn't stop himself from pulling her into his arms. The moment he did the small tremors became shudders, wracking her slender frame. He felt the tears start and held her tighter.

"Shh, sunrose." He pressed her head against his shoulder. It was like her, he thought, to handle the crisis with flying colors and only succumb to the strain afterward. "You did fine. You were perfect."

"I was afraid he'd push his way in. That he'd find you . . ."

His throat tightened unbearably. She'd done so much for him, with so little reason, and he'd done nothing for her except add to her grief. "He's gone, Kit. You handled him perfectly."

She gulped, trying to control her sobs. "He—he sounded so cold . . . hard. I really think he *is* capable of something horrible. He was so angry. . . . God, I was so scared. . . ."

"I know, sunrose. But you did it anyway. You sent him and that muscle-headed moron of his off with their tails between their legs."

Gus whined.

"Okay, okay. You and Gus, then."

It was a forced joke, but it seemed to turn the tide for her; after a couple of small hiccups, she bit her lip and stemmed the flow of tears.

"Do you... think he'll come back?"

Race looked down into her tearstained face, and couldn't find it in himself to lie to her; he'd lied so much already.

"Eventually, yes. But I think you threw him off the scent for now. He'll think he's safe as long as you don't know what you have. You think pretty fast, sunrose."

He smiled at her and reached out to brush away the last of her tears with the backs of his fingers. Her skin was so soft and smooth it made his fingers tingle with the urge to touch more than just her cheek. He smothered the thought before it gave rise to others that he couldn't afford, thoughts that he'd been battling for what seemed like forever, since the first day he'd seen her shed her bulky jacket to reveal a lithe, femininely curved shape, the sun streaking through the trees to turn rich chestnut hair to fire.

"I don't feel like I did," she said, her voice rueful now. "I think my knees were shaking the whole time."

"You were beautiful, Kit. *I* was the one whose knees were shaking, I was so scared for you, out there fighting my battles for me." And I felt so damned useless, he thought. "All I could think of was that if things went sour, I hoped to God Gus went for Walt, because I could take Whitney, but I wouldn't have a prayer against that gorilla."

"I didn't like the way he looked at all."

"You wouldn't like the way he cleans house either. He sure made a mess of mine."

She stared up at him. "He's the one? The one you saw in your place that night? And at Rick's?"

He nodded. "Whitney's favorite chunk of muscle." She shuddered, and he hugged her again. "It's okay. I don't think he'll be back for a while. He'll be worrying about the threat he knows exists first, not one that may or may not exist.''

"You mean you."

He hadn't meant to put it that way, but it was the truth, and he knew she was too smart not to realize it. He'd learned many things about Kit Cameron since the day he'd first seen her by the creek, many before they'd even come face to face. He'd learned that she was carrying a heavy load of sadness; it had been evident in the weary slump of her slender shoulders as she had sat on that rock, soaking up the rays of the spring sun as if she needed their radiant strength to replenish her own. He'd learned of her gentleness in the moments when he'd seen her with the big, shaggy golden-brown dog he'd kept such a wary eye on. He'd learned of her generous spirit—and, he supposed, of her courage—when she'd left him food while the rest of the mountain was hunting him. And he'd learned the lengths to which she would follow the course she'd chosen when she had given him her beloved father's shirt.

She was, he thought, an exceptional person. The kind of person who came along rarely in lonely, grim lives like his. He'd met one such person in Rick Parkson; he'd never expected to meet another. After his initial mistrust, he had come to understand why Rick had helped him; why Kit Cameron did so was beyond him.

"He'll keep hunting for you, won't he?"

He let out a long breath. "Yes. He has no choice."

"Then neither do we. We have to go to the police."

He felt as if he'd been kicked in the gut. She looked up at him, puzzled, and he knew she'd felt him recoil at her words.

"Race?"

"No."

"But we have to! My God, if he truly killed Dr. Parkson and he's still after you—"

"No."

"But—"

"I can't."

"Race, why? You can't let him get away with—"

"I can't. Just take my word for it, I can't."

For a moment she just stared at him. Then, slowly, "Is it . . . what you said before? When you thought Harve was here looking for you for something else?"

He almost told her then. The words he'd never said to anyone, not even Rick, were on the tip of his tongue for this amber-eyed woman who seemed to have taken over his life. For a brief moment he almost had himself convinced that she would understand. Then reality flooded back in, cold and harsh and unavoidable.

She was watching his face, saw the change. "Race, if it was so long ago . . ."

He fought back the words again, angry with this urge that had overtaken him, this urge to tell her everything. He knew his voice was flat, dead-sounding, but he couldn't help it. "It doesn't matter. Even if I could go to them, they wouldn't believe me."

"But even without whatever proof Rick had, surely you can tell them—"

"They won't listen. There's no way they would believe me. Not about this. I barely believe it myself."

She just looked at him, and he knew it was time. He'd kept her in the dark for far too long; she deserved part of the explanation, at the very least. And she needed to know what they were dealing with. She needed, he thought grimly, to be scared enough to be careful; she was too damned gutsy for her own good.

"How about some coffee? I think," he added gently, "you're going to need it. This is a long story."

In a few minutes they were sitting once again at the kitchen table, steaming mugs of coffee before them, the folder Whitney had been within feet of finding between them. He tilted the cup in his hands, as if the swirling, dark liquid could tell him where to start. Kit sat quietly, as if now that she knew he was going to tell her, she could wait. That alone amazed him; all things considered, she'd been more patient than he ever could have been.

"How much do you know about the center?" he asked at last.

Her brows furrowed. "Not as much as I should, I suppose, for all the years my father worked there. I know that it's where it is because it gives them two different belts of vegetation to study, both the forest and the alpine level that's above...oh, I forget."

"Eighty-five-hundred feet."

"Right." She wrinkled her nose. "I do words, not numbers. Anyway, I know they study plants and work on developing new strains that will resist diseases."

"What about your father's work?"

"Not much." She shrugged helplessly. "I mean, I know what my dad's work was, as a mycologist." A sad little smile curved her mouth. "I used to tell my friends my dad grew mushrooms. They never believed me."

Race reached over and gently laid a hand over hers. "Quite a description for one of the world's foremost experts on fungi."

"I think that's why I said it. I always hated that word. Fungus. Yech." She sighed, then seemed to steady herself, as if setting aside poignant memories. "So, I admit, I don't know much. Do I need to?"

"Sort of." He swirled the cup again. "Plant diseases are tricky things. To most people it seems like they just happen, but it really takes a pretty intricate set of conditions."

"The disease triangle? I remember my father telling me about that when I was in high school." She gave him a contrite grin that made his stomach knot and his heart swell with a wish to have known her then. "I wasn't above using my at-home resource to make my life easier when I was lost in the wilderness of eleventh-grade biology."

Then the smile faded, and the sadness crept back. Instinctively, his hand curled around hers, seeking to give what comfort he could.

"I'm sorry, Kit. I know this must be hard for you."

"Never mind," she said tightly. "Go on."

"Okay. If you know about the triangle, then you know there are three things that have to be present for a disease to occur. A pathogen, a favorable environment and a susceptible host."

She nodded. "And Daddy said time and temperature were variables."

"Right. Well, the center studied those things under laboratory conditions so they could determine how best to stop a disease before it got started, usually by changing one side of that triangle. You with me?"

"I think so. You mean by, say, killing off the virus, or whatever the pathogen is, or changing the conditions around it so that it couldn't multiply."

The grief, he saw gratefully, had receded, replaced by an alert concentration.

"Exactly. Or by developing a different strain of the host, one that isn't susceptible to that particular pathogen. Only in this case . . . Whitney went the other way."

"Huh?"

"Instead of developing a resistant host, he developed a stronger pathogen."

"Why on earth would he do that? And what does that have to do with anything?"

He sighed. This was going to be harder than he'd thought. "Let me start at the other end," he said after a moment. "About a year ago, I started noticing some weird things going on at the center."

"Weird?"

He nodded. "It was about six months after a big research project was dropped, without being finished."

"Why?"

"Dr. Whitney's orders. He said another center had taken it over. That wasn't strange in itself, since our main fungi expert—" he glanced at her, but she only nodded at the reference to her father "—had retired. But the supplies for the project kept coming in."

"Supplies?"

"Certain chemicals, specific types of imported soil. Things we had no other use for." He took a sip of coffee, then set down the mug. "At first I thought it was just a mix-up, that the suppliers hadn't gotten the word. I told Whitney, and he said not to worry about it. He'd handle it."

Kit tugged idly at a strand of hair, and Race couldn't help remembering how it had felt like living, warm silk against his fingers. His hand tightened around the mug.

"About that same time," he went on after a moment, "things started disappearing out of the lab. First it was little things, test tubes, PH-test kits, eyedroppers, chemicals. Silly stuff. Then it was an incubator, a microscope, big stuff."

He couldn't blame her for the bewildered look she gave him. "All this is over some stolen lab equipment?"

He sighed. "No. At first I thought that was all that was going on, so I reported *it* to Whitney, too."

"And?"

His mouth twisted into a travesty of a smile; it would be a long time before he forgot that confrontation. "He told me, among other things, that I was crazy. That there was nothing missing, that things were just out for repair. To stick to my own job and stop thinking I was—"

He broke off; she was going to know in a minute anyway, but somehow he couldn't tell her what Whitney had called him. "Anyway, he told me not to bother him again. That he had better things to do than worry about a broken petri dish that had been thrown out." He ran a hand over his hair. "But I knew something was up. He usually didn't...bother himself enough about me to get mad. And I knew that stuff hadn't been thrown out. Not enough to make up the difference in the inventory numbers."

"How can you be so sure?"

Here it comes, he thought grimly, plucking at the sleeve of her father's heavy shirt that he'd taken off and hung over the back of the chair. She's the daughter of a certifiable genius, and she herself graduated from Stanford in record speed, so she undoubtedly put the same value the rest of the world did on such credentials. It's time to blow your credibility with her right out of the water, Barkley.

"Because," he said flatly, "I'm the garbage man."

"What?" She gaped at him.

"You heard me," he said harshly. "I'm the guy who took out the garbage. And swept the floors, unloaded the trucks and washed Whitney's car."

He knew he sounded bitter, but he couldn't seem to help it. He avoided her eyes; to have her look at him with that polite, condescending expression was going to be more than he could stand. Twenty-six years old, and you've reached the glorious station in life of janitor, gofer and general flunky.

"And that," he added in the same flat tones, "is why the police would never believe me. They would have believed Rick. He's got ... he had the credentials. They'd never believe ... the garbage man." He stared at the rapidly cooling coffee. "I suppose that was why Whitney had to take Rick out first. He was the real threat. I was just a pest, a nuisance, too dumb to figure out what I'd stumbled onto."

"But ... you understood Dad's notes ... you know so much...."

"Osmosis," he said sourly, still refusing to look at her, even though he knew he was only postponing the inevitable. "You can't be around so much information without picking up some of it."

He heard the acid tone of his own words and tried to steady himself. "No, that's not fair. Rick taught me, taught me a lot. And he sent me to some classes, even when Whitney had a fit about it. 'You're not using the center's money to try to educate a janitor, for God's sake. We're not a charity,' was how he put it."

He was never going to be ready to see her look at him with that expression of disdain he knew so well, so he might as well face it now, he thought. He lifted his gaze from the coffee mug to her face.

She was looking at him, all right. But with a softness in her eyes that he didn't understand. "Perhaps that's what Dr. Whitney called it. But Dr. Parkson—and my father—called it finding the 'sparks of brilliance' that had gone unnoticed."

He gaped at her.

"I remember my father talking about it. It was one of the reasons he was so glad Dr. Parkson was to be his replacement. He thought he could do so much good. And he said that they'd already found some excellent people. Obviously he was right."

"I..."

He faltered, at a loss for words in the face of the way she bolstered his battered pride with a few honest, heartfelt words.

"No one else can define you unless you let them," she said softly. "My father taught me that a long time ago, when I was afraid he would love me less because my ability lay in words, not science."

"I wish... I'd known him."

"I think you did, indirectly. From what you've said, he and Dr. Parkson were a lot alike."

And they're both dead, he thought, pain lacing through him again. The words echoed so loudly in his head that for a moment he was afraid he'd said them out loud. Kit hadn't made the last jump, and he couldn't bring himself to prod her in that direction. Not yet.

"So, what *does* all this mean? And what does this—" she pointed at the folder "—have to do with it?"

He sighed and forced himself back to the ugly story. He flipped open the folder and thumbed through the clippings until he found the most recent one that had been attached to Rick's note. He scooted it across the table to her.

He watched her scan it, delicate brows furrowed. Then she looked up at him, clearly still confused.

"Here," he said, pointing to a paragraph midway through the wire service story. She looked again, reading aloud in a low murmur, as if hearing the words could help her understand.

"'The end of the ten-year-long war was hastened by the collapse of San Rafael's economy, which depended almost entirely on the rice crop that had been destroyed for the last two years by an annihilating disease.'"

She looked up at him again, a dawning realization furrowing her brow. "Are you saying, Whitney... had something to do with this? This disease?"

"The project Whitney pulled," he said quietly, "had to do with a specialized form of fungus that has only one susceptible host. A certain species of rice grass. The kind they grow in San Rafael."

"My God," she breathed.

"Yes," he said grimly, glad that she had caught on so quickly—not that he had expected any less from her—yet at the same time disheartened by her quick perception, given her lack of knowledge in the area. She was, he thought grimly, as smart as he'd thought. Or feared.

"When I finally worked up the nerve to go to Rick," he went on after a moment, "I found out he had been doing some wondering of his own. He'd come across an article in a college journal about this fungus that had struck San Rafael, and he wanted to be sure whoever had taken over the project saw it. But Whitney claimed to have forgotten what center it was."

"But he was the director—"

"Exactly. Not the kind of thing he would forget, having a major project pulled, or who had gotten it instead. Then Rick told me he'd had some things taken from his office. A couple of reference books and articles, and some of his own notes on the rice project."

He ran a hand over his hair, taking a moment to control himself; the realization of Rick's death was still raw. "He thought he'd just misplaced them. But when I went to him, he did some checking. The missing articles were on a similar type of fungus that killed off an entire corn crop and threw the state of Iowa into economic chaos several years ago."

"But what does that have to do with—"

"Nothing. Except maybe it gave Whitney the idea."

"The idea?" Kit swallowed tightly. "For this?" She gestured at the clipping. "The destruction of San Rafael's rice crop?"

He nodded. "And the end of that war."

"You're saying he developed this...thing on purpose? To do this? But San Rafael is halfway around the world! Why?"

"Money."

"How could he make any money out of a disease that destroyed their only cash crop?"

"Simple. He sold it to the other side."

It was late afternoon by the time he finished. He'd told her of Rick distracting Whitney long enough for him to get into the director's office and search for anything to back up what they had admitted to each other was a wild theory. He'd figured if there was anything, it would be in the safe in Whitney's office, and he'd been right.

"You're a safecracker, too?" Kit asked with a raised eyebrow as she leaned back against the hearth, her long legs stretched out on the bright Navajo rug, one hand idly patting Gus as he lay beside her.

Race winced at her words before he caught the gleam in the amber eyes that told him she was teasing. He felt the old familiar pain drain away.

"No. But I happen to be the guy who installed the thing. I guess he never worried about a mere janitor knowing about it. I never did understand why he needed it. Until I got it open and found what we'd been looking for."

"The evidence."

He nodded. "Notes, computer files, a list of dates...and a Swiss bank account number."

Kit stared into the fire he'd kindled as late afternoon approached; it grew chilly quickly in early spring on the mountain. "It seems impossible."

"I know. But Rick was able to follow the notes and make an educated guess at what Whitney had done."

"Which was?"

"A selective process. He used all the standard disease-control methods and kept the spores that survived until he had one so strong it would take months to figure out how to stop it, even with the most advanced research facilities."

"But...can you really control such a thing? I mean, how did they know the fungus would take hold, and when?"

"That was part of the plan. Some fungal pathogens only germinate in water. Like this one. And the rains come in San Rafael like clockwork in the spring, strong and constant. It's why they can grow rice. And it was enough to spread the fungus for miles."

"Lord," Kit breathed. "And he did all this at the center?"

Race nodded. "The lab at UC Davis is a lot bigger than ours, so Rick wanted them to take a look, to verify that it was as bad as we thought."

"So he sent you there?"

He nodded. "We knew Whitney would suspect me as soon as he realized he'd been found out, since I'd been the one to confront him. Rick figured I'd better be the one to leave. The lab there agreed with Rick's assessment that Whitney had developed a killer."

"Then they know . . . ?"

"Only that Rick wanted their opinion. They didn't know why." His mouth twisted ironically. "They didn't know it had been developed on purpose. They even offered their congratulations to Whitney for discovering it."

"Oh." She sipped at the latest in the long series of cups of coffee they'd drunk instead of eating; only Gus had his usual appetite. "It all seems so unreal."

"I know. Rick and I didn't put the last piece together until he remembered a tour group that had come to the center. Some UC students, along with a bunch of people from some foreign embassy. One of the delegate's sons was a student at one of the UC campuses."

"So?"

He pointed to the newsprint picture of the military leader of Anselmo, the other country embroiled in the long nasty border war with San Rafael. "That's the uniform the delegate was wearing. Because he didn't get involved much with the political ins and outs, Rick didn't realize it until he saw that photo."

"And when you read about the end of the war. . ."

He nodded. "That one sentence jumped out and hit us over the head. And the date of that tour was the first on that list of dates we found in the safe."

She sat staring at the stack of articles now spread out on the floor in front of the fireplace for a long time. Then, at last, she lifted her head and asked the question he'd been dreading ever since he'd realized that Rick had gone to Dr. Christoper Cameron with their theory.

"This must have been what my father was hinting at. Race... if Whitney thought my father knew something about this..."

He stared at the floor, saying nothing.

"Race?"

He began to gather up the pages, then shoved them back into the folder. When he didn't answer, Kit reached out and touched his hand. His head came up automatically, and her eyes searched his face.

"Kit..."

"Oh God." Her voice shook. Horror was darkening her clear golden eyes.

"Kit, don't." He took her hands and held them tightly.

"But, it couldn't be... It was only an acci—But, God, if he killed Dr. Parkson... he could have..."

He pulled her toward him. "Take it easy, Kit."

"You think he did, don't you? You think he killed my father!"

"I don't know."

"You do! That's why you looked so strange when you first saw that clipping. You knew then, didn't you?"

He let out a breath. "Kit, listen—"

"You knew!" Her hands curled up into fists, and she batted fiercely at his chest. "You knew he murdered my father, and you didn't tell me!"

"Easy, sunrose, easy," he said, pulling her hard against him. She fought him, surprising him with her strength. She twisted, trying to break his grasp. "We don't know that."

"But you believe it, don't you! Whitney, or that other horrible man... pushed him! He didn't fall." She shuddered.

"Shh," he soothed. "I know, Kit, I know. It hurts. God, I know it hurts."

She sagged against him then, little shudders rocketing through her. He didn't know what else to say; he knew there wasn't really anything he *could* say that would change what she was going through. And he knew exactly how she was feeling; he'd known it the moment she confirmed that Rick Parkson had been the victim of that hit-and-run.

He didn't know why Whitney had done it, especially so prematurely, before he and Rick had even put everything together. Perhaps just a combination of opportunity and preventive medicine, he thought. Whitney might be a charlatan of a scientist, but Race knew he'd had a healthy respect for Dr. Christopher Cameron's reputation. If he'd known Rick had gone to him and had been watching to see what Dr. Cameron would do, he might just have taken the chance that arose when Kit's father had clambered up to repair the roof.

She clung to him, seeming to take comfort from his touch, from the soft, meaningless words he murmured, from his gentle stroking of the firelit, silken tangle of her hair. He cradled her against him, leaning back against the front of the sofa, wishing the little shivers he could feel in her would stop, wishing he could do more, wishing he was somebody else, somebody who would know what to say or do to ease her pain. Somebody who could stop the tears that felt like acid on his skin.

"I'm sorry, sunrose. So sorry. I wish I could . . . make it not hurt so much."

She shivered again and clutched at him. "Just hold me, Race. Don't leave me alone."

"I'm right here, sunrose. I'm not going anywhere."

He held her for hours as the afternoon ticked away. He held her long after she at last slipped into an exhausted sleep. Only when the chill of dusk began to creep into the room, overpowering the heat from the dying fire, did he move.

He gently disentangled himself from her, easing her back against the sofa, and went to add wood and stir up the blaze. No sooner had it caught than he heard a tiny sound, the merest whisper of his name. He hurried back to her.

"I'm here, sunrose," he murmured, dropping back down beside her, hoping to soothe her back into sleep.

Only then did he realize that she was fully awake, her eyes wide and fastened on him. Slowly she lifted one hand and cupped his stubble-roughened jaw with her palm. He turned his head, driven by a need so strong he couldn't resist it, and pressed his lips gently against her palm. And he shivered when she traced his mouth, first with her thumb, then with her slender fingers. He watched, unable to speak, as she drew herself upward until she was bare inches from him.

"Race," she whispered, and the low husky note in her voice made him shiver again. He swallowed tightly.

"Don't, Kit. Don't do this."

Her hand slid downward until her fingers rested in the hollow of his throat; he felt his blood begin to heat, to pound heavily beneath her soft touch. Her fingers flexed, stroking the visible evidence of his response to her. Helplessly he let his head loll back, his eyes closing as his lips parted for the breath that was suddenly so hard to find.

And then she leaned forward to press her lips to that same spot, and he knew that she must have felt the sudden leap of his pulse. He lifted his hand, meaning to gently urge her away. Instead he found himself cupping the back of her head, pressing her to him.

At the feel of her tongue stealing between her lips to flick over his skin, Race couldn't smother the gasp that broke from him. And before he could stop himself he had shifted them both until his back was braced against the sofa and she was sprawled across him, his hands gripping her slender shoulders.

She never protested, never lifted her mouth from his skin, just trailed hot, sweet kisses along the cords of his neck to the angle of his jaw, lingered a moment in the strong curve there, then went on to nibble softly at his ear.

"God, Kit!"

It burst from him on a shuddering breath as his fingers clenched around her shoulders and he held her away from him. She looked down at him, her eyes wide and dark, her lips parted. The tip of her tongue crept out to moisten the soft lips that had just been tormenting him, and Race felt his body clench around a sudden shaft of searing heat unlike anything he'd ever known.

"Did I..." she began tentatively, then tried again. "Did I do something wrong?"

"No! Yes! Damn it, Kit, I can't play this game anymore. You've got me strung so tight I can't think."

"Game?"

"It's okay, I understand, but it's got to stop. I can't take much more."

"You understand...what?"

"Look, Kit, you're feeling vulnerable right now. Don't get in over your head just because that guy left you feeling...unsure of yourself."

Bracing her hand on his chest, she stared at him. "What guy?"

"Whatever his name was. That guy you were engaged to."

"Gary? What are you talking about?"

"You said he made you feel—"

"How he made me feel has nothing to do with this! This is about how *you* make me feel."

"Kit—"

"It's about how you make me feel things I've never felt. Things I *need* to feel, Race. Please."

Pain knifed through him as a shimmering image glowed in his mind, the image that had been haunting him all through these long nights, the image of Kit in his arms, her eyes hot and glowing, her hair flowing free, her hands on his body. An image he knew could never be real.

"Please, sunrose, don't say that. You don't know—"

"Why? Just because I've never felt this way doesn't mean I don't know what it means."

"Kit, stop. I can't give you what you deserve. I can't give you anything. Not even a promise for tomorrow, let alone anything else."

"I'm not asking for that."

"I don't think you know what you *are* asking for."

"I do. Just because I've never really...wanted a man before..."

"Kit, no. You can't want me."

Her forehead creased. "Why?"

"Because you're...who you are, for God's sake. And I'm who—and what—I am. You don't want me. Damn it, Kit, I never even finished high school."

For the briefest moment pain darted across her delicate features. "Is that what you think of me? That I can't see past whatever label people choose to hang on someone? That I can't see the real man you are?"

"Oh, Kit, I wish..." I wish it was true, he thought fervently. I wish what you see in me was true.

"I don't want to wish anymore, Race. I just...want."

He shuddered, heat coursing through him at her words, at the innocent hunger in her eyes. Tell her, he ordered himself. Give her the real reason, the one that will show her she can't do this, can't want this. Tell her what you really are.

And then she kissed him, and he couldn't tell her anything but yes.

Chapter 9

He'd never known anything like the fire that leapt through him at the first touch of her lips on his. He'd tried, in his effort to keep a tight rein on his response to her mere presence, to convince himself it hadn't been like this, that his body didn't leap to life at her touch and slip all restraints at her kiss. He knew better the moment he felt her tongue flick over his lips, stroking, as if she loved the taste of him. The thought roused him to a fever pitch faster than he'd known was possible.

It was like holding fire in his arms. She threaded her slender fingers through the thick hair at his nape, her long legs entangling with his as she deepened the kiss, making tiny little sounds of eagerness that sent darts of heat shooting through him. The feel of her slight weight bearing down on him as she twisted against him made him groan low in his throat, and he reached to pull her even tighter.

His tongue met hers, touched, teased, striking little glimmerings of heat, as if electricity were leaping between them. His hands slid down her back, clasping her waist and pressing down, shifting her hips so that she straddled him, gasping at the sweet pressure of her soft body against his rapidly hardening one.

Kit gave a low moan and arched against his chest. The soft fullness of her breasts seemed to sear him even through layers of cloth. Interfering layers; he wanted them gone. He wanted her skin, that soft, unbelievable silkiness, under his hands. And he wanted her hands on him, touching him in ways he'd never wanted a woman to touch him before.

His hands slipped up under the soft fleece of her shirt, and he smothered a groan at the proof that she was as silken smooth as he remembered. Eagerly, his fingers sought the catch of the lacy bra, his heated mind filled with a vision of her as she had been that day by the creek, leaning back on her elbows, head lolling back, offering the slender curve of her throat and the full, soft swell of her breasts beneath the thin shirt to the spring sun.

His hands had curled then at the thought of cupping that tender flesh; they trembled now at the reality. She had been a vision then, a wood sprite who had teased him with the impossibility of that dream; now she was here, alive and hot and soft beneath his hands, and it took his breath away.

He fumbled with the tiny hooks for a moment, wishing ruefully that he'd had more practice lately. Then, abruptly, he stopped.

After a moment Kit lifted her head, breaking at last the fiery kiss.

"Race?" she whispered.

He steadied himself, made himself meet her eyes. "It's been a long time for you, hasn't it?" he asked gently.

She bit her lip, staring at him like some tiny mountain creature expecting to be hurt. "I . . . does it matter?"

He let out a quick breath. "Only because . . . it's been a long time for me, too, and I'm afraid I'll . . ."

She was just looking at him, not understanding, her eyes wide and puzzled, her lips parted, still wet and swollen from their kiss.

"Damn it, Kit," he said hoarsely. "I don't want to hurt you. But you make me so hot, I haven't got any control at all."

He heard her quick little gasp in the instant her eyes widened. "I . . . do?"

His short laugh was harsh. He lifted her away from him for a moment, only then wondering when she had unbuttoned his shirt. He took her hand from where it lay against his chest and slid it slowly down his body.

"What do you think?" he said huskily, pressing her palm over his rising flesh, feeling himself pulse at the touch.

Slowly, instinctively, her fingers moved, stroking him, tracing his swollen length through the soft worn denim. He moved sharply, a low sound breaking from him as his hips jerked convulsively against her hand.

A tiny sigh drew his gaze back to her face. "You do want me," she murmured.

"Want you?" He stared at her, astonished. "I've wanted you since the first day I saw you."

"How could I know?" she asked simply. "You never said. All you did was tell me I couldn't want you."

He groaned as her hand moved again.

"I thought it was . . . just me," she said softly, "being silly, foolish, for thinking about you like that."

"You . . . thought about me?"

She nodded slowly, her eyes so hot and dreamy that Race thought he was going to explode just at the sight of them. And at that sweet, stroking caress she wouldn't stop.

"I . . . never imagined what a man would look like in my tub before," she said shyly. "Until you, that first time."

"Oh, sunrose," he groaned, catching her hand to stop the slow, lingering touch that was driving him to the brink, "if you'd come in to find out, you would have known then how much I wanted you. I was almost wishing you would."

He drew her hands up to his mouth and kissed them tenderly in each palm, then slowly, enticingly, on the tip of each slender finger. He felt her shiver, and it sent an echoing ripple down through his belly, adding to the pressure that had already built beyond bearing.

"Move it, dog," he growled at Gus without looking at the big animal. Somewhat to his surprise, the dog moved, going to curl up on a thick rug by the door.

Kit smiled softly, then leaned forward, this time to press her lips against his chest again and again. She stopped when she reached the edge of his shirt, lifting her head. He saw the tentative look in her eyes. In an instant he yanked off the shirt.

And almost wished he hadn't when she began again, pressing hot, wet kisses on him, letting her tongue trail over him, tasting, savoring, until he thought he was going to go out of his mind. Then, when the tip of her tongue found and circled first one flat male nipple, then the other, he nearly did.

The only thing that kept him from feeling guilty about the way he was clawing at her clothes, tearing them from her slender body, was that she was doing the same, fingers at his belt, pulling at the snap of his jeans. He tugged the sweats from her none too gently.

"Help me," she said softly, urgently, tugging at the zipper that wouldn't budge over the hardened swell of his flesh.

Only then did he realize that he'd been staring, frozen into motionlessness, at the sight of her slender body painted by firelight. She was everything he'd dared to imagine, from her long, trim legs to the lush, feminine swell of her pink-tipped breasts, high and full and so very tempting. The gentle curve from waist to hip was perfect, delicate enough to make her look almost fragile, yet womanly enough to remind his raging body exactly what the difference meant. The tangle of red curls beckoned him. She would cradle him so sweetly, and he would fill her with everything he could give her, he would—

His thoughts broke off abruptly as the stubborn zipper gave way for her, and she quickly freed him of the tangle of jeans and briefs. The feel of her hands, soft, caressing, on his naked flesh made him gasp in shocked pleasure. He was out of control; he couldn't deal with this. All she'd done was touch him and he was losing it.

"Kit . . . Kit, stop."

She stopped the sweet stroking, but she didn't release the tender grip of her fingers around him.

"I can't," she said huskily, with that natural innocence that sent wildfire leaping along every nerve. "Oh, Race, you're so... I didn't know a man could be so beautiful."

He groaned, wanting more than anything to take what she was offering here and now, to bury himself in her sweet warmth, to watch himself slide into her, to see her take him in until dark curls tangled with red....

"Kit," he gasped, "I... forgot. I don't—oh, please, stop—I don't have anything to protect you."

She paused then, giving him a brief moment's relief from that encircling, teasing caress that had him half-crazy, his body trembling with the effort to hold back.

"Wait," she said softly, then got up.

Wait? he groaned silently. I can't even move; where does she think I'm going? Never in his life had a woman done this to him, touched him with such care, looked at him with a reverence that made him feel humble and proud at the same time. He didn't deserve this, not from anyone. That it was Kit, bright, beautiful, gentle, brave Kit, made it almost impossible to believe. But he had to believe it; the taut, throbbing ache of his body left him no choice.

And then she was back, holding a small foil packet and refusing to look at him. "My father presented these to me, along with a very involved, scientific lecture that would have made no sense at all if I hadn't already known what he was talking about."

"Your father," Race said fervently, "was a very wise man."

He saw the flush of color in her face then and couldn't tell if it was from embarrassment about the little package she was holding, or from the realization that she'd been walking around nude in front of him. He reached out and lifted her chin with a gentle finger.

"Don't, sunrose. Don't be embarrassed. Not with me. Not when just looking at you, standing there with the light from the fire rippling over you, makes me—"

He broke off, shaking his head in a sharp movement that was somehow more eloquent than any words he could have said. He pulled her to him, hugging her, stroking her, fighting to go slow despite the exhilarating feel of her against him, naked skin to naked skin, as he'd wanted so desperately. He kissed her, long and deep, letting his hands roam over her, searching out every sensitive spot that made her gasp, made her quiver.

He cupped her breast and slowly ran his thumb over her nipple, groaning himself when he found it already taut and awaiting his touch. She made a tiny, shocked sound of delight, echoed when he moved to the other ready peak. The sound became a cry when he repeated the action with his mouth, catching the erect crest with his lips and flicking it with his tongue.

"Race!"

"Fair play, Kit. My turn."

He suckled her deeply then, and she arched in his arms with a moan. He savored for a moment the sight of her tightened rosy flesh, wet from his mouth, before he moved to her other breast and repeated the caress.

She was breathing in short little gasps as his hand slid down her body once more, teasing, stroking, at last parting the red curls in a circling movement that made her cry out again.

Race felt his entire body clench, felt the hot demand of need boiling up inside him at the feel of her; she was ready for him, slick and welcoming, and it was killing him to wait.

"Race, please," she gasped in a voice that left him no doubt that his waiting was killing her as well. With hands that were shaking he reached for the foil packet and opened it.

With a low groan he lifted himself over her, heat flooding him yet again as she opened her legs for him to slide between them. He felt her hands slide over his back, down to his waist, then his hips, clutching at him as he felt like clutching at her.

He eased himself down, sucking in a harsh breath as his swollen flesh brushed her stomach, then the soft, red curls.

He could feel her heat, the enticing lure, and knew he couldn't last much longer. He inched forward, giving a low, guttural growl as the tip of his distended male flesh parted those curls and touched the slick, feminine part of her that welcomed him.

She gasped, a quick, shocked sound of pleasure, as his hardened body stroked the sensitive spot his fingers had discovered and aroused, that central core that sent ripples of fire through her. He heard it, felt her arch suddenly, involuntarily toward him, and repeated the movement.

She moaned low in her throat, a single syllable, his name spoken in a way he'd never thought to hear. He wanted to hear it again and again, wanted her to keep that almost frantic grasp on his hips, wanted her to be as desperate for him as he was for her, so he began a slow, caressing rhythm, sliding his body against that sweetly responsive spot over and over.

It had the effect he'd wanted; she began to writhe beneath him, crying out his name on every quick breath, lifting her hips to prolong each caressing stroke. It also had the effect of driving him to the edge of madness. And when her hands slid down from his hips to clutch at the muscled curve of his buttocks, he went flying over that edge. With a harsh, throttled groan he shifted, changed the angle of his body, and entered her with one fierce thrust.

"Oh! Oh, yes, Race!" she gasped, clawing at him.

For one long moment he was motionless, unable to move, helpless before the onslaught of sensation that was flooding him, centering on those swollen inches of flesh that were buried so deeply inside her.

"Sunrose," he panted, "please...wait, just...let me feel you around me...."

But it was he who couldn't wait, and he began to move again, driving, plunging, savoring her every cry of pleasure as she rose to meet him. He forgot everything, forgot why he would regret this, forgot his fear of how she would feel about him when she learned the truth, forgot everything but the slender woman in his arms as he felt the hot, sweet convulsion of her body around his. Her soft amazed cry echoed in his ears as his own world exploded in a rushing, pulsing release that made her name rip sharp and sweet from his throat.

He couldn't seem to stop the little shudders that swept him. He knew he was holding her tightly, perhaps too tightly, his hands clamped around her shoulders as if he were afraid she would somehow slip away from him. Long after the initial incredible explosion had ebbed, little quivers of sensation rippled through him, making his body clench. But what was more incredible was that he could feel, with each little wave of echoed pleasure, her body giving a little convulsion of its own, as if in answer to his.

At last even that faded, and all he was aware of was someone murmuring her name, over and over. When he realized it was himself, he stopped, lifting his head to look at her. The thick, firelit hair was tousled, making the colors of the woven Navajo rug they lay upon look dull by comparison. Her lips were parted for breath that was only now beginning to slow, and her eyes were shining.

It sounded corny to him even as he thought it, but it was true. Her eyes *were* shining—with pleasure, with wonder, with joy. It was her joy that shook him the most. It was pure, honest, open, clean, just as she was, as if there were no clouds hovering over them, no problems that couldn't be solved. It was so fierce, so overpowering, that for just one second he let himself believe it, let himself bask in it. It was a feeling he'd never known before.

"I . . . you humble me, sunrose."

"Humble?"

Her voice, still husky, sent a feather skating along his spine, tickling, making the muscles ripple. He tried to move, to relieve her of his weight, but her arms tightened around him in protest.

"Why humble?" she asked, as if troubled by the word.

"You . . . give yourself so completely. So honestly. I didn't know . . . anyone could be like that."

"You make me like that. . . . I couldn't do anything else."

Something else came into her eyes then, something he couldn't put a name to. He only knew it warmed him to his very core, thawed the places that had been frozen so long that he'd forgotten they existed. And the moment he realized it, terror struck him. God, how would he survive leaving her? He'd let her in, let her burrow into him, melting the ice and replacing it with her sweet, gentle warmth. And already he knew that when he had to tear her out of that soft, warm place, it would tear him up as well, rip apart every vital part of him, every part he'd sworn was frozen too solid to ever be melted again.

"Thank you," Kit whispered, reaching up to touch his cheek.

"What?" he asked, startled.

"I was afraid... what I'd had before was all there was. You showed me..."

"No more than I showed myself," he muttered. "Lord, I thought I knew. I thought the...basics were all you needed to understand."

He looked down at her, at her flushed face, her still-swollen lips, her bright, clear eyes. And for a moment, just for a moment, he let it show, all the tangled emotions he was feeling.

"Then I ran into a mountain sunrose... and found out I didn't know anything."

She made a tiny sound that was half sigh, half moan, and put her arms around him to pull him down to her. He rolled to his side, taking her with him, pulling her into the curve of his body. He just held her for a long time, the snap of the fire an occasional random punctuation of their breathing.

"Race?" she said, much later.

"Mmmm?"

"Er... the floor's kind of hard."

Immediately contrite, he rose up on one elbow. "I'm sorry. Why didn't you say something?"

"I just did." She paused, taking a breath as if she were poised on the edge of a high dive. "I know it's early, but...there's a perfectly good bed in there," she said at last, gesturing toward her room.

The way she blushed when she said it, shyly avoiding his eyes, made something warm and tender expand inside him.

When he saw her bite her lip nervously, that something flexed, grew, until it became almost painful. He realized with a start that it was a fierce, passionate protectiveness. Only once had he ever felt anything like it. He choked off the memory sharply, aware that he was skating on ice much too thin to hold his weight.

"I'm disappointed," he said, forcing himself to sound merely teasing. "I thought you wanted to use me as a cushion."

Her head came up sharply, her eyes searching his face, her color deepening. And suddenly what had begun as a diversion became a need, rising fierce and hot and sudden.

"And believe me," he said hoarsely, his hand coming up to cup her cheek, "I can't think of anything I'd like more."

"You . . . can't?"

Her voice broke, the little catch sending a searing dart of fire through him. Words, he thought suddenly. I do words, not numbers, she'd said.

"Anything I'd like more than you draped all over me, naked, that silky skin of yours rubbing against me?" he asked in a low growl. "Anything I'd like more than those long legs wrapped around me, pulling me into you? Anything I'd like more than your breasts against my chest, your nipples hard and wet from my mouth? No. Nothing."

He watched her as he spoke, saw her eyes widen, then go smoky, the gold flecks in the amber glittering in the firelight. He felt her unconscious movement as she arched toward him, felt the searing contact of her breasts against his chest, felt the puckering of her nipples as he spoke.

Words were her magic, he thought. Perhaps he'd found a way to give back some of the miracle she'd given him. He leaned over and whispered in her ear exactly what else he would like to feel, like to do, like to have done to him. And by the time he scooped her up and carried her to the bedroom she was a writhing impassioned thing in his arms, pressing sweet wet kisses over him, responding fervently to his hot suggestions.

But his thoughts of giving to her came back at him like the echo of a shout on the mountain; by the time they lay down on the big four-poster, she was frantic, stroking him, kissing him, laying paths of white-hot flame with her mouth and hands over his body.

The fire he'd been trying to keep banked for her sake caught, flaring instantly out of control, and he knew nothing but a savage, raging need until, as she bucked wildly beneath him, crying his name, he let loose and erupted in a final blast of heat and light and pure sweet sensation.

He wasn't sure of anything when he woke up, not of what had awakened him, why he felt so utterly drained and relaxed, or why he seemed to be, for the first time in over a week, in a real bed. All he was sure of was that it was fully dark now. He stretched slightly, coming up against something warm and soft and silken.

Kit. He sucked in a breath as heat flooded him. Kit, hot and sweet and naked in his arms, wanting him as much as he wanted her. Crying out as he filled her, making him cry out as he sank into her welcoming body. As quickly as that it was back, that hot, wild need, and he reached for her.

The second ring of the phone shattered the quiet, telling him it had been the first ring that had awakened him. And with the sound, with the invasion of the outside world, the small cocoon of safety he'd found disintegrated. The memories of pleasure faded, beaten back by harsh reality. Safety had been only in his mind, he thought grimly. The haven had been a mirage he'd conjured up in her arms.

Kit stirred beside him, sleepily reaching for the phone. The moment she picked it up, he wished he'd stopped her. If it was Whitney again . . .

"'Lo," she mumbled into the phone.

He froze, waiting. Kit rubbed at her eyes.

"Yeah, I was asleep."

She smothered a yawn, and Race heard Gus stir on the floor beside the bed. "I know it's only nine, and no, I'm not sick, I just—"

He felt her stiffen and knew that memory had just startled her awake, as it had him. Her gaze flew to his face, and he read the emotions flitting across her features as clearly as if she'd spoken them: shyness, remembered heat, then doubt. A tiny chill curled through him. Was she regretting it already?

"No, Susan," she said quickly, her attention tugged back to the phone. Not Whitney, he thought in relief. "I'm fine. Really. I just felt like going to bed early."

That, Race thought wryly, was no less than the truth.

"Thank you," she was saying. "That's nice of you and Steve. But I can't." Her eyes flicked to him for the briefest of seconds. "No, I don't have other plans. I just . . . don't feel like doing anything this year."

Race heard the slight quiver that had come into her voice, and he propped himself up on one elbow to look at her.

"Really, please, I don't want a party. I'd rather be alone. Rain check for next year, okay?" A pause, then, "I know. I'll be fine. Thanks, though. I'll call you."

She hung up, and Race didn't think it was his imagination that she was avoiding looking at him. She tugged the sheet closer around her, as if afraid it might slip and reveal something. As if, he thought, there was one square inch of her beautiful body he'd missed in this long, exquisite evening. And just thinking about it was tightening his own body uncomfortably.

"A party?" he asked, trying to ignore the way her hair was falling in a tangled—by his hands—mass over her shoulders. "For what?"

"Nothing. There is no party."

"I gathered that. So what's this nonexistent party that you're taking a rain check on until next year?"

She sighed. "My birthday. Now can we drop it?"

He sat back, gaping at her a little. "Your birthday? Today?"

"Tomorrow. And I'd rather just forget it, if you don't mind."

She moved as if she were going to get up. He caught her arm, holding her back, realization suddenly dawning. "It's hard, I know," he said softly. "The first Christmas, the first Thanksgiving . . . the first birthday with that big hole in your life."

She stared at him, and he saw her lips quiver before she set her jaw, fighting it.

"Oh, sunrose," he breathed, reaching for her, pulling her to him. "I wish I could make it all right. I wish I could say there will come a time when it won't hurt at all anymore. But it would be a lie." And God knows I've lied to you enough already, he added in grim silence.

She sagged against him, little shivers rippling through her as she fought her own emotions. "It was hard enough before." She gulped out. "But now, knowing that he didn't just fall from the roof, that someone—"

"Shh," he soothed. "I know. But don't think about it now, Kit. We'll sort it all out, decide what to do, but in the morning. Just rest now."

He wondered, when she turned to him in the dark, if she was merely desperate for something to keep the horrible thoughts out of her mind. But then her hands began to slip over him, caressing, stroking, as if she were trying to memorize him, and it didn't matter why. It only mattered that she wanted him, and he was going to revel in it while he could; it would change soon enough.

Later, when she had slipped back into a deep, sated sleep, he found himself strangely awake. His body was satisfied, utterly content, but his emotions were strung out in a way he'd never known before. While his every muscle loudly proclaimed itself ready for a long rest, his mind was wound so tightly he couldn't relax, and he couldn't seem to slow it down.

After a while he gave up and slid out of bed, careful not to waken her. For a long moment he just stood there, looking down at her, at the slender shape barely covered by the sheet, at the silken mass of her hair spread out over the pillow. His gaze fastened on one slim hand, resting atop the pillow he'd just left, and he remembered that hand touching him, caressing, learning so quickly from his groans of pleasure how to stroke, where to linger tormentingly.

He didn't need to look down at himself to know how his train of thought was affecting him; he'd felt the aching heaviness, the pooling of rapidly heating blood, the moment he'd stopped to stare down at her. Shuddering, he turned and walked out to the great room.

He found his jeans and pulled them on, trying not to think about how her eager hands had stripped them off him, much as his own had divested her of the soft sweats. Unable to beat down the odd restlessness that had seized him, he began to pace, crisscrossing the room, stopping to stoke the fire, then resuming his pacing. Gus ambled out of the bedroom to watch him curiously. On one of his passes, he stopped to tickle the big dog behind the ears.

"Thanks, pal. You're as close to a guardian as she's got now. Thanks for deciding I'm good enough for her." His mouth quirked into an expression that was both wry and a little grim. "Even though you're wrong."

He resumed his pacing, then stopped to look out the front window at the meadow. He jammed his hands deep into his pockets, his fingers curling into tense fists. He scraped his knuckles on something in the left pocket and pulled back, drawing out his folding knife. He stared at it for a long moment, then glanced back through the window at the copse of trees across the meadow.

He turned around and reached for his shirt.

Race heard her in the moment before she stepped into the room and was grateful he'd already cleaned up the mess he'd made. Swiftly he flipped off the desk light, grabbed what sat on the desk and wrapped it in the heavy shirt she'd given him, and walked quickly over to the sofa.

He didn't understand the wide-eyed look of relief she wore when she stepped into the room and saw him sitting there. He looked at her, standing there clad only in the blue robe he'd been using. Even knowing it was her father's, and that she'd undoubtedly put it on in an effort to be closer to him, it gave Race an odd feeling to see her wearing something he had worn, even temporarily. Especially knowing that she, as he had been, was naked beneath it.

"You're here," she breathed.

His brows lowered. "What?"

"I thought . . . I woke up, and you weren't there."

He stood up abruptly. Her words stung deeply, in a way he didn't understand. "Did you really think I'd leave? Without a word?"

"You almost did, once."

"But that was..."

"Before?" she said softly.

He nodded; he couldn't think of anything to say.

"I wasn't sure...it meant that much to you. As much as it did to me, I mean."

"God, Kit!" He strode swiftly across the room, grabbing her shoulders. "How could you doubt it?" He hugged her fiercely. "Whatever else I may be, or may have done, don't ever doubt that last night was real. Last night was...the most incredible thing that's ever happened to me."

He felt the tension in her ebb away, and her arms came up to encircle his waist. "I knew it would be...special with you. But I never knew it would..."

"Would what?" he asked softly.

"Make me understand so many things."

He drew back; he wasn't sure what he'd expected her to say, but that hadn't been it. "Understand?"

"Why people write those songs. Why lovers look at each other that way that closes out the rest of the world. Why...my father never remarried after my mother died."

He stared at her, stunned.

"Oh, don't worry," she said. "I don't mean that I expect anything from you. I'm not *that* naive. But I just...wanted you to know."

He pulled her close again, emotion tightening his throat and making his voice hoarse. "You should expect everything, Kit. You deserve everything."

"I've already had more than I ever expected," she whispered against his chest.

Her simple words left him speechless; all he could do was hold her.

"Race?" she said after a while.

"What, sunrose?"

"You're sure...we can't go to the police?"

The old tension gripped him, tight, hard and low in his gut. "Kit, I . . . Yes."

"But—"

"Kit, I can't. If I did . . ."

"What?" she prodded when he stopped.

"They'd arrest me."

She stared at him. "But . . . whatever it was, you said it was a long time ago . . ."

He sighed. Tell her, he ordered himself. You'll never have a better chance. Tell her now. But when he looked down at her, when he looked into those wide, innocent eyes, he couldn't do it. Last night was too fresh in his mind, too precious, to destroy with his own hands. Not yet.

"I can't tell you, Kit. Just believe me, I can't go to the police."

"But . . . we can't just let him get away with this!"

He looked at her for a long time, hating the pain that marred her delicate features. "No. No, we can't," he said at last.

He let go of her and walked over to stand in front of the fireplace, staring into the fire he'd let die down with the rising sun. The silence stretched until at last, coming to stand beside him, Kit spoke his name quietly. He turned to look at her.

"I can't go to the police, but you can."

"Me? But I don't know anything except what you told me."

"But you're Dr. Christopher Cameron's daughter. They'll listen to you."

"But—"

"We have to find the rest of the evidence," he said suddenly, decisively. "You'll need to give them that so they can move quickly. Without what Rick had, they'll have to start their own investigation, which will give Whitney enough time to run. We can't give him that time."

Kit stared at him. "What makes you think they'll believe me, even with those papers? I didn't see anything, didn't hear anything. I don't even know enough to talk about it halfway intelligently."

"I told you. They'll listen because of who you are."

"But you're the one who—"

"I told you," he repeated, "even if I could go to them, they wouldn't believe a . . . janitor."

"Stop it!" she snapped. "You know, you're the one with the problem about that! You're a snob in reverse, Race Barkley, and if you don't know you're better than that, you should!"

He stared at her. "You don't do anything halfway, do you?" He lifted a hand and stroked a finger along the delicate line of her jaw. "Going to fight for me now, sunrose?"

"Well, somebody has to," she said, her chin coming up stubbornly. "You won't do it."

"Kit—"

"Well, you won't. You just keep putting yourself down."

He chuckled wryly. "Kit, I'm a janitor because it's the best job I could get and keep. You don't find much white-collar work without a college diploma, let alone without a high school one. That's not putting myself down, that's the truth."

Her chin came up higher. "Well, you're smarter than most of the college graduates I know, and believe me, I know a few. Len, for instance. He learned what he had to to get by and never did another thing." She eyed him steadily. "But you . . . you've never stopped learning, have you?"

Race stared at her; Rick had told him the same thing. He'd had no use for people with a piece of paper with some college's name on it and absolutely no capacity for logical thought. "You learn from everything, Race," he'd said. "You soak it up like a sponge. You're every teacher's dream."

Rick had almost had him convinced to complete the paperwork necessary for an equivalency test. He'd done it by dangling the carrot of a college education in front of Race's nose, swearing that they would work out the finances if Race would just try. Even when Race had known deep down it was impossible, Rick had made him want to try.

He'd lost more than just a good friend on that lonely mountain road.

Something must have shown in his face, because Kit was touching his arm, her eyes moist as she looked up at him. "I'm sorry, Race. I had no right to say that. Or to yell at you."

He laughed, a harsh, joyless sound. "If you don't, then nobody does. I wish..."

God, he wished so much, he who had given up on wishes when he was fifteen. He sat down heavily on the edge of the hearth, feeling older, more tired and more beaten than he could ever remember. And he had a storehouse of grim memories to call on.

Kit came down beside him, taking his hand in hers, saying nothing, just sitting there in quiet support. He was surprised at how it helped, yet wary of it at the same time; it only meant that it would hurt that much more when she turned on him, as he knew she eventually would.

"What are we going to do?" she asked at last.

"I'm going to find those papers. Then you can go to the police."

"Wrong. *We're* going to find those papers."

"No, Kit. I've gotten you too tangled up in this already."

"Exactly. I'm not quitting now."

"You don't understand. Wherever those documents are, I'm not going to be able to waltz right in and get them."

"Of course not. Where do you think they are?"

"I don't know."

Kit sighed, and he knew she was getting exasperated with him again. "Let me put it another way. Where are we going to look first?"

His jaw tightened.

"Look, what makes you think I'll be any better off here, what with Whitney showing up, clamoring for my father's notes?"

She had a point there, one that had been nagging at him for some time but that he'd managed to quash until now. "You have Gus—"

"You said yourself, he can't . . . stop a bullet." Her voice wavered a little at the image, but she got through it.

"Kit," he began, his tone holding weariness tinged with frustration.

"Race," she mimicked. Then she held up one hand, ticking things off on her fingers. "You'll never get anywhere in time if you try to walk. You need wheels. Mine. You need a second pair of eyes. Mine. If you run into any of the locals, or Harve, you'll need help. Mine. You need a weapon. Mine. You need a . . . watchdog. Mi—"

"Kit, stop."

It came out sharply, and she drew back a little. When she spoke again, all trace of lightness was gone from her voice.

"Don't shut me out, Race. If not for all those reasons, then because I deserve it. I've earned the chance to help put away the man who murdered my father."

In a few short words she had shattered his defenses. Everything she'd said was true, and he had no answer for her except the one she wanted.

"All right, sunrose. You're right. You've earned it." It was true. He would just have to see that she didn't get hurt. And he would have agreed to a lot more if he'd known his reward would be the smile she gave him then.

"Thank you," she said softly.

"I hope you know what you're doing."

She looked at him, amusement glinting in her eyes for the first time. "I was kind of hoping you did. What *are* we going to do?"

He let out a long breath and gave her a sideways look. "We," he said ruefully, "are about to become burglars."

Chapter 10

"Won't they have searched already?"

"Probably. But maybe they missed something." He looked at her in the dim light of the toolshed. "You don't have to do this, you know."

"But you do?"

"I have to try."

"Then let's get going."

He reached out, cupping her cheek, barely restraining himself from pulling her into his arms. But he knew if he did that, he wouldn't be able to stop there, so he contented himself with that small caress, then made himself turn away.

He picked up the small crowbar and added it to the collection of tools he'd gathered and placed in the soft canvas backpack Kit had dug out of a closet. A hand ax went on top of the crowbar, then a small coil of rope, and then one of the tarps that had been his only blankets on the nights he'd spent sleeping here. He unfolded it a little, wrapping it around the metal tools.

When he looked up again, Kit was watching him intently. "I admit I missed 'Burglary 101' in school," she said mildly, "but what's the tarp for?"

"Keep everything from rattling."

Dismay flashed across her face. "No one will be there, will they?"

"I don't know. Rick's family—" Pain dug at him again, and he had to stop to fight it down. It was strange to feel pain after all the years of numbness. He didn't like it. He never should have let Rick get so close. He'd forgotten the lessons he'd learned the hard way. Lessons he was going to have to learn all over again when he had to leave Kit.

"I'm sorry, Race."

"I know." He took a breath and tried again. "I don't think anybody will still be there. His brother's a state senator, so I don't think he'd have much time. To spend here, I mean. If he came at all. Maybe he just...had Rick brought home."

"Home?"

"Iowa." His mouth twisted wryly. "Rick and I were both from there. That's how we got to talking one day. He's from Ames, where the University is. I grew up in a town just down the road, small then and smaller now, I imagine. It—"

He broke off suddenly, sharply. God, what are you doing? He stared at her, knowing his shock must be showing in his face, but unable to hide it. He'd spent ten years hiding his past, guarding against any casual words that might tell someone too much, and then he went and blurted all that out to her. Damn, why couldn't he keep his mouth shut around her? He'd even given her his real name, not the name he'd been using since he'd come here. She knew more than enough, he thought grimly, to bring him down. And when she found out the truth, she just might decide to do it.

She was staring at him, saying nothing, but he could almost see the racing of her agile mind. She would put it together, he thought, sooner or later. She would start to question, to search, and eventually she'd find out. He could only hope it would be later, after he'd gone.

He returned his attention to the backpack with a jerky movement, reaching for the straps to close it. It's your own fault, he told himself roughly, over the swelling pain. You knew this was only temporary, like everything, every place, has been for the last ten years. It's your own fault for being fool enough to think this might be the end, that this might be the place where you could stop, rest, maybe even stay.

"Tell me something," she said then, not bothering to hide the hurt that tinged her voice. "Did Rick know as much about you as you do about him?"

He let out a short, compressed breath. "No. And it...made him as angry as it does you."

He yanked the straps tight and lifted the bag; the only sound was a very muffled clank. It would do, he thought. When he looked up at Kit again, she was still watching him, but whatever she was thinking was hidden behind a mask of calm.

"If someone *is* there..." she began.

"Depends on who it is."

After a moment she nodded.

"You want out? Now's the time."

He knew he sounded sharp, but he couldn't seem to control it; his thoughts were biting too deep.

"Did I say I wanted out? I merely wanted to know if we were going to jump right into being cat burglars."

The coolness of her voice stung more than anger would have. "Sorry," he muttered. "I'm just...edgy."

"And secretive." She gave him a halfhearted smile. "If you don't know by now that I trust you, that I believe in you...then I have no idea how to convince you."

Her words, low and sharpened with sadness, sliced through him, cutting loose all the sweet, hot memories of last night. Acid flowed after them, blistering already raw emotions. She'd trusted him with the most precious thing in the world, herself, and he was begrudging her the paltry gifts of his name and a tiny crumb of his bleak past.

"Kit, I'm sorry. I wish things could be different."

"You wish a lot of things, it seems." It wasn't a reproach, merely a rather wistful observation, but it hurt just the same.

"Yes, I do. Lately, anyway," he said tightly, then slung the pack over his shoulder by one strap. "Do you know the houses down on the lake road?"

She nodded. "I used to go to the beach down below them when I came up for the summer. Gus likes to play there."

"Good. It won't look strange for you to be there, then."

"No. Which one is it?"

"The third one down from the highway."

Her forehead creased. "The white one?"

"Next one back. The cedar house."

"The little one?"

She sounded surprised, and Race couldn't help smiling. He knew what she meant; most of the houses on the lake road were large, impressive affairs, taking up much more of the expansive—and expensive—lots than Rick's did.

"Yeah. The land, and the vegetation, were more important to him, so he kept the house small."

He saw her quick glance back at the neat, compact house her father had built, leaving untouched the trees and most of the meadow, and he agreed softly.

"You were right. They . . . were a lot alike."

"Yes. I think they were."

And Whitney had killed them both, Race thought bitterly as he climbed into the back of the Jeep, grunting a little in his effort to cram his long body into the small space behind the seat. Well, Whitney would pay. He would see to that. If not by legal means, then . . . He gave a mental shrug. He would be on the run again soon enough anyway; taking care of Whitney if he had to wouldn't make it any harder.

"Okay?" Kit asked as she tugged the blanket up to cover him completely.

"Sure," he muttered. "Good thing I'm not allergic to dogs."

"Hush. You'll hurt his feelings. Up, Gus."

He heard the quick bark, felt the Jeep give, then bounce back as the big dog leapt into the passenger seat. Then he heard the motor turn, catch, felt the clunk as she shifted into gear, and they began to move.

It seemed like forever beneath the heavy, Gus-permeated woolen blanket. The sun was up and beating down strongly, making it seem impossible that this was the same place that only days ago had been blanketed in snow. He swiped at a bead of sweat that dripped down his face and guessed that when he finally got out from under this hair-coated thing, it would be tough to tell him from Gus.

Except, he thought dryly, Gus is a lot smarter. He found the prize and stuck with her, come hell or high water. He would die before he left her. Me, I'll die afterward. The silent thought didn't sound nearly as improbable as it should have.

He felt the change immediately after a sharp right turn. He could hear the different sound of the wheels on the road, a rougher, louder sound after the smooth pavement. He could feel the bumps of an uneven surface. And the heat suddenly abated, as if a cloud had slipped in front of the sun. Or, he realized, as if they were in the shade.

We must be close to the lake now, he thought. Where the trees are thick and the roads narrow enough to be shaded from edge to edge.

Then it changed again. The road noise softened, but paradoxically the bumps were harder and more frequent. The pitch of the motor changed, lowered, as the Jeep slowed. The bumps became slow, rolling swells, and he realized that they were on a dirt road. He started to lift his head to look, catching himself at the last moment and ducking back under the concealing blanket.

He found himself pressed against the back of the Jeep, one arm caught painfully on the base of the tubular roll bar. They were going uphill, he thought, sharply uphill. Fear clutched at him for a moment; Rick's house was down the hill from the main road. Had she changed her mind? Had it all been a bluff? Had she just wanted him to go along so she could deliver him to her friend, the sheriff?

The Jeep slowed even more as the ground beneath them got even rougher. His body tensed, readying itself for the instinctive flight or fight response. Then the reality of what he'd thought sank in, and he sagged weakly. If it was true, he was finished. Through with fighting, through with running. If Kit had turned against him, he didn't have the strength to do either anymore. And more, he didn't care. The air seemed even chillier and the sky darker, but he wasn't sure if it was reality or the grim shadow of his thoughts.

When she stopped and shut off the Jeep, he couldn't bring himself to move. He didn't want to know.

"Race? Did you go to sleep in there, or what?"

The minute he heard her voice the ugly vision fled. She hadn't done it. She couldn't. Not Kit. He reached for the edge of the blanket and pulled it back.

The coolness, and the shade, were reality. He sat up, blinking. They were in the middle of a thick stand of pines, tiny pockets of snow lingering at the sheltered base of their trunks. And there wasn't a road in sight. He looked around. There wasn't *anything* in sight, except trees.

"Where are we?"

"Just below the houses on the lake road."

He glanced around again, then back at Kit. She shrugged. "There's a dirt road—a trail, really—that starts down by the beach. It only comes up a couple of hundred yards, to what used to be a picnic area before they improved the park down on the lake. Nobody uses it anymore. Anyway, we're about halfway up the hill from there. The houses are just out of sight, up through those trees." She gestured up the slope.

"Oh."

She looked at him quizzically. "What's wrong? Where did you think we were?"

"I…" He stopped, breathed a fervent, silent apology for doubting her, and said quickly, "I just didn't know there was a way up from the lake."

"Gus found it, really, one day when he took off after a rabbit. I didn't remember about it until we were on the way here. But you can't see this spot from either the houses or the road below, so I thought it would work."

"It's perfect."

"What about the other houses? What if someone's home and sees us?"

"You can't see Rick's house from either side. They'd have to be outside and practically on his property to see anything."

He scrambled out of the Jeep, reaching back to grab the pack.

"Race?"

He looked over his shoulder at her.

"Let me go first."

He straightened up slowly. "What?"

"I can see if anyone's around."

"Alone? No way."

"But if there's anybody up there, I can bluff my way out easier than you could."

"It's too risky."

"Not as risky as you being seen. I can always say I was just chasing Gus."

She reached out to scratch Gus's ears, her slender fingers tangling in the longer fur at the back of his neck. It made Race think of her fingers threading through his own hair, stroking, caressing, sending fiery ripples of heat throughout his body. Jaw tightening, he clamped down on his instantaneous response to his errant thoughts.

"What if it happens to be Whitney or his over-muscled sidekick?"

"Why would he come back, if he's already searched?" she asked reasonably.

"I don't know. But he might."

"Even so, what are the odds he'd be here today, now?"

Race let out a compressed breath, reluctant to concede the accuracy of her words. As if seeing his hesitancy at her answer, Kit turned to go, Gus close at her heels.

"Kit, wait."

She looked back over her shoulder. Race tried to think of words to stop her, any words. But something in her eyes, some soft warmth, made it impossible for him to speak.

"I'll be fine. I'll send Gus back for you as soon as I'm sure it's clear."

She started up the hill, and Race couldn't find his voice until she was too far away to hear his husky, "Be careful."

The five minutes before he saw Gus gamboling cheerfully down the hill seemed more like five hours. Countless times he had almost started after her, only the logic of what she'd said stopping him. She was right, he told himself; she would be safer than he would. The rationale did little good when arrayed against the unexpectedly fierce protective urge he felt for her. And it did no good at all to remind himself that it was a protectiveness like this that had blown his life to bits ten years ago.

The big dog came to a halt in front of Race, barked once, short and sharp, then turned and trotted a few feet back the way he had come, looking over his shoulder all the while. Race couldn't help smiling at the obvious summons and obediently began to move. Satisfied that his message had been received, Gus broke into a loping run up the hill.

Race found her waiting below the deck that jutted out from the house on the hillside.

"The door's locked, and I didn't see anyone. Gus didn't see or hear anyone either."

"He didn't?" Race couldn't quite hide his amusement at her phrasing.

"He would have let me know," she said simply.

She was right, he thought. The big dog was so protective of her that he would have instantly alerted her to any stranger's presence. And, after the scene at her cabin, the animal would have warned her if Whitney or his pet hulk were around. It must be nice if that someone had four feet and twenty pounds of fur. He almost laughed at himself, albeit bitterly, that he was envious of a dog. Instead he smothered a sigh and turned to walk up the hill along the edge of the deck that bordered the lower floor of the house.

Climbing over the railing, he inspected the wide expanse of glass that gave the living room of the house a 180-degree view of the lake below.

"Are you going to have to break a window?" Kit asked, having clambered over the railing herself after ordering Gus to stay close.

"I hope not," he muttered as he walked along the outside wall of the house. "Ahh," he said in quiet discovery as he stopped in front of a pair of French doors just around the corner. They were locked, but with the flat-bladed chisel he'd put in the pack it took him only moments to get them open.

Jaw tightening, he replaced the chisel in the pack and quietly swung the door open. They stepped into what was obviously a master bedroom. And into a house that had just as obviously been thoroughly searched.

"They *have* been here," Kit breathed beside him, looking in shock at the chaos around them; chairs overturned and cushions tossed, tables tipped over, the contents of drawers and shelves scattered.

"Yeah." His voice was grim. "I recognize the touch."

He'd only been in this room once, the first time Rick had brought him here, but he found his way to the main room easily enough. It was in much the same shape, although it looked a little less awful because of its larger size.

He let out a frustrated sigh; there was little chance that the kind of search that had taken place here had missed anything. Lips tightened into a thin line, he surveyed what had once been the warm, welcoming home of his closest friend.

"I'm sorry, Race."

Kit's quiet words stirred him to movement. "Yeah," he muttered, crossing the room to the bookshelves that filled one wall. Books were piled haphazardly on the floor in front of the oak shelves, tossed there in the furious hunt. A few were still on the shelves, lying at odd angles, some half open, others face down, pages crumpled. They'd missed nothing here, he thought grimly.

He walked over to the big ornately carved desk that Rick had told him had been a gift from his brother. "He didn't need it anymore," Rick had said with teasing pride. "He has a much bigger one in his state senate office."

Now the lovely piece of furniture was covered with more books and scattered papers, letters, notes and charts, all no doubt carefully scanned before being discarded into the pile on the polished surface. Still, he glanced through them quickly, clenching his jaw against the stinging of his eyes at the familiar writing. Race put the letters—mostly from Rick's niece, the daughter of his "famous brother," as Rick had always jokingly referred to William Parkson—in a neat pile, anger overwhelming his pain at the thought of Whitney handling these pieces of Rick's personal life.

"Race?" He looked over his shoulder; Kit was standing beside the breakfast bar that separated the living room from the compact kitchen. "I don't know if it means anything, but I think somebody wrote a phone number here."

He walked over to her and looked at the imprint of a number on a notepad beside the phone, left after someone had scrawled it on the top sheet and torn it off. Tearing the page off, he angled it toward the light from the kitchen window. The numbers became clearly visible.

Something must have shown in his face, because Kit asked quickly, "What's wrong?"

"It's mine."

"Yours? You mean your phone number? At the center?"

He nodded.

Her brows furrowed. "But I thought . . . wouldn't Rick already know your number?"

"He did."

He heard her breath catching as she made the connection. "Then somebody else wrote this?"

He nodded again. "It's not Rick's writing."

"But . . . Whitney would know it, too, wouldn't he?"

"Sure." His mouth twisted sardonically. "How else could he call me at three in the morning to replace a light bulb for him?"

Kit's eyes widened; then she muttered a short, sharp, unladylike word.

"Yeah," he agreed, his gaze going to the paper again.

"Well, if he didn't write it, and Rick didn't, who did?"

"And why?" Race added, his tone grim as he stared at the impressions as if they could tell him. "I don't—"

He broke off suddenly, turning on his heel and walking back over to the desk. He picked up the letters he'd straightened, stifling again a pang at the "Dear Uncle Rick" that headed the top one, and shuffled through until he came to the one he'd noticed only because of the difference in the writing. He held it up, comparing the boldly scrawled date to the numbers showing faintly on the otherwise blank sheet from the notepad.

"What is it?" Kit asked from close behind him.

Silently, he held the two papers so that she could see them. He saw her eyes flick quickly back and forth between the two, and the furrow between her brows deepened.

"They match. Who...?"

"His brother."

Her forehead smoothed out. "Of course. He *was* here, then."

"Apparently."

"They must have broken in after he left, then. Surely he wouldn't have left it like this."

"They waited," he confirmed with certainty. "They wouldn't take a chance on his brother reporting it. Somebody might begin to wonder why a supposed hit-and-run victim's house had been trashed. This way they're clear until somebody comes back here, maybe even after, if it gets blamed on vandals breaking into an empty house."

She just looked at him, the understanding that he had just told her that they would not be reporting the break-in either clear in her eyes. "It wouldn't do any good, Kit," he said. "They'd probably just think it was me again anyway." He sighed. "But why would Rick's brother want my number? He doesn't even know who I am."

Kit gave him an odd little smile he didn't understand, then put one slender hand on his arm and guided him back to where she'd found the notepad. On the wall behind the telephone were several framed pictures: Rick and his brother, Rick and his niece Rachel, but the one Kit pointed to was of Rick and another man, in grubby clothes, holding up a long string of fat lake trout. The two were grinning widely at each other, the friendship between them clearly written on their faces.

"That's what made me walk over here," she said softly. "I could hardly believe it was you. You look so…happy."

"I was," he said, his voice low and taut. "Happier than I'd been—" He heard how strained the words sounded and stopped abruptly. "But he still wouldn't have known who I was from that picture."

Kit pointed at a newspaper clipping that had been framed and hung above the picture. His gaze shifted, and he went suddenly still. He'd forgotten about the article in one of the University of California newspapers, talking about the mentor program Rick had begun. The picture was of the two of them, the caption describing Race as Dr. Parkson's "protégé."

If Kit had noticed that the last name printed there was Booker, not Barkley, she didn't say so. But he doubted that she'd missed that detail; she was too sharp.

He'd been worried about others who might be too sharp when he'd first seen the photo, immediately regretting the fact that he had used the name Race here, even with the false last name. But as time passed and nothing happened, he'd realized that the chance of anyone who knew of him seeing a small university paper was slim. And he looked very different from the skinny teenager who had fled into the darkness that long ago night.

"I wonder if he called?"

Her soft words snapped him out of his reverie, and he shook his head sharply.

"Who knows? It hardly matters now."

His voice was sharp, and he saw the sting of it in her eyes. He turned away from her; it hurt too much to see the pain

and know he'd caused it. He began to look through the rest
of the jumbled house.

He didn't mean to hurt her, but here, in this place that
brought home to him so powerfully that Rick was dead, he
could feel himself closing up inside, chilling over, retreating to that cold, lonely place he'd lived in for so long. The
place he'd run to when his world had crumbled ten years
ago. He'd been drawn out of it by Rick's attention and re-
gard, then coaxed further out by Kit's loving warmth, and
now he was cursing himself roundly for being too much of
a hungry fool to realize that his whole world would crum-
ble, would collapse into dust, when she learned the truth.

And he owed her the truth, he thought. What he should
have done was leave before he hurt her, but he hadn't. He
had stayed, even knowing he was getting in deeper with
every moment. And now there was no way to avoid caus-
ing her pain. He'd already taken too much from her. Far
too much.

So he owed her at least the truth. He should have told her
before now. And God knows he should have told her before they'd made love. It would tear her up, to know she
had given herself so completely, so sweetly, to a man who
couldn't have deserved it less.

But he hadn't told her, and with a sickening little jolt of
self-knowledge, he realized why. He hadn't told her because he'd instinctively known that the truth was the one
thing that would destroy the look of need for him in her
eyes, the one thing that would still her caressing hands forever. And he hadn't wanted that, hadn't wanted her to stop.
He had wanted nothing more than to bury himself in her,
to lose himself in her sweet warmth, to forget, for a moment, the truth of his life, the truth of himself.

Kit was the first, the only, woman he'd ever met who had
the power to give him that peace. And in return she had
bestowed on him the power to wound her deeply, to give her
more heartache than anyone should have to bear. He saw
it in her eyes, felt it in her touch, and every time it ripped
at him a little more, until he wondered how he could even

stand to be with her, knowing that he would, however unwillingly, inevitably use that power.

His thoughts tumbled like a rockslide down the mountain as he mechanically continued to search the tossed room. He paused momentarily when, after inadvertently kicking something hard that lay beneath one of the scattered sofa cushions, he reached down to find a 35-millimeter camera. He stared at it for a long moment, brows furrowed. The back of the camera flapped open, and he turned it over.

"What's wrong? Did they break it?"

He nearly jumped, she had approached so quietly. He gave her a sideways glance; if she was still hurt or angry at his sharpness, it didn't show. "No," he said after a moment. "At least I don't think so. But it's empty."

"Do you think they took the film?"

He shrugged. "Or maybe it was already empty. It's just that I don't remember the camera. Or Rick even having one here." His eyes flicked back to the photos on the wall. "He always had somebody else take the pictures. He always said that after taking photomicrographs of every stage of hundreds of experiments, the last thing he wanted to do was take pictures at home."

"Photo-whats?"

"Photomicrographs. Photos taken through a microscope. Rick was always careful about documenting everything, even if he wasn't sure the experiment was of any significance."

With one hand he righted the coffee table, then set the camera carefully down on the polished surface. He didn't want to go on, but the words seemed to come despite himself.

"He just wasn't as careful with himself." Bitterness laced his voice.

"Oh, Race..."

Her hand came out to touch his arm. He knew she meant it to be comforting, and that she could do it after he'd snapped at her made him shift uncomfortably beneath a growing burden of guilt. That the gentle touch sent an in-

stant jolt of heat rippling through him, that it started a series of vivid images from last night racing through his mind
until his entire body clenched at the force of his reaction to
them, made the guilt almost unbearable. God, she deserved better. Better than what she thought he was, let alone
what he *really* was.

He had to tell her, he thought. Soon. Then there would
be no tears when, as soon as he'd done what he had to do
to put Rick's murderer away, he did the other thing he had
to do: take himself out of her life. He couldn't change what
he'd already taken from her, but he could make sure that he
didn't take any more. Never mind that the thought of leaving her tore him into raw, bleeding pieces inside; this horrible guilt was worse. He'd thought he'd known all there
was to know about that particular burden, but he saw now
that he'd known nothing. Only this decision to do what he
should have done long ago brought any easing of that heavy
weight of self-blame.

She would want him out then, he told himself, and her
anger would see her through what hurt there might be. He
only hoped she wasn't too hard on herself for being foolish enough to get involved with a man who wasn't worth a
single strand of the silken fire of her hair.

"Race?"

Her voice was soft, tender with compassion, and only the
knowledge that he would soon put an end to using her
strength, her gentle honesty and her sweet hot fire to warm
himself enabled him to face her.

"It's all right, sunrose," he said quietly. "Let's finish up
and get out of here."

The "before we get caught" was unspoken, but her quick
nod told him that she understood.

The remainder of their search was fruitless, but he hadn't
expected anything else. Whoever had been here before—
and he had little doubt that it was the hulk—had been too
thorough.

The ride back to her cabin in the afternoon sun was even
more stifling than the ride there had been.

"I'm sorry you have to do this," she'd said as he'd climbed in and she'd made sure the blanket covered him completely. He'd felt an odd little twinge at the realization that he hadn't even really thought about it. Had he been hiding out so long that he took even this kind of stealth for granted?

"Believe me," he'd said dryly, "this is nothing." And he'd winced at the look she gave him, a look of curiosity mixed with apprehension that made him think of how very much worse she would look if he at last satisfied that curiosity.

When they pulled off onto the gravel drive, he knew something was wrong the moment he heard the low, menacing growl rumbling up from Gus's throat. He heard the scratching of the dog's feet on the seat, then Kit's voice as she restrained the dog with a few soft words.

"No, Gus, stay."

He barely managed to stop himself from instinctively sitting up to see what had the big dog so angry. He'd decided to risk a whispered question when Kit solved his dilemma.

"Easy, Gus," she said, loud enough for him to hear, yet as if she were explaining to the dog. "That's Len's new car, so he must be here somewhere. I know you don't like him, but it would be rude to chew on a harmless visitor. We'll just get him to leave."

The tension drained from him. Damn, she was quick, he thought. But then, as the Jeep pulled to a halt and he heard footsteps on the porch as a masculine voice called out to her, his tension returned.

"Hi, kitten!"

Kitten? Bile, acid and burning, rose in his throat so strongly that he nearly missed the underlying alarm in the man's voice.

"God," Kit muttered under her breath, "I hate that name."

The bile receded, but the memory of that undertone of tension remained. He heard the heavy footsteps again, on the gravel now, then felt the Jeep shift as both Kit and Gus left it. He heard Kit's quicker, lighter steps, heard Gus's restrained grumblings, and knew that she had hurried to intercept Len. The golden boy, he thought grimly. What the hell was he doing here?

"Hey, sweetheart, I was about to leave you a note."

Trying to ignore the repugnance that shot through him at the casual endearment, he concentrated on the voice itself. The dismay was gone now, but there was still an odd undertone there, he thought. Tension? Nervousness? Fear? He wasn't sure what it was, only that it was there, and he didn't understand why.

"About what?"

Kit's question came in a steady, even tone, but Race didn't miss the note of unease. It was odd, he thought, how much more you could hear when you weren't able to see.

"Er...I...just to say hello," Len said, floundering a little. Then he seemed to think of something. "You said you wanted a ride in my new car, remember?"

He sounds relieved, Race thought, like an actor who'd remembered his line. The image bothered him, but then, everything about this guy bothered him, even though he hadn't laid eyes on him yet.

"I'm sorry, Len. It will have to be later." Race heard Kit's hesitation, then she said quickly, "Gus isn't feeling real well." A rather ominous tone crept into her voice. "And he gets so cranky when he's sick, he's likely to just bite anybody."

Race smothered a grin at the sudden sound of crunching gravel, as if Len had taken a hasty step back. Then, as if to cover his timidity, Len's voice came again, energetic and hearty.

"How about this weekend, then, babe? I'll take you out to the swankiest club on the south shore, a little dinner, some Dom Pérignon, a moonlight drive along the lake, just you and me. Nothing but the best for you, kitten, what do you say?"

The golden boy, Race's mind repeated as he listened. The one who had it all. The one who could give it all to Kit.

Everything she deserved. Everything he could never give her.

He didn't even hear their next words, so desperately was he trying to smother the sound of pain that threatened to burst from him. Kit was out there, in the mountain sun, with the golden boy. Where she belonged. While he was here, cowering beneath a blanket that was more fur than wool, hiding in the dark like some animal fit only for the underworld. Where he belonged.

The ache of the comparison was so strong that he couldn't stop himself from looking. Inching upward, he lifted the edge of the blanket. Turning his head so that he could see with the minimum of exposure, he peered out.

Len Porter was indeed a golden boy. Tall, blond, handsome, with a cocky grin, a law degree and the world at his feet. Not to mention the huge, white, expensive car he was so obviously proud of. And eyes that were fastened on Kit with an ardent avidity that made Race wince with abhorrence. The golden boy, he thought again, as if his mind had somehow stuck in a raw, painful groove.

The sound of tires on gravel mercifully ended his painful introspection. He heard the swift, light steps as Kit came back; then her low husky voice made his efforts to pull himself together that much harder.

"Race? It's all right, he's gone."

Slowly he made himself sit up. He started to speak, but when he realized that the only thing he wanted to ask was what her answer to Len had been, he stopped himself. In silence he clambered out of the Jeep and walked past her into the cabin.

Although she looked at him in concern, Kit held to the silence she sensed he needed. He paced the great room, stirred the fire on the hearth to life and added wood, then paced some more. Gus seemed unable to settle down either, making low, unsettled noises as he inspected every corner of the cabin as though he'd never seen it before. Sometimes man and dog would have to dodge each other as their restless paths crossed. At last Kit retreated to the kitchen. She returned a few minutes later with two steaming cups of chocolate and a pleading look in her eyes.

"Please, Race. Sit down. You look exhausted."

As if her saying it had destroyed the last of his resistance against it, he felt the fatigue flood him. He took the cup she held out to him and none too steadily sat down on the sofa. The sofa he'd slept on, before she had let him into her bed. Again the memories, hot, sweet and vivid, rose up to swamp him with streaming rivulets of sensation. He shuddered, watching the echo of it in the rippling of the liquid in the cup. He quickly set it on the end table, afraid he would begin to shake so badly he'd spill it.

After a moment Kit asked quietly, "What do we do now?"

"I don't know."

It was flat, it was harsh, but it was the truth. He didn't know. And he was too tired to think about it now. He hadn't gotten much sleep. . . .

Damn you, he swore at himself. Stop thinking about last night. Stop remembering. Stop feeling. Stop wanting. Stop it all, because you're not going to get any more. It's over. You're not going to take what you want. You're not going to use her anymore.

"Race, what's wrong?"

She'd set her cup down sharply and was staring at him in dismay.

"Nothing," he grated out.

"But you look so—"

"Stop it, Kit. Stop worrying about me. Worry about yourself for a change."

"I am," she said in a tiny voice. "And I'm worried about you. I'm worried about . . . us."

That tiny pause, that hesitation before the tentative declaration that there was an "us" for her to worry about, made his throat tighten unbearably. God, what he wouldn't give to have the right to be half of that "us," the right to belong to Kit, to have her belong to him, in that mutual sharing of love and caring that he'd only imagined existed.

And it doesn't exist, he told himself sternly. Not for you.

He knew that in his weariness he'd let too much show in his face, because Kit made a tiny sound and then shifted on the sofa to throw her arms around his neck.

"Please, Race, don't look like that! You're scaring me!"

He stiffened, ordering his body not to respond to the feel of her, the sweet scent of her, ordering it not to react to the memories that filled him with swirling heat. It was a losing battle, and he knew it. Yet it was one he had to win. With a fierceness that spoke volumes of his pain he pulled away from her, staggering slightly as he got to his feet. Gus looked at him, tilting his big head, from where he'd finally settled beside the front door. You were wrong about me, buddy, he silently told the dog. Dead wrong.

"Race . . . ?"

"Don't, Kit. Don't do this to yourself."

"Do . . . what?"

"You deserve better than this. Better than . . . what I'm putting you through. You deserve that golden boy and everything he can give you."

"That gold—Len?" She started at him, tears brimming in her eyes. His throat tightened again at her determined courage as she fought them back. "I wouldn't want Len if he could give me the moon and the stars."

"He's got it all, Kit. Looks, charm, a college education. A law degree, for God's sake. You'd be a fool to pass up a man like that."

Her chin came up, and a spark of anger glinted through the tears. "I'd be a fool," she said slowly, "to pass up the man who *can* give me the moon and the stars."

He couldn't stand the way she was looking at him, as if he were the answer to all her dreams. He wanted to forget the decision he'd made, he wanted to grab her and hold her forever, to make love to her until she cried out his name, until he was hoarse from his own groans of pleasure.

And he would wind up hurting her even more when, as it must, the end came, he told himself bleakly. With the last of his fading strength, he stiffened his resolve.

"I'm not that man, sunrose," he whispered. "I'm not who—or what—you think I am."

"I know you're a good man, an honest man, it's just—"

"You don't know anything!" He hated himself for doing it this way, sharply, in anger, but it was the only way he could make his determination hold out long enough. "I'm not good *or* honest, Kit Cameron."

She drew back from him a little, looking at him with a sudden wariness that clawed at him, sharpening his voice even more.

"Then what are you?" she asked tightly.

He set his jaw. "I'm exactly what you thought I was that day the sheriff showed up here."

Her eyes widened, and she shook her head slowly, uncomprehendingly. "What do you mean? What are you?"

He met her gaze levelly. "A killer, Kit. That's what I am."

Chapter 11

It was done, Race thought grimly. He'd told her, and any moment loathing would replace the wide-eyed shock on her face. Abhorrence would fill her, pushing out the soft, tender feelings she'd had for him. Kit Cameron was a kindhearted, compassionate woman; she would have nothing to do with a murderer.

But the change in her expression didn't come. She just shook her head slowly, in mute denial. It made him angry, and he didn't know why, whether it was because she was so foolishly trusting, or because she was making this so much harder on both of them by forcing him to make her believe what he was saying.

"It's the truth, Kit. It's the thing I didn't tell you. It's why I can't go to the police."

Her face was pale, and her lips moved, but no words came. She shook her head again; this time he couldn't tell if it was in denial or protest.

"Ironic, isn't it?" he said harshly. "I can't turn in a murderer because I'm one myself. You wondered, didn't you? Why I thought the sheriff might be after me, even after ten years? Didn't you think of the one thing there's no statute of limitations on? The one thing that the law will be after you forever for?''

"Race, no..."

"Yes," he snapped, his own agony sharpening his voice. "Yes, damn it! I told you you wouldn't want me, not if you knew. Well, now you do, and you know I'm right."

She gave a quiet moan, and Race felt himself cringe as he looked away from her. He walked to the hearth, scraping at the fieldstone with the toe of his boot. Gus lifted his head to look at him, but Race barely noticed. That bitter acid was churning inside him, and he knew if it ever ebbed, there would be nothing left but a hollow, corroded shell, emptied of any heart, soul or feelings.

"I'm sorry." It broke from him involuntarily. "I should have told you. I know if I had, you never would have..." His voice broke, and he finished lamely, "I should have told you." He still couldn't look at her. "You had a right to know. Especially before we...before you let me...touch you."

"No."

It was barely a whisper, but it cut Race to his core, to what was left of his tattered soul. "I'm sorry, Kit. I just couldn't lie to you anymore."

"I don't believe it."

The words were stronger this time, but no less painful. A short laugh broke from him, harsh and humorless, a barren cold sound.

"God, you give your trust completely, don't you?" He drew a ragged breath. "It's true, Kit. It isn't a mistake. I wasn't framed or anything else. I killed a man. And I ran. And I've been running ever since."

"It must have been an accident—"

She broke off when he whirled back to face her. "Damn it, Kit, stop trying to sugarcoat this! It was no accident. It was intentional, do you understand? I meant to kill him, and I did."

She stared at him, and he saw her shiver as she huddled on the couch. He saw her effort to pull herself together, saw her square her shoulders and straighten her quivering body.

God, she had more raw courage than anyone he'd ever known, he thought. Certainly more than he'd ever had. And then, quietly, steadily, she spoke one simple word.

"Why?"

He blinked, brows furrowing. "What?"

"Why? Why did you kill him?"

He just stared at her; of all the things he'd expected her to say, that question had not occurred to him.

"I know you must have had a good reason," she insisted.

"How?" he choked out. "How can you know that?"

She met his gaze, her eyes full of pain and confusion, but with both of those emotions overshadowed by softness.

"Because I know you," she said softly, simply.

Her quiet faith, her unnerving trust, robbed him of what little strength he had left, and he dropped down to sit on the edge of the raised hearth. He stared into the fire.

"Is there ever a good enough reason to...kill someone?" he whispered, his voice taut with strain.

Kit was off the sofa and at his side in seconds. "What happened, Race?" She reached out to touch him, then drew back, as if she'd sensed that it would be more than he could bear right now. "You said ten years.... God, you couldn't have been more than a boy then."

"Fifteen. Old enough. I should have been able to think of another way to stop him."

"Who was it? What did he do to you?"

He lifted his head to look at her, knowing she couldn't help seeing the moisture in his eyes and the way he had to blink rapidly to hold it back. He wasn't sure he cared.

"Why are you so sure he did something to me?"

"I told you. I know you."

He shuddered, and she did touch him then, placing one slender hand gently on his knee. He could feel the words bubbling up inside him, burning his throat, and he knew he was going to tell her the story he'd never told anyone. He couldn't help himself, not when she was touching him, not when she was looking at him like that.

"It wasn't me," he said slowly. "It was... He was... I..."

He couldn't find the words. He'd kept this bottled-up inside him for so long that now he couldn't seem to lower his guard to let it out.

"Who was he?" Kit asked gently.

He took a deep breath and tried again. "My stepfather."

Her breath caught. "What did you have to... stop?"

"I... He was..." He took another breath and tried again. "I almost didn't go in the house that day. I came home from baseball practice, and his car was there, even though he was supposed to be at work. I heard them, even outside." A shiver rippled through him, and Kit's hand tightened on his knee. "They were always fighting. He was big, and he had a rotten temper. I always felt guilty, because I thought she'd married him because she couldn't support me alone. She'd never worked, and after my dad died she didn't know what to do...."

It was coming out all mixed up, he thought, but Kit only nodded.

"They were arguing that day. He was shouting. He hadn't started hitting her yet. I didn't understand at first what he was saying. He was calling her names and accusing her of...having an affair with somebody." He laughed, low, harsh, sour. "It was so absurd. She was so afraid of him she'd barely talk to anyone but me. I wanted to tell somebody, to report him, but she wouldn't let me. She kept saying at least we had a home. Then I wanted to hit him, hurt him back...but she stopped me. Said it would only make it worse on her."

He shuddered, forcing himself to go on. "Anyway, he was standing there calling her those awful names. She denied it, but he wouldn't believe her. I'd never heard him so mad. I wanted to leave...but I was afraid of him, too."

"Of course you were. You were only a boy."

He let out a compressed breath. Kit reached for his hand, wrapping her slender fingers around his. He knew he should pull away, but that precious touch was much too necessary to him.

"I thought about going in through the patio door, to avoid them. Then I heard him start to hit her. I ran inside, I thought maybe I could...distract him or something, I guess. He'd done it before, but he always stopped when she started to cry...like it was some kind of sign that he'd won, when he'd made her cry."

"But this time he didn't stop," Kit guessed quietly.

He closed his eyes, seeing it all again, his mother cowering in a corner, his stepfather raining down heavy, thudding blows with angry hands, then fists.

"No. He just kept hitting her. Again and again. I yelled at him, but...then he grabbed a lamp...a big, heavy brass one. He hit her with it...in the head...."

He shuddered, barely feeling Kit's arms come around him, hugging him, so vivid was the horrible memory.

"I hit him," he choked out. "I still had my baseball bat in my hand, and I hit him. Hard. He went down but...I couldn't seem to stop...."

"Oh, God, Race..."

"I just kept hitting him...until he didn't move at all anymore."

Her arms tightened around him, and through the painful mist he heard her ask softly, "Your mother?"

He shook his head, for a moment unable to form the words. "She...she was dead. I could tell...she was so pale, and still. She was just lying there, all crooked...." His voice broke, and he had to swallow heavily before he could go on. "I called the police...so they would find her and...take care of things. Then I ran."

"But why?" It burst from her incredulously. "He was beating your mother! My God, Race, he killed her! You had no choice!"

With a soft, short expulsion of breath, he let his head loll back wearily.

"He was a big man in that little town, Kit. He owned the bank, was on the town council. Nobody would believe he went home at night and beat his wife."

"But if he'd done it before, surely she must have gone to someone...."

"She did, once. To the doctor in town. He did exactly what he was supposed to have done. He called the police. Who called my stepfather."

When he didn't go on, Kit's brows lowered. "What happened?"

He smiled crookedly. "He admitted she'd been beaten."

Kit gaped at him. "What?"

"He said he knew all about it. And that something was going to have to be done about the one who did it."

"The one—you mean he blamed someone else?" He didn't think his expression changed, but Kit's eyes widened in shock. "You?" she whispered. "He blamed you?"

"I was a big kid, almost as tall as he was. It wasn't hard for them to believe. Especially when they had a 'pillar of the community' to tell them so." The trite phrase rolled sardonically off his tongue. "My mother tried to deny it at first, but he threatened her. He told her he'd turn me over to the juvenile authorities the next time she said anything to anyone. But that before that, he'd show her what a beating really was." Weariness flooded him, and only the feel of Kit's arms around him enabled him to keep going. "He used me as a weapon against her. I wanted to leave, to just get away, but I was afraid of what he'd do to her...."

"Oh, God, Race, how awful for you. Both of you."

"So you see why I couldn't stay. They'd never believe that...I had to do it. They'd just think he'd tried to stop me from hurting her and I'd killed him."

"So you've been on the run ever since," she whispered.

"Yes." His mouth twisted. "Until now. And look what I've accomplished. Your father's dead, Rick's dead, and I've hurt you."

"Race, stop. I—"

"It's all right, I understand. There's no room in your life for...someone like me. Someone who did...what I did."

"It wasn't your fault!"

"It just seems to happen wherever I am," he muttered.

"But you—"

"Bring trouble with me. So it's about time I took it away with me. You've done enough, put up with enough."

"But it wasn't your fault!" she exclaimed again. "You aren't a murderer, it was self-defense, or something, you—"

"You don't understand, Kit," he said gently. "I could have stopped. I didn't have to hit him anymore, not after he went down. He wasn't hurting her anymore, but...I just kept hitting him. I couldn't seem to stop. I killed him, and I didn't have to. That's murder in anyone's book."

"Not mine," she said fiercely. "After everything you went through, after what he did to you, to your mother, he deserved it!"

For the first time, helpless to stop himself, he let himself do what he'd been aching to do since she'd come to him. He embraced her, pulling her close.

"God, sunrose, you don't stint on your loyalty, do you?"

"I just know it wasn't your fault. If I could have saved my father, I would have killed, too, without a second thought."

He buried his face in the silk of her hair. He couldn't believe this. He'd thought she would turn from him in disgust when she knew the truth. Even if he could justify his initial action, he'd never been able to rationalize the way he'd continued to hit a man who was down. The fury that had been unstoppable then seemed practically crazed in the calmer aftermath, and it had frightened him. "I don't think you could, Kit. Not like I did. But . . . thank you."

There was a long, silent moment before she drew back in his embrace to look at him with brimming eyes.

"Did you really think I would hate you? Once I knew the whole story?"

He sighed. "I didn't think...you could accept it. Not the way it happened, not when...God, Kit, I didn't have to kill him, but I did. I did, and I swear I'd do it again. I hated him, and all I could think about when I was hitting him was that he wouldn't ever hurt anybody again. I should have stopped, but I didn't. How can you want...to be with someone who's capable of that?"

"You mean someone who's capable of enough love to risk his own life for it? Someone who's paid the price for that love every day of his life since? Someone who gave up the life he should have had to save someone he loved? You want to know how I can want someone like that?"

"Kit..."

"Well, I do. I want him more than I've ever wanted anyone. More than I knew I *could* want anyone." She took a quick breath, lips parted, and Race felt a tiny glow of heat begin deep inside him. "You did what you had to do, Race. And even if you can't stop blaming yourself, don't expect me to blame you for something you had no control over. He was an evil man, a cruel, brutal bully, and he reaped what he'd sown."

"Ah, sunrose..."

"I'm sorry you had to dredge up those ugly memories, but I'm glad you told me. I'm glad you trusted me—" She broke off, staring at him, as if she'd seen something in his face. "You didn't trust me, did you?"

He let out a weary sigh. "I just knew I couldn't lie to you any longer."

"What did you expect me to do? Turn on you? Throw you out? Call Harve and turn you in? Is that what you expected?"

She sounded almost angry, and he was too exhausted to deal with it. "I expected," he said with tired numbness, "to lose you like I've lost everything else I ever cared about. And if that sounds self-pitying, I'm too damned tired to care."

An odd look came over her face, a look that was tender yet shy. But her eyes were aglow with that golden warmth, and her voice was husky with the sound that matched it as she reached up to touch his cheek.

"You look tired," she agreed softly. "So why don't we go to bed?"

He stared, knowing he was gaping at her but unable to stop. "I...how can you still...?"

"You're not a killer, Race. You were a boy who did the best he could to protect the person who should have been protecting him. And you got sucked up into this mess now through no fault of your own. It's already cost you your best friend—"

"And you your father," he reminded her grimly.

"That wasn't your fault either."

"If I'd kept my nose out of this—"

"You couldn't have done that."

"Sure I could have. I could have just emptied the trash and kept my mouth shut. But no, I had to be an idiot and confront Whitney—"

"Whitney's the idiot for not seeing past some silly personal caste system to who you really are. He brought this on himself, and he's responsible for Rick's death. And my father's."

She ran her thumb along the line of his jaw, and one slender finger crept over to trace his lips. Fire leapt through him, and involuntarily his lips parted for her touch. His tongue flicked out to taste, to gently stroke the tip of that caressing finger. He saw heat flare in her eyes, and the knowledge that he could still make her want him, despite what he'd told her, sent a brilliant flare of hope to that cringing place deep inside him that had been certain the truth would drive her away.

"Kit?" he gasped as she ran her fingers in a stroking motion down the cords of his neck.

"You're tired," she said softly. "You need sleep. And I think I might know just how to make sure you get some."

He groaned as her fingers lingered over the hollow of his throat, where his pulse began to hammer. And he sucked in a quick, harsh breath as those fingers moved to undo the top button of his shirt. It took all his will to give her a last chance to think about it again. He grasped her slender wrists and held her hands away from the second button she'd been reaching for.

"Kit . . . are you sure?"

She looked up at him, her eyes hot and golden now. She made no effort to pull her hands free. Without a word she leaned forward and, nuzzling aside his shirt, pressed her lips to the bare skin of his chest.

With a final sigh of joyous surrender, Race lifted his arms to enclose her, pressing her head tightly against his chest. He felt the flexing of her fingers as she worked at the remaining buttons of his shirt, then the hot precious caress of her hands as she slid them over his chest.

His body tightened with fierce suddenness as her fingertips brushed over his nipples. She felt his sudden tension and repeated the movement. He groaned as the flat, brown circles of flesh puckered. Then he felt the tickle of her lashes against his skin as she shifted to look at him.

"You . . . like that?"

He gave a short, sharp chuckle. "Sunrose, there's only one way I could like it any more."

"What way?"

"Do it with your tongue."

She colored slightly, but her eyes glinted as the flames from the hearth danced. She reached for the edges of his shirt, but he beat her to it and stripped it off quickly. She moved her head, her tongue creeping out to tentatively glide over the disk of flesh her fingers had teased.

Race groaned as he looked down at her, not quite certain how the sight of the pink tip of her tongue caressing that flat nub of flesh could be so utterly arousing. That it was he couldn't deny; his body was already throbbing, demanding release from the suddenly too-tight confines of his jeans.

She had moved to his other nipple, flicking it with more assurance, sending little darts of fire racing along nerves that seemed to lead straight to the pulsing, hardening core of him. He caught the reflection of the flickering firelight on his own flesh, on his nipple wet from her mouth, and a stab of white-hot sensation went through him, so fierce it made him nearly double over under its force.

"Race?"

"Kit, you're driving me crazy."

She smiled, a soft, satisfied smile. "Good. It's only fair."

She began to trail soft, wet kisses over him, from nipple to nipple, then down his chest. She blazed a path over the smooth flatness of his belly, and he felt the muscles there ripple with her passing. She ran her tongue around his navel, and a low, harsh sound burst from him.

Kit lifted one hand, then hesitated as it hovered near the snap of his jeans.

"Race?" she whispered.

Hearing the note of shyness in her voice, he grabbed her hand and pressed her palm against him, arching his hips up to increase the pressure on his swollen flesh.

"Don't ever ask, sunrose. You don't ever have to ask to touch me."

She blushed, but the look she gave him was one of pure pleasure. "Then I won't," she said huskily. "I'll just ask if I can do it without all these clothes on."

For answer he reached for the waistband of his jeans, releasing the zipper with one swift yank. He lifted himself to work out of the worn denim and his briefs, then nearly collapsed when Kit took advantage of his movement to encircle his newly freed hardness with slender, stroking fingers.

He groaned, and she stopped, startled at his hoarse cry, but when he convulsively arched himself into her hands she began again, stroking him from base to tip, and lingering there to rub his exquisitely sensitive flesh.

He kicked free of the entangling clothes and shoes, then reached for her.

"Please," she murmured, stopping him. "Let me. You made me feel so... wonderful, I want to... I need to..."

He understood the words she didn't say. He saw them in the touch of shyness amid the flaring heat in her eyes, felt them in the slight hesitation every time she touched him someplace new. She needed to know that she wasn't in this alone, that he was as hot, as eager, as wanting, as she was. And that, he thought ruefully, gasping as she found another wildly inflamed collection of nerve endings and he shuddered in response, shouldn't be hard to prove to her.

It wasn't until she gave a slow, stroking caress up the inside of his thigh, a caress that ended with a tentative cupping of taut, rounded flesh that was so sensitive he groaned deeply at the feel of her hand there, that he realized the

oddness of lying there naked before her while she, fully
clothed, ministered sweetly to his clamoring, aroused body.

It was as if she were tending to his pleasure with no
thought of her own, and when, at that moment, she lifted
her eyes to his, something in her gaze made him feel like
some sort of god, placed on a pedestal to be worshiped by
a beautiful handmaiden. Then she lowered her head to trail
kisses across his belly down to his hip, making him trem-
ble, and he thought it was much more likely that she was the
goddess and he merely the offering to her.

When her lips brushed over his distended flesh a throttled growl ripped from his throat and he reached for her.
She pulled away, shaking her head. He fell back, closing his
eyes as he drew a harsh breath, trying to regain control. He
owed her this, he thought. He owed her anything she
wanted. And he loved what she was doing to him. He just
didn't think he could stand it for long.

"Race?" It was a quiet, tremulous sound, and his eyes
snapped open. "Don't you like...?"

"Like?" He groaned softly. "Sunrose, that doesn't even
begin to cover what you're doing to me."

He looked at her for a moment, at the pink that stained
her cheeks, as if it were she who lay so exposed, so vulnerable. And in a way, he supposed, she was. He swallowed
hard before he spoke softly.

"It's just that...it's difficult to just lie here when I want
to touch you so much. Besides..."

"Besides what?" she prompted when he didn't finish.

Honesty, he ordered himself. You've lied to her for the
last time. "I'm feeling a little...alone here."

She looked puzzled for a moment; then her gaze swept
over his naked body and understanding lit her eyes. The
color in her cheeks deepened, but she never hesitated. She
sat back and tugged her sweater over her head, then released the catch of her bra. Satin gleamed in the firelight for
a moment before it fell, freeing her breasts.

Race's hands curled into fists, and a low, harsh sound
rumbled up from his throat. It was all he could do to stop
himself from grabbing her, from pulling her down so that

he could touch, could taste, that soft, tender flesh. She heard the sound, and her hands halted on the snap of her jeans.

"Please, don't stop now," he ground out.

As if given new impetus by his plea, she quickly wiggled out of the tight tan denims, taking the small swath of satin panties with them, along with her heavy socks. For a moment she just sat there, the firelight dancing over her, and Race sucked in a quick, deep breath as his stomach knotted at the sight.

"Is that...better?" she asked shyly, not looking at him.

"That," he breathed with a heartfelt earnestness, "is the most beautiful sight I've ever seen."

Her head came up then, her eyes meeting his, and he saw the shyness fade as the golden flecks seemed to shimmer again with renewed heat.

"In that case," she said, a husky note coming into her voice, making a shiver run down his spine, "where was I?"

Involuntarily, the hard, taut muscles of his buttocks clenched, lifting him slightly, as if to remind her exactly where she'd been. He tried to stop it, it felt so much like begging her to continue that sweet caress, but then she bent to him and he was lost. She tasted him tentatively, then, as he gasped at the hot, sharp jolt of pleasure, more assuredly, until he was moaning her name.

She hovered over him, then shifted to straddle him. The movement brought her within reach, and he couldn't resist the lure of her breasts. Her nipples were already taut, as if her ministrations to his body had thoroughly aroused her own; he found the thought incredibly inflaming. His hands went up to cup and lift the full curves, his thumbs rubbing the crests. The rosy peaks stiffened further, and with a little cry she arched her back, thrusting them forward against his hands. He recognized the movement, the same kind of convulsive jerk his hips gave every time she touched his swollen, aching shaft.

This proof of her response sent a darting little thrill through him, and he repeated the stroking of his thumbs again and again. And when she arched even further, he caught those tight little peaks and tugged at them. She cried out his name while he smothered another gasp as her movements brought the soft tangle of reddish curls at the apex of her parted thighs into heated contact with flesh already tight to the point of bursting.

He was unraveling much too quickly. With a swiftness born of that knowledge he moved one hand to part those curls, to prove and test soft feminine folds. When his fingers met slick, wet heat, when he found and stroked that tiny, central core, she shuddered.

"Oh, Race!"

"Now, sunrose? You want me now?" I sure as hell hope so, he thought wildly as she moved against his hand.

"Please," she moaned. "Yes, now."

"Then take me," he whispered hoarsely, "because I don't think I can wait another second."

Her eyes widened, but something she saw in his face must have reassured her, because after a brief moment she moved. She shifted her body, lowering herself, and after a moment's hesitation she reached between them to gently guide him into her waiting heat.

He'd meant to let her do it, meant to give her the assurance taking the lead would bring her, but at the first fiery clasp of her body around his, he lost all track of his intentions. With a low, strangled groan he rose up off the floor, his hands going to her hips to impale her upon him in one fierce movement. She cried out in shocked pleasure and straightened her legs so they extended behind him, bringing her full weight against his hips as he sat upright, his arms wrapping around her.

"I'm sorry," he gasped, rocking her slightly as he extended his own legs before him for balance, "but I just couldn't stay still. Did I hurt you?"

"No," she whispered. "Oh, no." As if for emphasis, she twisted sinuously in his arms, rubbing the hardened tips of her breasts against his chest.

Slowly he became aware that the instinctive rocking movements he'd begun when he was afraid his sudden thrust had hurt her were sending hot little rushes of plea-

sure along his already sizzling nerves. The tiny increments
of penetration and withdrawal seemed much too small to
cause such fierce sensations, but the longer he did it, the
more intense they became, until his breathing was harsh
and ragged against the silken skin of her neck.

Finally he made himself stop, not sure that what was so
pleasurable for him, with her full weight driving him so
deeply inside her, was as good for her. But the tiny moan of
protest she made when he stopped the gentle rocking made
him wonder.

"Kit?"

"No, don't stop. It feels so good. You're so full inside
me, I want..."

"You want what?" he asked softly, his voice rough with
the realization that it had indeed been as good for her.

"I want it to last forever," she said in a breathless little
burst of words as he lifted his head to press a nibbling kiss
in the soft curve of her neck and shoulder. "But I want...to
go flying, too."

"You will," he promised fervently. "I promise, sunrose."

It took every ounce of his self-control to keep that
promise. He rocked her gently on him, savoring her moans
and the tightening of her arms around him. He shifted
slightly, changing the angle of his body, and reveled in her
sudden gasp of his name. He increased the pressure, con-
centrating intently on her every response, all the while ordering his own body to retreat from that rapidly
approaching boiling point.

"Kit," he panted, his hands, then his lips, going to her
breasts again. Her hands went around his neck, pressing his
mouth to her harder as she repeated his name over and
over.

He didn't think he was going to make it. He was strung
too tightly, she was holding him too close, caressing him too
sweetly with that slick, hot, feminine flesh. He clenched his
jaw against the rising tide, fighting to hold back, to take her
with him. When he felt it begin for her, felt the deep, fierce
clenching of those inner muscles, he knew he couldn't wait.

The sound of his name, breaking from her in a clear, rapturous cry as she went rigid in his arms, sent him spiraling up and out in a flare of bright light and heat. He fell back to brace himself on his hands as his hips arched upwards, lifting her as he drove into her, pouring himself into her in an explosion he felt to his toes.

"Yes," he cried hoarsely. "Oh, *yes!*"

He collapsed, barely able to move his arms to make sure she was cushioned from the floor by his body. She quivered in his arms, or maybe it was he who was shaking; he didn't know and didn't care. He knew only that he wanted to hold her like this forever and refused to acknowledge that he knew he couldn't.

He was so languorous he didn't know how long had passed when she lifted her head from his chest.

"Race?"

"Mmm."

"We're on the floor again."

He opened one eye sleepily. "Umm-hmm." He closed it again.

"Wouldn't you rather be in a nice, soft bed?"

"Umm-hmm."

When he made no effort to move, she gave him a nudge. One eye flickered open again.

"I said I wanted to *be* there, not that I could get up and go there."

She giggled, then looked startled, as if she'd surprised herself with the sound. He opened both eyes then, the simple, light sound pleasing him in a way he didn't quite understand. In a sudden, controlled surge he gathered her in his arms, rose to his feet and started toward the bedroom. The giggle came again, as he'd hoped it would, and he couldn't help the wide, pleased grin that spread across his face.

She went suddenly still, her eyes wide with wonder as she reached up to touch one corner of his mouth.

He quirked an eyebrow at her. "What?"

"I've never seen you really smile before," she said simply. "It's wonderful."

He felt himself flush, but turned his head to press his lips to the palm of her caressing hand. He nudged open the bedroom door, then crossed the room to lay her with exquisite care in the center of the big four-poster. She snuggled into the thick quilt, then held out her arms invitingly. He moved to go to her, already feeling the renewed thrum of desire as he looked down at her slender, naked body.

"What is it?" she asked when he stopped suddenly.

"I forgot something. I'll be right back."

He had forgotten, he thought, probably because it was such a poor attempt at marking the special day. Nevertheless, it was all he had, so he quickly went back to the great room and dug into the side pocket of the backpack of tools.

He was aware of her eyes on him the moment he walked back into the room. It was still light out, but gray, and she'd lit a candle. The single small flame cast a warm little circle of light. She watched him cross the floor, and he felt her gaze like a physical caress, his body responding as if it had been. He didn't try to hide it; if she didn't know by now that she could turn him on with a look, she never would.

He tried to ignore the rapid tightening of his body as he sat on the edge of the bed and looked at her, his right hand out of sight behind him.

"I know it's not much," he began, "but..."

"What?"

Slowly, feeling more than a little silly, he drew out the small object he'd brought back. Wrapped in shiny aluminum foil and tied with a rather limp bow from a scrap of fabric from his already torn shirt, it looked pathetically shabby to him. He wished he'd never done it, or at least hadn't brought it to her. Although maybe the candlelight helped, gleaming on the shiny wrapping.

"I... meant it for your birthday." He heard her quick intake of breath. "I mean, you're alone because of me. You could have been with your friends, but—"

She lifted one slender finger and pressed it to his lips, hushing him. "I can never be alone if you're with me," she whispered.

His throat tightened around a sudden lump. He couldn't speak, so he just handed her the package that suddenly didn't seem quite so pitiful.

She opened it quickly, with an eagerness that made that lump in his throat larger. She lifted out the small wooden carving with as much care as she would have used to handle fine crystal and held it up.

"It's Gus!" she exclaimed in delight, cradling the four-inch tall statue in her hands. "Oh, Race, it's really Gus! It's perfect. That's just the way he holds his head when you ask him a question, and his ears perk up just like that—"

She stopped suddenly and looked from the carving to his face, her eyes widening.

"You did this? You carved it yourself?"

He shrugged.

"That's what you were doing last night, wasn't it? No wonder you're so tired . . ."

He looked away, more pleased than he could ever have imagined at the reception given his small effort, yet unable to meet the overwhelming warmth in her eyes.

"It's beautiful, Race. It's the most wonderful gift I've ever received."

He looked at her then, a denial of that excessive praise on his lips, but when he met her steady gaze, he knew that she meant it as nothing less than the truth. She read his look and spoke softly.

"It is. Because you've given me something of Gus to keep forever. Because of the thought that made you do it. And the time and effort and talent in the work. And because—"

She didn't finish, didn't say, "because it's from you," but he read the words in her face and in the gentle touch of her hand as she reached out to take his.

With gentle care she set the carving on the bedside table, then tugged him down beside her. He went, letting her tug the quilt over him, then pulled her close into the curve of his body.

"Happy birthday, Kit. I'm sorry it . . . turned out like this."

"I'm not," she whispered, letting one hand come to rest on his chest, fingers flexing as if responding to the steady thud of his heart. "It turned out better than I ever would have hoped it could."

He wished he could find words that would comfort her, that would ease her through the pain of this first birthday without her father, but he was so tired he couldn't think anymore. So he just held her close, hoping that she would understand.

At first it was the deep, restful sleep he so badly needed, but as the day faded, the demons rose up to haunt his dreams again. His mother, lying so limp and pale, the feel of the bat in his hands, the fear as he fled the certain doom he knew awaited him if he were caught. Then it was Rick, lying helpless on a deserted road, his life draining away.

And then came the worst of all, Kit, turning from him as he'd expected, pushing him away, disgust at being touched by a killer clear on her face, scorn in her voice as she told him to go back to being what he was, a failure, a man who—

He awoke with a start to find Kit close above him, concern creasing her forehead.

"Race, wake up. It's just a dream."

He stared at her, searching her face as if he expected to find some trace of that disgust, that scorn. But this was the real Kit, the loving, generous woman, and there was nothing of either. With a little choked sound he grabbed her, pulling her against him so tightly he was afraid he would hurt her, yet he was unable to stop himself.

"God," he whispered tightly, "I thought . . . I dreamed you hated me, pushed me away. . . ."

"I would never push you away," she said softly, burying her face in the strong curve of his shoulder. "I couldn't. I love you."

He went suddenly still, those three little words hitting him with an impact that left him breathless. A grand, joyous vision of a life spent with Kit by his side unrolled before him, and he savored it for one brief ecstatic moment before reality flooded back. He couldn't have it, he knew he couldn't, and the pain of losing the sweet fantasy he'd never really had a chance at knifed through him with lethal force.

In desperation he clutched at her, driven by pain as much as need and desire. He made love to her fiercely, almost savagely, as if he could change the inevitable ending by the sheer force of his passion. Although he knew she couldn't understand, she responded to what she must have felt in him, to the need, the drive, if not the reason, and she clung to him fervently as he thrust long and deep and hard, until he sent them both soaring on a rising tide of liquid golden heat that inundated them both in an explosive burst of drenching pleasure.

He tried once, afterward, to lift his weight off her, but his drained, spent body refused to cooperate. He tried to speak, to apologize for crushing her, but she only murmured soothing words and smoothed a hand over his sweat-dampened hair. It was the last thing he remembered until, as darkness settled in, he came sharply awake again. The candle had burned out, and the room was shadowed and still except for Kit's quiet, rhythmic breathing.

He sat up slowly, turning the idea over and over in his head. Kit stirred beside him, then opened her eyes sleepily.

"Race?"

He let out a long breath as he turned his head to meet her gaze. Something in his expression made all grogginess fade from her face.

"What's wrong?"

"I think I know where Rick might have put the evidence."

Chapter 12

"Gus, hush."

Kit whispered the words urgently into the darkness, and the big dog's excited whining ceased. There was a quiet clank as Race lowered the backpack from his shoulder to the pine-needle cushioned ground. They had found the low white shape of Rick's car easily enough, and he was grateful that it was back here by the fence of the tow yard. He looked up at the chain-link barrier, considering.

"Are you going to cut it?"

He shifted his gaze to her shadowed face. She'd seen him add, along with a flashlight, a pair of wire cutters from the toolshed to the pack, so the question wasn't a surprise. What was surprising was the calmness with which she asked it. Just as her calm consideration of what to wear on this escapade, resulting in her selection of the black knit pants and sweater, black boots, and the black knitted cap that hid the burnished sheen of her hair had surprised him.

Her reactions ever since he'd told her his dismal story had been a surprise to him. He'd expected her to be repelled, but she had still welcomed him, had soothed those deeply buried hurts with generous understanding. He'd expected her to see the smallness of the wooden gift he'd given her, but she had seen only beauty. He'd expected her to hate him, but she had told him she . . .

He had to stop this, or the memory of those sweetly murmured words was going to incapacitate him, and he had a job to do.

"Doesn't this bother you in the least?" He managed to sound faintly amused.

"Sometimes," she said quietly, "the ends *do* justify the means. So are you going to cut it?"

"I'd rather not. I don't want to leave a calling card if I don't have to. Besides, I don't know if these cutters are heavy enough. This is a pretty sturdy fence."

"Over the top, then?"

He saw her move, saw her head tilt back as she looked doubtfully up at the curling strands of barbed wire atop the fence.

"It's not that bad," he said. "It's pretty mild, as barbed wire goes. I'd guess it's mainly there to keep animals out."

She turned back, the dim light catching the luster of her eyes as she looked at him. "I thought barbed wire was barbed wire."

He began to lift the tools out of the pack. "There are different sizes of barbs, different spacing. Depending on what you're trying to keep in." He glanced at her, his mouth twisting with grim humor. "Or out."

She stared at him for a moment. "You're amazing," she said at last. He lifted a brow at her. "Is there anything you don't know about?"

"Sure." Like what I'm going to do if I'm wrong about this. And how to get myself out of this corner I'm in. Most of all, how am I going to live without you, after this is all over?

That he would have to was certain. If they were successful in putting Whitney where he belonged, there would be a flood of publicity; you didn't bring down a well-known state university professor on charges of meddling in foreign wars without the world noticing. And he didn't dare get noticed. Sometime, somewhere, somebody would put two and two together and come up with a one-way ride to an Iowa prison for him.

And if they weren't successful, and Whitney and his muscle-bound cohort stayed loose, his own life wouldn't be worth one of Gus's whiskers around here. Less, he thought wryly, watching Kit scratch behind the dog's ears.

At last he lifted out the tarp he'd wrapped everything in to keep it quiet. If he folded it double, he thought, it would cushion the barbed wire enough to let him climb over. He spread it out, folded it, then sat back on his heels and looked at Kit.

"Kit, you've got to wait here."

Her chin came up instantly, and he knew they were going to have the same heated discussion they'd had on the way over. That they were in the tree-shadowed darkness of the woods behind the tow yard and forced to do it quietly did not lessen the heat.

"I am not going to just sit out here, waiting."

"I'll be fine. You said there was no guard dog, and Gus sure isn't acting like there is."

"Then we'll both be fine."

"Kit, there's no need for you to climb over this stupid fence—"

"You need someone to watch, in case somebody shows up."

"At two in the morning?"

Even in the dim light he could see her stubborn expression. With an exasperated breath, he reached out and grabbed her hands.

"Listen to me, Kit. If anything does go wrong, you've got to be safe. You're the only one who can go to the cops, the only one they'll listen to. Even if you don't have the papers, they'll look into it. At the least Whitney will have to run. It's not much, but it's something."

"So if something happens to you, you expect me to just take off running, is that it?"

"I expect you to do what you have to do. What you know is right."

For the first time he saw that he'd stopped her automatic comebacks. He pressed his advantage, knowing he had to convince her now.

"You have to, Kit. It may be the only way to make him pay for what he did."

He didn't mention Dr. Cameron, but he knew by the sudden tautness in her face that she was thinking of the day she'd come home to find her father sprawled lifelessly on the ground.

"I'll be back in ten minutes," he promised. "If I'm not, or if anything happens, you take off out of here." She started to protest, and he quieted her with a gentle squeeze of his hands over hers. "Please, Kit. I can't do what I have to if I'm worried about you."

He felt her relax slightly and moved quickly, wanting to be over the fence and gone before she could change her mind. He tossed the folded tarp over the sharp-pronged wire and scrambled up and over.

He headed at a low crouched run for the white car. He'd told her as he'd yanked on his clothes in the dark of the cabin about the stereo system he'd installed in Rick's car, and about how they'd talked about the empty space behind the inner door panels, where he'd put the speakers.

"I showed him what a great hiding-place it was. Told him that a lot of people used it for guns, drugs, whatever." He'd stopped then, his mouth twisting ruefully as he watched her. "He looked at me the same way you are. Wondering how I knew all that. I'm not sure he believed me when I said I'd read it somewhere."

She'd said nothing as she tucked her hair up under the knitted cap, but he wondered now if she had believed him either. It didn't really matter, he supposed. He was still here, sneaking into a yard full of stored and impounded cars, skulking around like a thief.

He knew within moments of reaching the car that he was too late. One quick sweep with the beam of the flashlight showed him all he needed to see and his hopes crumpled into dust. The inside of the car strongly resembled the interior of Rick's home, except this was even worse. The seats had been slashed, padding strewn about in clumps, the dash ripped apart, the carpet torn from the floor.

And, he noted grimly, the door panels were pulled loose and sagging. They couldn't have known that Rick might use the space around the stereo speakers, but it hardly mattered when they'd obviously been determined not to miss any possible hiding-place in the car. And they hadn't; if Rick had hidden the damning papers here, they were gone now. And he had little doubt as to who had found them; this had all the earmarks of one of Walt the hulk's decorating jobs.

His shoulders slumped. It was over. This had been his last chance. Oh, Kit could go to the police, but even if they believed her without proof, it would take them forever to get moving. They would spook Whitney the first time they talked to him, and the man would pack up the tidy fortune he'd made by playing God in a small war halfway around the world and take off for somewhere bright and sunny to live the good life.

Gus's trumpeting bark was his first warning. He jerked around and saw the beam of another flashlight, bouncing as the person carrying it began to run across the tow yard. Smothering a curse, he flipped off his own light and dodged to the back of Rick's car. The man kept coming.

Just when Race knew he was going to be discovered, Gus let out another string of furious barks, this time from further up the fence. The man stopped in his tracks. He turned and headed in the direction of Gus's outburst.

Atta boy, Gus, Race muttered silently, slipping out from behind the car and crossing the shadowed area of the yard, back to where the tarp lay over the top of the fence. Just keep him busy for another thirty seconds, boy....

He was up and over, grabbing the tarp as he dropped to the ground outside and headed for the trees. He felt the flashlight go, but didn't wait. Kit was there, and he was so glad to see her that he didn't ask her why the hell she was running along the fence instead of heading for the Jeep to get out of here like he'd told her.

"Are you all right?" she asked anxiously.

"Yes."

He heard her quick breath of relief. "When Gus barked, I saw the other light, and I didn't know what to do, so I took him up a few yards and told him to keep barking."

He hugged her swiftly. "You did great, sunrose. Call the big lug, and we'll get out of—"

A sudden shout and a sharp loud report were followed by an animal yelp of pain.

"Gus!"

Kit was on her feet in an instant, and Race had to grab her around the waist to stop her from heading straight toward the sound.

"Kit, stop. You can't go over there."

"Let me go!" she cried. "Gus is hurt!"

"Kit, don't." He tried to calm her, but she was beyond that.

"I have to! He's hurt, didn't you hear?"

"I heard," he said grimly, realizing that all she was thinking of was her injured friend, not that what they had heard had been a gunshot. She struggled with him, trying to pull free.

"Let me go." She struck out, catching him on the jaw. It stung, but he only tightened his grip. Damn it, she was stubborn, he thought, panic rising in him as he imagined what could happen to her in the dark with a man so careless—or so vicious—that he would shoot at a dog he could barely have seen.

"Kit, stop!" he hissed.

"I have to go, can't you see?"

"Kit, hush! He'll hear—"

"I can't leave him! I love him!"

"And I love you, damn it! You're not going over there with some guy running around with a gun he's too damned eager to fire!"

She went suddenly still, staring up at him. Only then did he realize what he'd said. Your timing, he told himself with bitter mockery, has always been impeccable, Barkley.

"Stay here," he ordered quickly, before she could speak. "I'll get him."

"But—"

"Sunrose, you couldn't carry him anyway. Stay here," he repeated, then took off at a low run through the trees.

He figured he had a few more seconds while the guy who had apparently been guarding the yard decided whether he was going to go outside the fence, and before he got there. When he got close to where he thought the sound had come from, he called in a low voice that was barely audible, but that he knew Gus would be able to hear. If, he thought grimly, the dog was able to hear anything at all.

For a moment he was afraid his last thought was right, and he dreaded the thought of going back to tell Kit that the last, dearest thing in her life had died to save him. Then he heard it, a low whimpering. He scrambled through the carpet of dead pine needles, wincing when he put his knee down on a fallen sharp-pointed cone, but too grateful to find the big animal alive to really notice the pain.

He heard the clank of metal on metal and knew the guard had decided to come out and see what he'd hit. Knowing he had little time, Race whispered reassurance to Gus, who was panting heavily as he lay on his side, then hoisted the dog up and over his head to rest on his shoulders. It was an awkward effort; he would bet the dog weighed at least a hundred pounds, and he was trying hard not to hurt him, but that was difficult when he didn't know where he was injured. But Gus was a trouper and never let out a sound above that soft whimper as Race went at the fastest pace he could manage through the thick belt of trees.

He met Kit a few yards from the Jeep. Headed his way, he noted sourly, worry for Gus written on her face.

"You don't listen very well, do you?" he grated out, shifting Gus's weight. "Why didn't you stay by the Jeep?"

"Why did you go back for him?" she countered quietly.

He looked at her blankly for a moment. He tried to shrug, but it was impossible with Gus draped over his shoulders. "Because you love him," he finally said, knowing what he was admitting and not caring.

He heard her make an odd little noise that sounded almost like a sob. Yet her voice was steady enough as she asked, "Is he badly hurt?"

"I can't tell. And we can't look now, we've got to get moving. That guy's on his way out here."

He laid the animal gently in the back of the Jeep and then, for the first time, climbed into the front seat.

"You'll have to drive," he told her. "You know this area a lot better than I do."

She nodded, the trembling of her hand as she turned the key her only outward sign of emotion. In silence she maneuvered the Jeep through the trees and out onto the main road. Only then did she speak, and then only to say rather inanely that she'd used the Jeep for the off-road travel it had been designed for more in the last two days than she ever had before.

Race recognized the effort to distract herself and put a gentle hand on her arm. "I think he'll be all right, Kit. He had the strength to make a sound so I could find him, and he's still conscious. Is there a vet around here?"

She nodded. "Dr. Myers, down on the south shore. He treated Gus last year when he got stung by a wasp."

"Can you reach him at this hour?"

A nod again. "His clinic is next to his house."

"Let's go, then."

After a few minutes she spoke again.

"The papers?"

"Gone," he said flatly. "If they were ever there. Somebody beat me to the car."

After a moment she nodded. "That would explain the guard, if somebody had already broken in. There's never been one there before that I know of."

"Figures."

He knew he sounded bitter, beaten, but he couldn't seem to help it. Kit looked at him, brows furrowing in concern, then turned her eyes back to the road. She drove intently, her attention shifting only once, when a car pulled up far too close behind them. She tapped the brakes, and the car dropped back. She studied the rearview mirror for a moment, then shook her head.

"Crazy people out at this hour."

Race didn't answer. Able to turn around, he'd gotten a better look at the car before it had dropped back and been swallowed up by the darkness. Enough to think that maybe he'd seen it before. But he couldn't be sure, and he didn't say anything about his guess to Kit. He told himself it was because he wasn't sure, not because he was afraid to see what her reaction might be. He kept an eye on the distant headlights.

Gus whimpered, and Kit upped the speed of the Jeep, her hands curling tensely around the steering wheel. She slowed only when they reached the clinic, to negotiate the driveway with the least jostling possible for the wounded dog. Race watched the road behind them while she was intent on the maneuver; his jaw tightened when he saw the car that had been behind them slow, then keep going.

"What . . . will we tell him?" Kit asked as she eased the Jeep to a stop. "Dr. Myers, I mean."

"I don't know. Maybe that somebody mistook him for a deer or something."

That, as it turned out, was exactly what she told the sleepy-eyed doctor. Race carried the dog inside, then retreated to the door of the examination room as the man, his white coat looking a little absurd over baggy pajamas, looked the dog over. Kit, of course, stayed close to Gus, stroking his big head and crooning over him as he patiently endured the veterinarian's probing.

"Hmph," the man snorted at last. "Trigger-happy hunters. Shoot before they even know what they're shooting at even when the season's over." Then he reached out and patted Kit's hand. "But he'll be all right. Went right through the fleshy part of his right hind leg, and he's bled some, but leave him here for a few days and he'll be right as rain."

As they walked out of the clinic into the night, Kit quietly asked if he would drive. He took the keys she handed him, and she didn't say another word as they walked to the

Jeep. Yet somehow Race knew what she was thinking, knew that she was hearing yet again his admission that he loved her.

He hadn't meant to tell her that way. In fact, he hadn't meant to tell her at all, knowing it would only complicate an already impossible situation. But he had, and now his insides were knotting up as he wondered what she was thinking.

He'd only driven a mile or so when, as he glanced at her out of the corner of one eye, he realized she was trembling. He quickly pulled the Jeep to the side of the road and turned to her.

"Kit? He'll be all right. The vet said so."

She looked at him, eyes wide and troubled. "It's not... I... I can't... You..." Her voice sounded impossibly tiny as it trailed off. She bit her lip, shaking her head in frustration, then tried again. "I'm sorry. I'm not making any sense. I'm tired and cold and worried, and I..."

Her voice faded away again, and she lifted her hands helplessly.

"Poor sunrose," he whispered, reaching out to cover her hands. "We'll get you some rest... and don't worry about Gus. He's tough. He'll pull through."

She looked at him for a long moment, searching his face, before she said quietly, "It isn't Gus I'm worried about."

Race stiffened, fighting the emotion that flooded him. It had been so long, so damned long, since anyone had worried about him that he didn't know how to deal with it. Rick had been curious, and probably a little hurt that he knew so little, but Race doubted he'd ever been worried. That Kit was, even after she knew the whole grim story, awed him.

"Do you think," she asked, glancing up the road to where a small twenty-four-hour coffee shop sat, a small oasis of activity in a quiet nighttime world, "that we could get some coffee? Or just something warm. I need..." Again her voice faded away. "I'm sorry," she whispered. "I forgot, you can't... go in there, can you?"

"I think I can stand the light of public scrutiny for a while," he growled.

"I didn't mean—"

"I know you didn't."

"But maybe—"

"It'll be all right, Kit. It's only a cup of coffee."

He wasn't sure if he really thought it would be safe, or if he just didn't care anymore. He'd had to accept a lot of limitations on his life since the night he'd fled that gruesome scene. And he had accepted them; the alternative to going up against a system carefully stacked against him by the very man he'd been trying to stop had been far too daunting for a scared fifteen-year-old.

A few minutes later he sat staring at the cup of coffee before him on the table. On the edge of his vision he saw Kit's delicate hands curved around her own cup, savoring the heat. It felt strange to be sitting here with her so conventionally, like the other people in the small café. It seemed forever since he'd done anything so routine, so normal. Not, he thought wryly, that he would ever have considered sitting here with the likes of Kit Cameron normal for him.

The customers began to drift away, off to their homes after a night out, he supposed, with nothing more complicated facing them than going to work in the morning. Soon they were alone at the small corner table, only an occasional new face coming through the doors, letting in a draft of chill air that swirled around their ankles.

"Race?"

He looked up. He'd been wondering when she would speak and what she would say; she'd been quiet for a long time. He braced himself, even though he wasn't sure for what.

"Do you ever think about . . . going back? Getting it all straightened out?"

He stiffened. He hadn't expected this. "Straightened out?" he asked tightly. "You mean spend the next twenty years or so in jail?"

She winced but didn't waver. "But if you told them what really happened . . ."

He dug a groove into the white foam of the cup with his thumbnail. "I told you who he was. There's not a chance in hell they'd take the word of the guy they already think beat up on his own mother."

"But you've never been in trouble since, and it's been so long, maybe they . . . I mean, don't they think about things like extenuating circumstances?"

He let out a long sigh. She was trying so hard, trying to make everything all right, to convince herself everything would work out if he just went back and told the truth. He knew the feeling; he'd caught himself trying to believe it himself more than once over the last ten years. But then the ugly memory of being dragged into the police station and accused of being responsible for the bruises that marked his mother's face, of his stepfather nobly saying they just wanted to take him home and get him "straightened out," would leap viciously to life in his mind, and he knew better. The whole town had talked of nothing else for weeks but how kind, how generous, how understanding, Henry Lytton was, to refuse to press charges against the obviously wild boy who wasn't even his own son. And when Race's mother had tried to tell the truth, it had earned her another beating, once more blamed on her son. From then on he had endured abhorrence from the adults, wariness from his peers, and he'd begun to discover how truly alone it was possible to be.

At least, he thought he had. The thought of how alone he would be without Kit made him shudder with a dread he'd never felt in all the long years of running and hiding.

"You know," he said, barely aware of saying it aloud, "I always thought I couldn't stand jail . . . that's why I ran . . . but I don't know anymore."

"You don't?"

He looked at her, and something in her face, some combination of pain and concern, drew the words from him, slowly, torturously.

"I guess you don't have to be in a jail to be in prison. If I have to go on without...after this, maybe I might as well be in jail."

He hadn't finished that "without you," but he knew from the look that flickered lightning-fast through her eyes that she'd heard it as clearly as if he had. He half expected her to call him on it, to demand a repetition of his declaration of love, but again she surprised him.

"What do we do now?"

"You go home and get some rest."

"You know what I mean."

"Yes." He let out a compressed breath. "And I don't know."

"If they did find those papers..."

"They'll know I can't prove a thing now."

She bit her lip. "But they'll still know you know."

"Yeah."

"And if they didn't find them, nothing's changed. They'll still be after you either way. Because they don't know you can't go to the police."

He didn't try to deny it; he knew she knew better. She just looked at him, realization dawning in her eyes.

"You're going to run again, aren't you? You have to. Even if you had the proof, you couldn't stay around and risk the police finding out who you are during the investigation."

"Kit—"

"That's the real reason you wanted me to go to the police, isn't it? It wasn't because they wouldn't believe you, but because they might check you out first."

"Kit, please—"

"You knew all along that you'd have to leave, no matter what happened. Didn't you?"

He crushed the now empty cup in his fist.

"Didn't you?" she repeated.

"Yes."

He couldn't look at her, couldn't face what he knew he would see.

"Well," she said after a moment, her voice oddly even, "when you said you couldn't even promise tomorrow, you weren't kidding, were you?"

They were the last words she spoke. He wished she would get angry or cry or do something, anything, except keep that tightly controlled silence. She remained silent as they finished their coffee, went back to the Jeep and drove to the cabin.

He should leave now, he thought, while she was upset enough with him that she would let him go without a qualm. She would get over it in time, he told himself. Maybe Len would console her, he told himself brutally, and she would soon forget him. That he would never forget her, that he would spend the rest of his life loving her, even knowing that she would rightfully hate him, was already a cold, hard lump of knowledge somewhere deep inside him.

When he pulled the Jeep to a halt at the head of the gravel drive, he turned to look at her at last. The moon had cleared the ridge, sending down a silvery light that seemed to rob the color from everything. Except her hair. Even the moon couldn't seem to rob it of its copper fire. It was bright and vivid and warm, and warned him grimly of the coldness to come.

She lifted one hand slowly, to touch his shoulder. He didn't understand the look in her eyes until she drew her fingers away and looked at them. He saw the brownish stain and realized that some of the blood from Gus's wound had stained his shirt.

Her father's shirt, he corrected himself. He glanced down at the blotch, then back at her.

"I'm sorry about the shirt," he began. "I—"

"You saved Gus for me."

He shrugged. "He saved me. If he hadn't started barking when he did . . ."

"You didn't have to go back for him."

"I've . . . gotten kind of used to him."

She just looked at him for a long moment, her eyes boring into him until he thought she must be looking at his very soul. And then it came at last, the question he'd been waiting for.

"Did you mean it?"

He had too much respect for her to pretend not to understand. He answered levelly, knowing he was making things worse, yet unable to give her anything less than the truth.

"Yes."

"You love me."

"Yes."

"And I love you."

He shivered, the words sending a feeling he couldn't even name rippling through him. She took it as answer enough.

"But you're leaving."

"I don't have a choice."

"I know. But I do. If you'd ask."

"Ask . . . ?"

"Ask me to go with you."

He stared at her, his eyes widening in shock. "Go . . . ? You? But your life is here, your friends. . . . I'm not . . . I couldn't ask you to leave all that."

"You're not worth it? Is that what you were going to say? Well, I think that's my decision. And if you can't see your own worth, then you need someone around who does. Someone who can see past the position fate has forced you into."

"Kit," he said desperately, trying to smother the burgeoning hope that had soared in him at the suggestion he had never even dared to voice, "you don't mean it. Think about it, the way I live . . . it's no kind of life for you. You deserve so much more—"

"You know," she interrupted conversationally, "I am getting sick and tired of being told what I do and don't want, what I deserve, and what I mean or don't mean. If that college degree you're so zeroed in on means one thing to me, it's that I'm quite capable of doing my own thinking. And making my own decisions."

"Kit—"

"But I guess that's all academic, isn't it? You didn't ask, so I don't have a decision to make, do I?"

She turned on her heel and strode across the porch. Race gaped after her. He'd never dreamed she would even consider leaving this place she loved. She'd had more than a taste of the kind of life he led during the last two weeks; she had to know it was an impossible life for her.

That she'd thought about it, that she'd apparently just been waiting for him to ask, stunned him. Was there a chance? Was it possible that he could escape that long grim life without her that he'd foreseen unrolling before him in all its dark soulless eternity?

As she reached the front door and opened it, he leapt up onto the porch and hurried toward her. As she flipped on the inside light he lifted a hand to reach for her, wanting urgently to see her face, to read the truth in those gold-flecked eyes, when he asked her if she'd meant it, if she would really—

Her short, sharp cry stopped him dead for an instant. Then the fear that had been laced through the shock in her voice galvanized him, and he crossed the last three feet in one quick stride.

"Kit?"

She looked at him then, eyes wide and dark, stark in her suddenly pale face. He looked past her into the cabin and knew that any choice he'd ever had, any chance at a brighter future, was gone now. They'd been here, had invaded her sanctuary, her home, and had left nothing but destruction behind them.

Chapter 13

Kit was ready to explode. It was evident in every quick, sharp movement she made, in the taut line of her clenched jaw, in the angry fire that lit her amber eyes. Race knew it, even before she at last whirled on him.

"Are you going to say something or just walk around looking furious?"

It took a moment for him to respond. The last thing he remembered really feeling was a fierce tug of emotion when the first thing she'd done was to run and see if the wood carving of her beloved Gus was uninjured. She'd found it tossed on the floor but undamaged, and it had been tightly clutched in her hands ever since.

"There's nothing to say. It's over."

"Over?"

She was staring at him as if he'd gone crazy. I haven't, he answered her look silently. I've only now regained my sanity. Crazy was me thinking I could do a damned thing about any of this without paying the price. The price I should have paid a long time ago.

"Come on," he said finally, abruptly. "Grab some clothes and whatever else you'll need for a few days."

Her stare widened. "What?"

"You can't stay here."

"This is my house, and those jerks are not going to drive me out of it—"

"Kit, they know."

"Know what?"

"That you know. And that you and I . . . connected."

"But how—"

"Your father's notes. And the clippings he had."

She paled, glancing over at the desk where she'd locked the file; the drawer was open, with splinters of oak around the lock.

"And," he added dully, feeling more of a fool than ever before in his life, "I put the lab results from Davis in there."

"And they knew that Rick sent you . . . ?"

He nodded. Kit bit her lip, and he could see her searching desperately for a way out. "But if they have Rick's papers from the car, they must know that we have no evidence, so there's no reason to come after us!"

"Me, no. Alone, I'm no threat to him. But with you as your father's proxy . . ."

Her lips parted for a quick, strained breath. Her eyes were wide, dark and troubled. "What are we going to do?"

He sighed, but the decision was already made. It had been made for him the moment Whitney had connected Kit to him, the moment he had moved his evil hunt into her home, into her life.

"We're going to do what you wanted to do all along."

"What I . . . ?"

"Go to the police."

She had, at last, quieted down. He didn't know if it was in frustration at his lack of response, or in final realization that this was, indeed, the only thing left to do. He couldn't run, not and leave her alone to face Whitney's deadly threat. It was his fault she'd been connected with him; he wasn't about to desert her now. And he wouldn't ask her to run with him; she deserved so much more than a life like his had been, a life on the run.

A life, he admitted at last, that he was heartily tired of. A life that now, without her, would truly be as much of a prison as the cage they would put him in. *Stone walls do not a prison make, Nor iron bars a cage,* he thought, the quote swimming up out of the numbness that seemed to have enveloped his mind. If his heart was in a cage, what did it matter where his body was?

He wasn't surprised to find he didn't really care about going to jail anymore. Paying the price for what he'd done so long ago seemed insignificant compared to Kit being in danger. He had to hope that there was enough evidence to at least make the police listen. The break-in at Kit's and the trashing of Rick's car at the tow yard should make them curious. It was all circumstantial, but coupled with the Cameron name, it had to make them look. It better, he thought grimly. It was all they had.

"Race?"

He glanced at her, then away. He drove the Jeep carefully, with more concentration than it needed. He braced himself for another round of protests; odd how now that he was going to do what she'd wanted in the first place, she didn't want him to do it. But when she spoke, it was to ask something so simple it took him aback.

"Where are we going?"

"I want to stop by my place for a minute." He heard her quick intake of breath. "It should be okay, especially at this hour. I don't think they'd expect me to walk right back into the hornet's nest. My place is on the outer perimeter, and there's a back way up. I'll go on foot. You can stay in the Jeep, and if anything happens—"

"I can run?" Sarcasm laced her words.

"Kit—"

"Why on earth do you want to go back there?"

"There are . . . a couple of things I want to pick up."

"Now? Can't it wait until after the police catch Whitney and it's safe?"

He didn't answer. His hands tightened on the wheel until his knuckles whitened. The silence stretched out until it was broken by a tiny, choking sound.

"God," she gasped out, "you think you'll be in jail by then, don't you? That they'll lock you up before you have a chance to get anything."

That was exactly what he thought, but he didn't want to discuss it with her now. "There are only a couple of things I want," he repeated tightly. "It won't take long."

She didn't speak again, and it wasn't until he'd parked the Jeep in the shadows of the trees behind the center that he realized she had clamped her hands between her knees, as if to keep them from shaking.

"Kit," he said softly, reaching out to turn her chin with a careful finger. She was pale, her eyes shadowed, and she was biting her full lower lip viciously, perhaps needing the pain to distract her. With his thumb he gently tugged her lip free, then leaned over to kiss the indentations of her teeth in the soft flesh. He felt her shiver and drew back.

"Give me ten minutes, then beat it," he said, then slipped out of the Jeep.

He was almost to his own back door when a sound behind him made him whirl, then go down into a defensive crouch.

"Damn it, Kit, I told you to wait!"

"You already know I don't listen well. Besides, I can watch for you."

"Get back to the Jeep," he said, his voice taut with the strain of keeping it low.

"No," she said simply. "Are we going in or what?"

Smothering an oath at that stubborn tone he recognized all too well. Race crept up to the door, key in hand, only to find it already unlocked. Inside, he tripped over something in the dark and swore again, this time at having lost the flashlight in the scramble at the tow yard.

"The hulk really left a mess," he muttered, stepping over the chair that had been overturned.

"Do we dare turn on a light?" Kit asked into the darkness.

"We'll have to," Race said, wincing as he mashed a toe into something solid and unmoving. "I know this place, and *I* can't find anything."

It took him a few minutes to find the small lamp that had been on top of the battered table he'd used as a desk. He set it on the floor, then tugged at a large cushion from his worn sofa, now ripped open, and leaned it against the lamp to block the light from the only window in the room. Then, holding his breath, he turned it on.

The sudden flare of light seemed blinding, but a quick glance toward the window showed him that not much would escape that way. They had, for some unknown reason, left the curtains intact and closed.

A small sound from Kit made him look over at her; she was staring in dismay at the wreckage of the room. Nothing was right side up, and every inch of the floor seemed covered with books.

"I warned you, it wasn't much to begin with," he said stiffly.

"No," she said quickly. "It's not...it's just...you weren't kidding about reading a lot, were you?"

The light note in her voice was forced, but Race appreciated the effort just the same. Seeing the place that, such as it was, had been the closest thing he'd had to a home in this condition would have made him furious if he'd been in any kind of shape to feel anything. But he'd put his emotions on hold the moment he'd realized what he had to do, and he didn't dare let them loose now.

"Race?" He turned to look at Kit. She was standing next to the phone. "There's a message here."

He glanced at the answering machine, seeing the small green light blinking. He didn't want to know, didn't want to hear it, whatever it was, but knew he had no choice.

"Play it," he ground out.

Kit reached out and pressed the button next to the light. The machine whirred, beeped, and then a deep masculine voice issued from the small speaker.

"Hello, Mr. Booker. This is William Parkson. I...my brother...well, he was very fond of you. He spoke and wrote about you often. He had planned to... Well, I'd rather tell you in person. I'd like to meet with you while I'm here, if you wouldn't mind. Please call me. I'm at the Lakeside Inn."

"He *did* call," Kit said softly.

Race tried to suppress the sound that rose in his throat, afraid it would come out as a whimper. But Kit, as usual, sensed his pain; he could hear it in her voice.

"Oh, Race, I'm so sorry."

"Don't," he said tightly, knowing the resolute hold he had on his feelings couldn't take much more. "Please."

She didn't say any more but began to tidy what she could of the mess.

He took a deep breath and after a moment turned back to the bookcase before him. He searched through the books until he found the one he wanted; it had been a gift from Rick. Vaguely aware of Kit still trying to straighten some of the rubble, he walked to a far wall and stood there for a moment.

"Damn."

"What?" Kit came up behind him.

"I wanted that picture," he said, staring at the blank space on the wall. "But we don't dare take time..."

"You mean this one?" she said softly, gingerly holding out something that clinked with the sound of broken glass. It was his copy of the photo on Rick's wall, of the two of them and the string of lake trout. Leave it to Kit to guess the one other thing he'd want from this place, he thought. He reached out to take it, then froze.

"I'm sorry they broke the glass," Kit said, "but the picture's only torn a little on one corner. It can be—what's wrong?" she finished, as if she'd realized his stillness was due to more than the damage to the photograph.

"I...that wasn't there before."

She stared at the frame, then looked up at his face.

"What wasn't?"

"That." He gestured toward the writing on one corner of the framed picture. She tilted her head to look.

"'Here's to the biggest fish of all,'" she read softly. "'This is the proof we can catch him.'" She lifted her gaze to his face. "Rick's writing?" she asked in a tone that told him she already knew the answer.

He nodded a little numbly. He knew the inscription hadn't been there before. So why, after the picture had hung on his wall for nearly a year, had Rick done it now? And apparently while Race had been gone?

Kit had been carefully picking broken shards of glass out of the frame when her fingers stopped in mid-motion.

"Race?" He looked at her, his mind still searching for an answer to the puzzle. "Remember what you said about Rick documenting all his experiments? Even the unimportant ones?"

His brow furrowed. "Yeah. Why?"

She bit her lip again, then said tentatively, "Then wouldn't he...maybe...document something *very* important...even if it wasn't exactly an experiment?"

His brows lifted sharply, and he sucked in a breath. "Damn. Of course he would." And then, as a memory flitted through his mind, he swore again. "The camera," he breathed.

"The one at Rick's house, right? That's what I thought."

He nodded. "It had a macro lens on it. Like the ones they use here."

"For what?"

"Close-ups," he said, confirming the guess he'd seen in her eyes. "But if he photographed those documents, he must have hidden the negatives somewhere...." He stared at the picture she held, reading again the newly written words. "'This is the proof,'" he murmured.

Their eyes met over the shattered glass, and without a word Kit turned the frame over. The tiny staples that held the cardboard backing in place were bent. Race couldn't remember if they'd always been that way, but there was a gouge in the backing that he definitely didn't remember, and he felt his pulse begin to hammer.

He saw Kit's fingers slide over the backing, then her eyes shot up to his face.

"There's something here," she said hoarsely.

Race jammed his hand into his pocket for his knife. Before he could reach it, a noise behind them made him spin around, leaving the frame in Kit's suddenly trembling hands.

"Well, well, now, isn't this convenient? Both of my problems come home to roost."

Martin Whitney stepped into the room, a small but deadly automatic held carefully in his right hand. Race froze, seized with a sudden terror that somehow it was going to happen again, that the one person left in the world that he loved was going to die because he wasn't able to stop it.

"Don't feel bad," Whitney said conversationally. "It was only logical that you'd show up back here eventually. I was certain there was nothing at Parkson's house, so it had to be here. When I learned you were headed for the veterinarian's office—"

"Gus!" Kit gasped, fear for her dog flooding her face.

"Oh, don't worry," Whitney said smoothly. "That beast of yours is fine. I'm actually quite grateful to him. I had my suspicions that you knew more than you let on, Miss Cameron, but I wasn't certain until I heard that the guard they stationed at the police impound yard after our little visit shot what he was certain was a wolf late last night."

Kit called him a name Race wouldn't have thought she even knew. Whitney looked startled, and Race felt pride swell up inside him; his little sunrose was tough all right. He took advantage of Whitney's surprise to sneak a half step forward.

"Temper, temper, Miss Cameron," Whitney cautioned. "It's unfortunate for you that that rather . . . pedestrian vehicle of yours is so recognizable."

"Leave her out of this," Race cut in harshly. "She doesn't know anything."

"Oh, I doubt that. Miss Cameron is too much her father's daughter."

Anger flared in Kit's face, and Race knew she was remembering that this was the man responsible for her father's death. He also saw by the fire that flashed in her eyes that she was about to call him on it.

"You've got all the evidence back," he said hastily, to cut her off before she accused Whitney outright of murder. "You know there's not a damned thing we can do."

"Oh, I have it, all right. It's already been destroyed. But you could make things quite uncomfortable for me. I'm about to . . . shall we say, close another deal, and I certainly can't have the sheriff poking around."

"What is it this time, Whitney?" Race used a sarcastic gesture to mask another small advance. "A little root rot for the corn crop in Bhutan? Or the wheat crop in Pakistan?"

"Shut up," Whitney snapped. "I'm sick of having to deal with you. You're nothing but a garbage man who thinks he's smart enough to comprehend the complexities of true science. Why Parkson wasted so much time on you I'll never know. My God, you never even made it through high school! I only allowed him to hire you because I knew you were too dumb to get in my way."

Race absorbed the insults silently, the tightening of his jaw the only outward sign of the inward pain he felt at Whitney's slashing attack. He couldn't look at Kit. She was finally being forced to see the reality of what he was, the truth of his wasted life, and he didn't want to see the disappointment in her face.

"But he did get in your way, didn't he?" Her quiet words rang with pride and soothed the wounds Whitney had inflicted in a way he'd never thought possible. He wanted to savor it, but he forced himself to use her distraction to inch forward again as she went on. "He figured it all out, and he made a fool out of you."

"Shut up!"

"But you'd already doomed yourself, Whitney, because you were too blind to see true intellect when it was right in front of you."

"So," Whitney sneered, "he's deluded you, as well. Pity, I thought you were smarter than that."

"Let her go," Race snapped. "She can't hurt you."

"On the contrary, Booker. It's you who can't hurt me. No one would take the word of a mere janitor against mine. But the daughter of Dr. Christopher Cameron is something else again."

"You didn't have to kill him."

Kit's taut words were out before Race could stop her. Whitney's brows rose, and Race could see him assimilate the fact that she knew what had happened to her father. He groaned inwardly; Whitney had no choice now.

"I would have had to have it done sometime." Whitney gestured with the weapon. "Walt simply took advantage of a convenient situation—"

"Like you did with Rick?" Race cut in sharply, one eye on Kit's pale face.

"That was a necessity," Whitney said blandly.

"A necessity?" Race hissed. "Damn you."

Whitney abandoned his pretense of nonchalance. "Get back," he snarled, leveling the gun at them. And suddenly, beneath the urbane exterior, flashed a cool hardness, and any remaining doubts that Whitney himself was capable of killing vanished.

"Why?" Kit whispered, shaking her head in pain. "Did you need money that badly? Enough to kill for it?"

"Money?" Whitney laughed harshly. "That had nothing to do with it. I was sick and tired of playing second fiddle to Parkson, that arrogant bastard. Sick of hearing what a genius he was, just like Cameron. Lording it over me just because I've been too busy running the center to do any research lately."

His lips twisted harshly as he glared at Race. "He gave you more respect than he did me. You! You're nothing! A nobody! You never even—"

"Doc? You in here?"

Kit gasped at the sound of the voice. Race saw hope flare in her eyes. Before he could warn her, she cried out.

"Len! Be careful, Whitney has a gun!"

The tall blonde sauntered into the room, an expression that could only be described as a smirk on his tanned face.

"Of course he does. I got it for him."

Stunned, Kit swiveled her gaze to Race. Then she closed her eyes, a tiny moan escaping her, and he knew his knowledge must have been clear on his face.

"Something wrong, sweetie?" Len said bitingly.

"You'll have to forgive her," Race snapped. "She thought you were a friend."

The anger in his tone disguised the sickness that had risen inside him at her reaction to the golden boy's betrayal. Did she care more than she'd said?

"Friend?" Len reached out to touch Kit's cheek; it was all Race could do to keep from lunging at him. "To the lofty Ms. Cameron? Oh, there was a time when I would have enjoyed that. And much more."

His lips lifted into the smirk he'd worn when he'd come in, only now it had a distinctly cruel edge as he spoke to Kit.

"But that was before I discovered what a bitch you were. It was bad enough having my folks on my back all the time, but I'll be damned if I was going to let you sit in judgment on me for how I spend my life."

"I . . . never meant to do that," Kit whispered. She sounded so shaken that Race couldn't stop himself from reaching for her hand to squeeze it reassuringly.

"So," Len stepped back, looking at them, "that's the story. I should have known there was an explanation."

"Of what?" Race grated out. "Why she didn't fall for your irresistible charm?"

"Oh, he has teeth, does he?" Len looked at Race as if he'd found him under an overturned rock. "You're right, Doc. Above himself, isn't he?"

"Shut up!" Kit cried out. "How dare you, you slime! He's worth a hundred of you!"

"Kit," Race said warningly, wary of Len's sudden tension even as her words warmed him, soothing his momentary doubts.

"It was you behind us tonight, wasn't it?" Kit asked suddenly, and Race could almost see her agile mind beginning to work again. "And then you went back to my house and broke in, didn't you?"

"Had to get those papers, darlin'. Figured I'd have time while you were at the vet's with that mangy mutt of yours," Len drawled. "When you didn't come back there, I headed here."

"And you weren't just leaving a note the other day, were you?" Kit's anger was rising as she spat out the accusation. "That's why Gus wouldn't settle down. He knew you'd been inside. And all this tagging after me was just to keep an eye on me, wasn't it?"

"You don't think I hung around because of *your* irresistible charm, do you?"

Kit ignored the jibe. The way she quickly brushed off the insult reinforced Race's confidence in her, you couldn't insult someone who didn't care what you thought.

"That day I saw you down on the lake road, you were leaving here, weren't you? I wondered what you were doing around here." She shook her head. "How, Len? How did you get involved in this?"

Len seemed suddenly aware that he'd admitted a great deal and backed up a step.

"I'd say," Race said slowly, "that he was part of the connection."

"Shut up," Len snapped as Kit looked at Race questioningly.

"Remember the student I told you about?" he said to her quietly. "The one who was related to the embassy delegate from San Rafael? I looked at that news clipping again, after we talked that day. He was from UC Berkeley. Just like the golden boy here."

His gaze switched to Len. "A friend of yours, Len? Hanging out with the elite, hoping some of it would rub off? Berkeley was the connection, wasn't it?"

Len's face told them that Race's guess had hit home. It would have been easy enough for Whitney to peg the indolent student as a brother under the skin, Race thought. A local boy with access to a relative of San Rafael's diplomatic staff and a penchant for money-for-nothing made a plum ripe for picking. The new car, cash flowing like a mountain stream despite Len's lack of a job...it wasn't hard to figure out.

"Why, Len?" Kit whispered, her voice breaking. "My God, my father... my father was *murdered* over this!"

"What? You're crazy, he fell."

"He was pushed," Race said flatly.

Len's eyes widened, and his blond head jerked toward Whitney, who had been watching their exchange with mild amusement.

"He fell," Len insisted, waiting for Whitney to confirm his words.

"Don't be a fool, Porter. He would have put it together sooner or later, just like Parkson did."

"So you killed them both."

At Race's flat words Len's gaze jerked back. His face was twisted in disbelief. "No," he said shakily. "That's not possible." Len turned back to Whitney. "You said there'd be no danger."

"And there is none, to you. Which is all you really care about, isn't it? Now let's stop this foolishness and get moving. We have things to do."

"He means," Race said softly, keeping an eye on Len's stunned face, "that now you have to kill us, too."

"No!" Len paled.

"Think about it. He never would have admitted to anything if he hadn't known we wouldn't be around to tell anyone. And now you're in it up to your neck, Len. You can't say you didn't know what he was doing—"

"Quiet!"

Race had been so intent on Len that he hadn't seen the swift movement that coincided with Whitney's shout. The barrel of the gun gouged his flesh as Whitney backhanded him across the face with it, and pain flashed hot and white behind his eyes. Stunned, he couldn't dodge the second blow, or the third. Reeling, he staggered back against the desk. He couldn't see, but he sensed Whitney closing in for another strike. He tried to regain his balance, but his ears were ringing so loudly it seemed impossible.

"No!"

He heard Kit's cry over the dizzying hum and tried to stop her, but he couldn't seem to focus. He sensed rather than saw her move, throwing herself at Whitney, heedless of the gun, and panic seized him. He staggered to his feet, arms flailing, cursing his spinning head.

When his vision cleared it was to see Len holding Kit back and a furious Whitney bending to pick up the glasses that, judging from the marks on his cheeks, Kit had clawed from his face. Another bloody, vicious slash marked the man's neck, and Race wondered what on earth had caused it.

"You can't do this," Kit was saying, twisting in Len's arms to look at him. "Whatever else you've done, you're not a killer, Len! Olive and Jack could never raise a murderer!"

Something like pain flashed across Len's face. He was wavering. And just as Race had, Whitney saw it.

"Enough!" The man took a step forward and raised a hand as if to deliver the same kind of blow to Kit's delicate face that he had inflicted on Race.

Race didn't know that the strangled roar of rage he heard had come from him; he only knew that if that blow landed, Whitney had breathed his last. He launched himself forward, barreling into the startled man.

The explosion that echoed in the room as Whitney went down under a hundred and ninety pounds of muscle and sinew sent a quiver of terror down Race's spine. He tried to look but caught only a glimpse of Kit and Len falling in a tangle to the floor before Whitney caught the side of his head with a wildly flung elbow.

His terror verged on panic; what if that wild shot had hit her? If this man, who had already taken so much from both Kit and himself, was responsible for her being hurt, or even . . . His terror turned to fury.

He levered himself up. Whitney squirmed, trying to free himself, trying to lever himself into a position where he could use the gun he still clutched. Pinning the hand that held the weapon against the floor, Race stopped him with a blow that sent his glasses flying again. The image of a wounded Kit glowing horribly in his mind, he hit him again and again, until Whitney let out a howl of pain.

"S-stop!"

"You bastard!" Race spat. "You didn't give her father a chance! You didn't give Rick a chance!"

He raised his hand again. Whitney whimpered, cringing, blubbering pleas spilling from his bloodied lips. Race began the downward stroke of another fierce blow. Then, as a wave of nausea rose inside him, he jerked his hand sideways so that it bounced harmlessly off the downed man's shoulder. He ripped the gun out of Whitney's trembling fingers, then released the pinned hand. He threw the gun away from him in repulsion. It clattered off into a distant corner.

Race shoved himself off the broken man, shuddering. He'd been about to do it again. He'd come within a whisker of continuing to thrash a beaten man after the danger was over. God, maybe there really was something wrong with him, maybe Kit just didn't see it, maybe—

Kit.

He whirled, his dread easing slightly when he saw her move. Len was oddly still, and she was pushing him off of her. Race scrambled across the floor to her side.

"Are you all right?" He couldn't help the tremor in his voice any more than he could help the shaking in his hands as he reached for her.

Kit nodded slowly as she sat up, free now of Len's limp body. "I . . . I think the shot hit Len. . . ."

Race looked quickly and found the spreading stain on the blond man's left shoulder.

"He'll be all right," he said gruffly. "It's not in a real bad spot."

"I . . . I'm glad." Race stiffened. "He . . . pushed me out of the way. If he hadn't . . ."

Race relaxed. He owed the golden boy one, he supposed. Although he wasn't going to be in any position to pay him back, he thought grimly. Whitney groaned, and Race glanced over his shoulder to see the man clutching at his bloody neck. He looked back at Kit.

"He's lucky whatever did that didn't hit the jugular."

"That's what I was trying to do." Kit's voice was shaky but unapologetic, and Race stared at her.

"You . . . did that?"

"He was hitting you with that damned gun. I thought he was going to kill you. What did you expect me to do?" She shivered. "I wish I'd killed him."

He couldn't deal with the emotion those words roused in him, so he asked simply, "With what?"

She looked around for a moment, then, with a hand that trembled slightly, reached behind her for the picture frame that Race realized she'd hung on to. She picked out a large shard of glass, smoothly finished on the squared edge, razor sharp along the curving break.

"One of these," she said, sparing Whitney a savage glare. "I wish I hadn't missed."

"Kit—"

"I won't deny it. He murdered my father. I wanted to kill him. So I guess that makes me as bad as he is."

"Kit, no." He pulled her into his arms, cradling her gently, trying to soothe the quivers he felt running through her. "You could never be like he is."

"If I'd been a better aim with that glass, he'd be dead. And I'd be a murderer."

"Stop it, damn it!" Race tightened his arms around her until he could almost feel her heartbeat. "You're *not* a murderer. Even if you'd succeeded, it was only what he deserved. He's the murderer, Kit, not you."

"I know," she said softly, unexpectedly. "I just didn't think you did."

He stiffened, unable to move as her words sank in. Before he could react, she spoke again.

"If you were a killer, you would have used that gun just now. In the heat of the fight, who would blame you? But you didn't use it. Just like you didn't bring Dad's gun here with you. You didn't even take it inside at Rick's house. Because you don't think that way. You're no killer."

He stared at her. He could have used Whitney's gun, he'd been furious enough. But he hadn't. And he hadn't even thought about bringing her father's gun inside, here or at Rick's. Why not? Was it simply that he wasn't used to carrying a weapon? Or was she right, was it because his mind didn't run along that track?

"They're here, Race." His gaze snapped back to her. She tugged at the back of the frame and held up a clear plastic negative holder. "The pictures Rick took. We have all the evidence they thought they destroyed. Harve will have to believe us."

He let out a breath. They *would* believe it now. He could leave. Kit could handle it. He could go back to a life on the run, waiting for disaster to happen all over again. Only this time he would be doing it with a vital part of him missing. He'd be doing it without Kit.

"You're no more a murderer than I am, Race," she said softly. "They have to see that. We'll make them see it."

Her faith was so simple, so shining, that for a moment he almost believed it. Then he looked around the ruins of what had once been his home, at the chaos around him, so reminiscent of that night all those years ago, and the hope drained out of him.

There was nothing left. He had no more hope, no more strength. It didn't matter anymore. Nothing did, except Kit. Without her, he'd be spending the rest of his life in hell anyway.

For one last, long, precious moment, he held her close. He let himself savor the feel of her, the closeness. And then, with a feeling of pain he'd never known before, he silently told her goodbye. He began to build up the walls he'd let down to let her in, distancing himself from her once more. After a while, with the greatest effort he'd ever made in his life, he let her go and walked to the phone.

The heavy clang of a jail cell door had to be one of the most distinctive sounds in the world, Race thought. And when he'd heard it close on him, in the last moments of twilight of a day that had left him in numbed exhaustion, the only thing he could think of was how strange it was that the sound he'd dreaded all these years was so much quieter in reality than it had been in his nightmares.

It had been hours before he'd heard that clang. The sheriff's deputy who had arrived had taken one look at the scene and immediately radioed Harve Brooks. Kit had quickly whispered, "Let me talk to him," when the portly man arrived. And selfishly, because each passing minute helped him build those walls a little higher, Race let her.

"You need a doctor, son," were his only words to Race, spoken with an intent look at his bruised face. Race shook his head.

"Okay, Sam, you get these two—" he gestured at Whitney and Len "—out of here. Stay with them every step of the way, until I find out exactly what we got here."

The deputy nodded, and Brooks turned back to them. "You two won't mind coming down to the office with me now, will you? I'm sure there's a mighty long story behind all this."

As Race had known it would, the name Cameron carried a lot of weight, and once in his office the sheriff listened carefully to Kit's story. With a magnifying glass he examined the negatives she handed him and made notes as she told him everything that had happened since the day Race had rescued her from the fallen tree limb. Almost everything, anyway.

Brooks gave him a cool, sideways glance at one point, and Race knew that, although he hadn't interrupted Kit's story to say so, the man knew he had been the elusive burglar he'd spent so much time chasing. Race didn't speak, merely let the acknowledgment of the sheriff's accurate guess show in his eyes, and the man turned back to Kit without a word.

When she was done, the sheriff turned to him and asked for his version. He gave it, much as he had given it to Kit in the cozy warmth of her cabin. He saw the sheriff's eyes narrow assessingly as he went through some of the more technical explanations, but again he listened to the end. And then, after making more notes and studying his pencil for a long, silent moment, he had raised his gaze to take them both in.

"I guess that just leaves me with one question."

Here it comes, Race thought.

"Why," he said, leaning back in his chair, "didn't you come forward with this before?"

Race heard Kit's breath catch in her throat as she turned suddenly frightened eyes on him. He wanted to reach out, to touch her, to tell her it was all right, but he didn't dare. He was training himself for life without her, and he couldn't weaken now. Taking a long, deep breath, he forced himself to meet the sheriff's eyes.

"I'm sure there's a reason," the man said, zeroing in on Race. "I'd certainly like to hear what it is."

Race closed his eyes. Then opened them. His hands tightened on the arms of the chair. He looked at the sheriff again. And then, in a flat, dead voice, he told him.

That had been—he glanced at his wrist automatically before he remembered they'd taken his watch away, as well as his belt, knife and boots—he didn't know how long ago. Two days? Three? Did it matter? He lowered his arm.

He'd had that knife a long time, he thought. It was the only thing he had left from his father, his real father, because it was the only thing he'd had with him that long-ago night. Yet somehow their taking his boots was the worst, reminding him with vicious certainty that he wouldn't be needing them to walk in the woods for a long, long time.

He'd tried to tell himself he was glad it was over, that he'd felt relief when he'd told the sheriff he was no doubt wanted in Iowa for the murder of Henry Lytton. But in truth he hadn't felt gladness or relief, or anything else, since the moment he'd let go of Kit.

Kit. He hadn't seen her since the sheriff, with a gruff order that Race had best "come along with me until I check this out," had taken him away. He'd heard her protests, but he hadn't had the nerve to look at her.

You knew it would happen, he told himself. And he had. He'd known that she would realize, when she saw the reality of it, of what they would do to him for what he'd done that long ago night, that she was lucky to be rid of him. Yet somewhere, in some stubborn corner of his mind, her fervent words echoed.

"You're no more a murderer than I am, Race. They have to see that. We'll make them see it."

If she'd meant it, he told himself wearily, sitting on the edge of the narrow bunk, she would have been here. At least once. But she hadn't been, and he'd better get used to it. He'd made his decision, he'd stayed when he could have run, so he had no room to whine about it now.

He rested his elbows on his knees, his hands dangling loosely as he stared at the floor whose randomly patterned tile had become all too familiar now. He could still feel the bruises every time he moved his head, but they were healing. A mark of time passing, of days survived, like hash marks on the wall, he thought.

He should try to sleep, he supposed, it *was* dark out. Not that it mattered. Dark, light, all the hours in here were the same: endless.

He heard a dog bark. It sounded like Gus. Then he laughed at himself, but the sound trailed off into a groan. It seemed impossible that the sweet tender hours he'd spent in Kit's arms had ever really happened. This cold, small cell was reality; Kit Cameron was just a beautiful dream conjured up out of a masochistic, lonely imagination. She was—

She was here.

He froze, not daring to look, but he would know that scent, rose-sweet with a touch of spice, anywhere. He heard the clank of the barred door being unlocked, and in that instant he cringed inside; for all his wishing she would come, now he hated the thought of her seeing him in here.

Then she was kneeling beside him, looking up at him with golden eyes already brimming with tears.

"Why didn't you just stay away?" he said hoarsely, hating the way he sounded.

"God, I'm sorry, Race, I knew you'd think I deserted you, but I had to go right away. I just couldn't stand to think of you in here one minute longer than you had to be."

He laughed, or tried to. "Try years. Get out of here. This is no place for you."

"Not until you meet someone."

"What?" His head came up then.

"Sir?" Kit's voice was light as she turned to one side.

Only then did Race see the man who had come in with her. Tall, spare, his dark hair sprinkled with gray, he looked oddly familiar. He stepped forward and held out his hand.

"I've been wanting to meet you for a long time, Mr. Booker. I've heard a lot about you."

Booker? Something was trying to break through the numbness, trying to register on his weary mind.

"I think," the man went on, "my brother mentioned you in every letter we've received in the last year."

Rick. That was who this man reminded him of. And at last the obvious broke through. But what an Iowa state senator was doing here, in a California mountain jail, he couldn't begin to comprehend. Slowly, a little unsteadily, he stood up. "You're..."

"William Parkson. And I want to express my family's sincere gratitude to you for bringing down the animal who killed my brother."

Race lowered his eyes. "I didn't... Kit was the one..."

"Miss Cameron has told me the whole story, Mr. Booker—" The man broke off with a sad smile. "I'm sorry. I'm rather used to that name, since that was how Rick always referred to you. You were...very important to him, you know. I think he looked on you as the son he never had."

Race's throat tightened beyond speaking; his numbness was retreating rapidly before a surge of pain.

"I'd like to talk to you sometime about my brother. But right now, I believe Miss Cameron has something for you."

Only then, when he let himself really look at her, did Race realize that the expression on her tearstained face was joy. Exultant, rapturous joy. It washed over him, soothing, healing, even though he didn't know the reason for it.

"Kit...?"

Silently, tears brimming anew, she handed him a letter that looked as if it had been clutched in her trembling hands for hours.

"What...?"

He could only stare at her. He glanced down at the letter, with just his first name written across the front, then back at her. At last, as if the effort to keep them in became too much for her, the words tumbled out.

"Open it, Race! Please!"

"Who...?"

She bit her lip, as if to try to stop herself again. Then, on a quick little rush of breath, it came out.

"Your mother, Race! It's from your mother!"

Staring at her, he drew back a little. She was wound up, certainly, but...

"She's alive, Race!" Kit cried. "Please, believe me. Just open the letter. You'll see!"

He tried to step back, to distance himself from this insanity. He came up against the bunk. Losing his balance, he sat down abruptly. Kit was immediately kneeling in front of him.

"Go ahead," William Parkson urged. "I had my office track down all the papers you'll need later, but your mother's letter should come first."

Race gaped at both of them.

"It's true, Race," Kit insisted. "She was hurt, badly hurt. It's why she didn't come in person. She doesn't walk very well. But she's alive. She's been trying to find you for years."

Race couldn't speak; he could only shake his head in stunned disbelief.

"It's true, son." William Parkson's voice was quiet yet assured. "Once your mother recovered enough to realize she was free of Lytton's brutality, she told everyone the truth about what had happened. And that you had never laid a hand on her in your life. Oh, they didn't want to believe her, but she wouldn't stop. Then they found that Lytton had been playing it a little loose with the bank's books, and everybody began to look at things a bit differently."

"You're free, Race," Kit whispered. "They ruled it justifiable homicide a long time ago."

He stared at her, his heart hammering with hope, his mind telling him it couldn't be true. But when he looked at her face, when he saw the elation, the love, there, he had no choice but to believe.

"Sunrose," he choked out, lifting his arms, and she went to him like a fox to its lair, quick and home and safe.

Epilogue

"Are you sure you're all right?"

Kit looked with concern at the woman beside her, who was wrestling awkwardly with her cane.

"I certainly am, dear. I mean, really, if you can walk in your condition, I can certainly walk in mine! Besides, I wouldn't miss this for the world."

"Neither would I," Kit said softly, turning her eyes to the front of the big stadium, to the rows of people in all their ceremonial robes. But only one concerned her, and despite the crowd, she knew exactly where he was.

When they called his name, followed by the list of honors, Kit thought she was going to burst into tears of joy and pride. He would pay back William Parkson with interest, she thought, even though the congratulatory telegram that had come this morning had told them to consider the remainder of the loan a graduation present.

The publicity after the Agricultural Center scandal had had far-reaching results, not the least of which was the airing of Race's tragic story and the truth about his part in the discovery of Whitney's activities. The influx of support, from financial to job offers, had been overwhelming.

But, as she'd known he would, Race had chosen the path he'd always wanted: he'd gone back to school. And along the way, with a single-minded concentration that awed her, he had stuck to the other goal he'd established.

"We'll write your father's book, sunrose," he'd told her quietly. "That's just as important to me."

She had hugged him hard, and when the book that made headlines in scientific circles had been released, and Race had seen the dedication she had secretly inserted, to Dr. Richard Parkson and the man he'd loved as a son, it had earned her an even fiercer hug in return. And a night of long, sweet love that had resulted in more than just satisfied exhaustion.

And now as, the ceremony over, he headed toward her with the coveted degree in his hand and the mortarboard cocked at a jaunty angle, his face alight with a love that made her eyes brim with tears, Kit knew the last shadow had been banished. He would decide now what he would do, and she rejoiced inwardly that this man who had had so few choices in life had so many now. And she would be beside him; she'd made certain he had no more doubts of that.

Excitement fairly crackled around him as he came to a stop before them. He hugged them both fiercely, tugging the black robe out of the way. Then he grinned at them, waggling his precious burden.

"Not bad for a former janitor, huh?"

"And modest, too," Kit said dryly, but with nothing less than pure love in her eyes.

"Well, at least I made it before thirty," he said with a grin at her teasing and a look no less warm for her in his own eyes.

"I'm so very proud of you," the older woman said, tears spilling over.

For a moment Race just looked at his mother. There had been some rough moments in the beginning. She had had to face her own guilt about not having had the courage to stop things before they came to such a disastrous ending, and Race had had to confront his own buried anger over the same thing, but with Kit's gentle help and support they had worked through it. And now there was nothing but love in the look the two exchanged.

"Come on, ladies. Let's go. We've got dinner reservations at—"

"Er, Race?" Kit said, a little oddly.

"What, sunrose?" He hugged her again, albeit carefully.

"I hate to ruin your plans, but do you remember that deal we made with a certain someone? About not making an appearance before you graduated?"

He pulled back, eyes widening. He swallowed heavily and nodded.

"Well, he kept it. To the letter."

"Now?" His voice nearly squeaked.

"Right now," Kit said, catching her breath as her body sent her an unmistakable signal.

Race paled. "Damn. Where—what—"

"Just go get the car, son," Elise Barkley said calmly. "We'll meet you at the curb."

"But—"

"Go," she insisted as Kit gasped. "Unless you want your son born on the Stanford football field."

Race wheeled around, then turned back. He planted a swift fierce kiss on his wife's cheek.

"I love you, sunrose."

"I love you," she answered. "Remember that, in case I forget in the next few hours."

Race remembered, Kit never forgot, and in the hours just after dark, Race held Christopher Richard Barkley in his arms, heedless of the tears that filled his eyes, aware only of his tiny son and the woman who, against all odds, loved him.

* * * * *

A SENSATIONAL NEW LOOK

To keep pace with this thrilling series of suspense, adventure and passion, we are introducing new covers in July.

So look out for the bright new fuschia-pink covers.

From: July 1994   Price: £1.95

A NEW LOOK FOR THE

Look out for the bright, modern, new covers on the Silhouette range this July.

INTRIGUE

Romantic tales of danger, mystery and suspense that will keep you gripped page after page.

4 titles every month at £1.95 each.

DESIRE

A selection of provocative and sensual love stories for today's woman.

6 titles every month at £1.90 each.

SILHOUETTE

SILHOUETTE RANGE

And be sure to try our exciting
new line—INTRIGUE

SPECIAL EDITION

Satisfying, realistic romances which feature all the joys and sorrows of love.

6 titles every month at £1.95 each.

SENSATION

Exciting stories which feature a thrilling mix of suspense, adventure, drama and passion.

4 titles every month at £1.95 each.

YOU'LL BE INTRIGUED BY OUR NEW SERIES

Intrigue, the new series from Silhouette, features romantic tales of danger and suspense.

The intriguing plots will keep you turning page after page as the gripping stories reveal mystery, murder and even a touch of the supernatural.

4 titles every month, priced at £1.95 each, from July 1994.

SILHOUETTE

Intrigue

$\mathcal{S}$ilhouette Sensation

COMING NEXT MONTH

WITHOUT PRICE Dee Holmes

Terrified by the attempted kidnapping of her nephew, Katherine Brewster accepted protection from tough, sexy private investigator Sloan Calder. They were to pretend to be a married couple, but that pretence was likely to be just as dangerous as evading the bad guys. After all, they'd both learned the hard way that "happily ever after" didn't exist.

A ROSE FOR MAGGIE Kathleen Korbel

Allison Henley was raising a child with special needs—alone. She could never hope to have another child, and she certainly couldn't risk falling in love again. But sexy carpenter Joe Burgett was handsome, compassionate and strong—and falling in love with Allison. He wanted children of his own. What could they do?

ONCE UPON A WEDDING Paula Detmer Riggs

A terrible accident had left lawyer Jess Dante scarred forever, in body and soul. Yet a needy, newborn little girl found a way into his embittered heart. The only future he could offer her was to adopt her, and for that he needed a wife. The only woman he could consider marrying was Hazel O'Connor; would she consider him?

RECKLESS ANGEL Maggie Shayne

Toni del Rio was in over her head. Witnessing a mob hit she'd had to pretend to be dead and allow herself to be kidnapped. Although undercover FBI agent Nick Manelli wasn't about to kill anyone, he had to hide Toni or they would *both* be dead. Alone together in close quarters, Toni couldn't help fantasizing about her rugged captor...even *before* she decided he couldn't be a gangster!